T0148269

2012...
THE YEAR JESUS (YESHUA)
FINALLY CAME BACK TO EARTH

A Fictional Tale of His Physical Arrival Back to Modern Times

DANTE P. CHELOSSI JR.

Order this book online at www.trafford.com
or email orders@trafford.com

Most Trafford titles are also available at major online book retailers.

Author of two prior books titled as follows . . . "Allah's Jihadists" and "Truckee River WaterBabies"

Printed in the United States of America.

ISBN: 978-1-4669-5220-1 (sc)
ISBN: 978-1-4669-5222-5 (hc)
ISBN: 978-1-4669-5221-8 (e)

Library of Congress Control Number: 2012914580

Trafford rev. 08/09/2012

 www.trafford.com

North America & international
toll-free: 1 888 232 4444 (USA & Canada)
phone: 250 383 6864 ✦ fax: 812 355 4082

ACKNOWLEDGEMENT

I would like to thank a nice young lady named Dakota Daetwiler. She is a very special person with phenomenal artistic talents.

I commissioned her talents to paint for me a large painting, as I had also done with my other two books, with a different artist, that I wrote prior to this latest book.

I always take these paintings and then turn them into the covers for my books.

Looking at the paintings have always been able to give me some additional inspiration to get over the final hump, and "Get-R-done.

Dakota, she did such a wonderful job on this latest painting, that I was inspired enough to finish this book well ahead of schedule.

This cover that she did for this book was beyond my greatest expectations.

Truthfully, I am not exaggerating about her talents as an artist.

She is so humble about her artistic talents when you meet her in real life, and tell her how impressed you are with her artwork.

Amazingly, she finished this painting in less then two weeks!!

I explained to her exactly what I wanted, and even though she was only a short time away from becoming a new mother, she got on this project right away . . . WOW!!

A little background on this talented artist . . .

She is 24 years of age.

She was born and raised in Humboldt County, California

She started her own business selling her artwork at age 22.

The business took off beyond belief.

She has been doing art since she was little, and loves working with different mediums such as . . . acrylic, molding gel, and Swarovski crystals, as well as 24K gold flakes in some of her paintings.

She prides herself in her very affordable pricing, quality work, and unique ideas.

If you would like to view anymore of her artwork besides the book cover that she did for me, or contact her, here is where you can find her beautiful work . . . dakotasdesigns@hotmail.com or . . . www.facebook.com/dakotadesigns

I am so impressed with her work that I have already asked her if she would be willing to do a painting for my next book, my fourth, which I will begin working on next spring of 2013. Thanks again Dakota!! Your work is very much appreciated. Dante' P. Chelossi Jr.

DEDICATIONS

I would like to dedicate this latest book that I have written, my third, to my loving wife . . . Sprite Marie Chelossi, and all of my zoo of animal children who often drive me crazy, but I love them . . . my dogs . . . Texi who is shown with me on the authors photo on the back cover, and the rest of the Chelossi pack of canines . . . Archie, Oreo, Esher, Ophra, Cinco, and Cinnamon . . . my cats . . . Tiki and Reka . . . my Parakeet birds . . . Teal and Benny . . . and my newest animal children . . . my chickens . . . Latifa, Midnight, Tarzan, Sambo, Sunshine, Lucy, and finally Ethel.

It is a wonderful thing to be able to come home to my sweet little wife, and all of my animal children. It helps to give to me the motivation to pursue my goals and pursuit of mutual happiness. I feel very happy to have such a wonderful group who I know really truly cares about me. They are always there for me, and I will always be there for them as well.

CHAPTER ONE

D r. Darnell ("Darny") Colma was an archeologist specializing in ancient middle eastern cultures.

He was especially interested in the era of the biblical times.

Dr. Darny was very well known in the academia world, as a person who was obsessed with using the field of archeology to prove to the world, that some things noted in biblical times, were not exactly what they were supposed to be.

Theology type people abhorred him, because they thought that he was out to prove, that many of the things they spent their lives believing in, were not true.

His obsession clashed with their obsession.

For thirty seven years, Dr. Darny, and the people who worshiped a man who lived in the ancient biblical times, verbally fought, and disagreed openly and privately.

This biblical man of ancient times was known as "Yeshua."

The name Yeshua, throughout time since his death almost two thousand years ago, was eventually transformed into the name that is very well recognized today as . . . "Jesus."

The name . . . "Jesus" did not even exist as a word during that time period in ancient times.

Even though Yeshua was at the time, a very common name used by many people to name their sons, this particular person who had this name from birth was considered special.

He became very well known in his times because of the things that he supposedly did, and said.

Years after his well documented death, he became a martyr for the people who called themselves "Christians."

A book that became the Christian holy book was written many years after the death of this special man called Yeshua . . . Jesus.

This book survived many centuries, and a few thousand years, to become a book, that people would die for the text written between it's covers.

There were many wars fought, and much blood spilled upon the Earth because of the text between the covers of this holy book.

This book is known throughout the world as the "Holy Bible."

Dr. Darny often liked to make references to any number of Gnostic texts, that were readily available, to all who might be interested in reading them, to prove some of his points of views in regards to particular texts within the Holy Bible.

But . . . Dr. Darny also was very sure, that there existed other ancient papers with text, that could give him more proof, to show that his academic obsession was not wasted time on his part for most of his adult life.

So here was Dr. Darny, in what could be called, his "final pasture," making one last effort to hopefully find some new ancient documents to finally put to rest about what is the real truth about this special man called Yeshua . . . Jesus, who lived and died over two thousand years ago.

The year A.D. that the obsessed Dr. Darny was toiling about in the mountain range of an Egyptian desert was 2012.

It is still only early spring, a few weeks before summer time.

This mountain range was pock marked with many caves that had already been thoroughly searched over the millennia by ancient and modern people.

Dr. Darny had found an area in this mountain range that he thought, did not have enough caves dug into it.

This area had what appeared to be, a huge landslide of sandstone boulders from ancient times.

It was his hope, along with some of the students, and hired workers that were helping him, that maybe if some of these boulders were to be moved from where they sat on the side of this particular mountain, that he had chosen in this mountain range, there might very well be an undiscovered, and unsearched cave behind one of them.

His well paid workers engaged their physical efforts tirelessly, and very meticulously, moved each boulder, one by one, in the hopes of finding one of these theoretical possible caves.

Nobody dared to suggest that maybe this effort was possibly a waste of every ones time, partly because of the Dr. Darney's reputation of prior academic success in his field of expertise, and the bottom line good money, that was paid to all who helped him.

His work crew had worked on a particularly large boulder for almost two weeks, and was now clearing the area far down below the mountain, because they were going to dislodge this ancient boulder on this day, and roll it down the slope of the mountain.

Once all of the people down below were safely out of danger from this boulder when it rolled down this mountain slope, the large sandstone rock would be separated from it's resting spot, from a time when this special man Yeshua . . . Jesus, may have walked the Earth.

After almost an hour of clearing people from the path, that this boulder would travel, the time had finally come, to witness this unglorious event, out in the middle of nowhere, and far from the nearest civilized area of a living population of people.

The head of the hired work crew was named "Habaz."

He stood with Dr. Darny about thirty feet away, directly to the side of this boulder ready for the order to be given to dislodge the giant rock.

His work crew had the boulder completely ready for it's separation from the mountain, and awaited their command from Habaz.

Dr. Darny told Habaz to go ahead and dislodge this ancient sandstone boulder.

Habaz gave the signal to his crew to give the final push for dislodging of the giant boulder.

With one great push by twenty five men, the boulder tipped forward, and started it's decent downwards on the steep slope of the mountain from where it sat for over two thousand years.

It tumbled and rolled, quickly picking up speed, and causing other rocks to follow its path downward, pushed by the invisible strength of gravity to the bottom of the mountain to a flatter area of ground.

It came to rest at a new spot, where it would surely sit forever into all eternity.

To the utter amazement of all the people near the area of where the giant boulder once sat before it's dislodging, there was indeed a cave!!

Dr. Darny was completely flabbergasted at this moment in time.

No words could come out of his mouth, even though he was screaming in his head a flood of silent verbal celebration.

One of his students by the name of Suzie Howser began screaming her surprised delight.

She jumped towards Dr. Darny, and gave him a huge hug, and continued to scream her happiness about seeing a cave, less than thirty feet away from where they all stood in happy shock.

Not a single person went even an inch towards this newly discovered ancient hole in the mountain.

The cave was about eight feet at it's highest point, and close to twelve feet across.

All eyes were upon Dr. Darny, waiting for him to be the first man to set foot in this cave, in over, possibly . . . twenty centuries!!

Dr. Darny regained his composure, and was finally able to speak aloud to everyone around the area.

"We have a cave!!"

"Habaz!!"

"Is it safe for me to enter?"

Habaz walked over to the entrance to the cave, and turned on a large halogen flashlight, and pointed it in the direction of the inner confines of this ancient man made hole.

He did not step inside, because he knew that it would be his boss, Dr. Darny who would have that honor.

As Habaz looked at the inside area of the cave from where he stood at it's entrance, he could see that the cave went into the mountain for an estimated distance of forty to fifty feet.

There appeared to be no more loose rock near the entrance.

He quickly concluded that it would indeed be safe for Dr. Darny to enter inside of the cave.

Habaz hollered politely over at Dr. Darny: "It appears to be safe for entering boss!!"

Dr. Darny motioned for Suzie Howser to walk at his side, and they both calmly walked over to where Habaz stood, still aiming the flashlight into the cave.

Habaz handed the flashlight to Dr. Darny, and stepped back away towards where the rest of his crew stood, wide eyed at what they saw before their eyes.

Dr. Darny slowly entered into the cave, with Suzie now following silently, and closely behind him.

He swept the bright halogen light back and for, up and down, slowly on all walls, the ceiling, and the ground below their feet.

All that he could see for the first few steps, were the many rough gash marks, left behind from the people who dug this ancient cave.

He and his student companion walked to almost the full length of the cave before they could see what appeared to be a bunch of ancient pottery pots.

Dr. Darny's heart skipped a few beats upon seeing the pots.

Suzie gasped, but still did not say anything aloud.

Dr. Darny spoke in a low tone to Suzie: "Do you see what I see?"

Suzie answered back to him: "Yeah . . . Dr. Darny, I see what appears to be some ancient pottery pots in that corner of this cave."

"My goodness Dr. Darny, what have we found here?"

Dr. Darny flashed a smile in the darkness of the cave and answered her: "Well, Suzie, lets find out!!"

They both walked over to the ancient pottery and stopped just short of where they still stood, untouched for who knows how long . . . centuries? . . . millennia?

Dr. Darny squatted down a looked closely at the clay pots.

To his amazement, and utter delight, none appeared to be broken, or even cracked.

All of these pots had lids on top of them, and they appeared to be sealed with a waxy substance.

Dr. Darny counted the pots out loud: "One, two, three, four, five, six."

Five of the pots were of medium size, about twenty inches tall, and eight to ten inches across.

The sixth pot was smaller, it was only about twelve inches tall, and seven inches across.

This sixth pot also was different from the other pots because it did not have a handle as the other five did.

Dr. Darny handed the flashlight to Suzie, and very carefully picked up this pot from the ground.

They both looked at the surface of the pot at what appeared to be ancient written text.

Neither one of them could recognize these ancient writings.

Dr. Darny turned to Suzie and told her to get the other students, and bring them back into the cave, and to tell Habaz to set—up more lighting in this area of the cave.

He told her that he would just stand there in the dark and wait for her and the others to come back.

He wanted a few private moments to be by himself, and relish this special moment in his life.

He had a feeling deep within his intellectual brain that was extremely exhilarating.

He felt like he was floating in outer space in a timeless vacuum.

The darkness of the cave helped to influence the feeling that he was experiencing.

He stood there in the dark for several minutes with an earlobe to earlobe smile upon his face.

He thought to himself . . . Could this be the moment in his life that he had often dreamt about.

The dream to finally discover some ancient proof, that would substantiate everything he had adamantly preached in regards to his personal opinions, and to quiet the many doubters and naysayers throughout the world.

Several flashes of lights crisscrossed the area of the cave where he stood, as Suzie, and the other students began to approach him.

Dr. Darny could feel the excitement of the students as they came closer to him.

Dr. Darny raised his arms to stop the students a few feet from him and the ancient clay pots.

Habaz was now close by with a few workers, setting up a large telescopic light on a tripod, and aiming the light at the area where Dr. Darny and the students stood.

A long electrical cord was fed out to a gas generator outside of the cave to run this lighting system.

A few minutes later, and the back of the cave was as bright as the daylight sun outside of the cave.

Dr. Darny, Suzie, and the rest of the students analyzed the ancient clay pots.

All of the other pots had the same ancient writing on their surfaces as the one that Dr. Darny held in his hands.

After an hour of meticulous hands on analysis of these ancient clay pots, and photo's and video taken to document this spectacular find, Dr Darny finally decided that it was time to move the pots outside of the cave, and package them for transport to the ancient antiquities department at the National Museum of Egypt.

Once these ancients clay pots were safely inside of a lab at the museum, Dr. Darny and a team of specialists would then take the time to first decipher the ancient language on the surfaces of the pots, and then open them to see what the contents would reveal.

CHAPTER TWO

The date was April 11ᵗʰ, 32 AD.

It was early afternoon on a very hot and sunny day.

Blood dripped down to the ground to form a small puddle at the feet of Ossismi and Mary.

Ossismi was an ancient scholar who came from the ancient area of the world known as "Gaul."

He would be the one and only person who would be writing an actual text account of the crucifixion of a well known person of the times known as "Yeshua."

In modern times this name would be changed to the name of Jesus.

But the reality was that this man being crucified by the Romans was indeed named "Yeshua."

Ossismi was very careful and meticulous in the actual description of what Yeshua looked like as a man of their times.

He described Yeshua as a man with the skin color of a very dark ebony, and the hair with the same texture as that of the wool of a sheep.

If a modern day person were to see this man named Yeshua in person, they would say that he looked like an average black man with an African decent.

Ossismi was a friend of both Yeshua and Mary since being invited to witness their wedding in the town of Cana years earlier.

Since that time, Ossismi was unofficially granted permission by Yeshua and Mary to write about the teachings, accomplishments, and various different events of Yeshua's life.

Yeshua, on numerous occasions, emphasized that these writings would one day be important for people to read long after his death.

Ossismi had fled from the Roman conquered province of Gaule Lyonnaise or "Gaul" (Modern day France) because he was one of the few people of that area who was educated, and knew how to write text upon papyri.

Anyone with these talents were considered threats to the Romans of those times.

Mary Magdalene, who stood beside Ossismi, was from a small city named Migdal Nunaiya.

Her nickname was Mary Migdal because of where she came from.

The town was known for it's ship building and fishing.

This is where she had met Yeshua when he was visiting friends who were local carpenters.

Mary and Yeshua were granted permission for marriage from her family, after knowing each other for two and a half years.

As Mary and Ossismi stood there watching the blood drip from above where Yeshua was secured to two crossed post's by iron spikes, She cried openly, and he communicated with the dying man.

As Yeshua spoke, Ossismi wrote text to document all that was said.

Ossismi was not as open in his writing as Mary was with her crying, because if a Roman soldier were to see this, he would surely experience the same fate as Yeshua.

There was an anonymous person nearby who acted as a lookout for Ossismi to warn him if any Roman soldiers were coming.

He would then have enough time to hide the papyri underneath his clothing.

Mary had told Yeshua that she was carrying his child in her womb only a few weeks before this sad day.

Yeshua asked Ossismi for four favors before he died.

He asked him if he would be with him and document his last words before his death.

He asked him if he would transport Mary out of the region because he feared she and his child might be harmed by the Romans when they found out who she and her child were.

He asked Ossismi if he would bring Mary back to the lands where he had fled from for the child to be born and raised under his protection.

Lastly, Yeshua wanted Ossismi to place all of the text that he had written from this last day and all of the previous days since their wedding, in sealed pottery, and hidden in a cave in the mountains where many kings had been buried from centuries past.

Ossismi promised Yeshua that he would carry out all of these promises for his friend.

Ossismi and Mary stood at this area with Yeshua for another three hours before he finally said his last words: "When I do return, It will be when all of the children of God are close to perishing permanently from our world, I am now departing and will journey to the place of good souls . . . "Nevaehruo" . . . Farewell."

Upon saying this, Yeshua closed his eyes, and passed on into another world of non physical entities.

Yeshua had been alive since his birth for 33 years, and almost halfway in this year to becoming 34 years old.

Before dying, Yeshua had given a clue as to when he might return back in physical form upon this world.

He had said: "I will return when the time is twenty years subtracted from twenty centuries into the future, it will be a time for reckoning, and judgment for all of the children of God."

"I will be the judge who will decide their fates when that time arrives."

Ossismi wrote this text in his native language of "Transalpine Gaulish" . . . often referred to as the "tongue of Gaul."

He spelled the actual text in Aramaic, but as it was pronounced in the tongue of Gaul.

He did this, so it would be hard for anyone to translate, if he were to lose the important papyri before putting them safely into a cave.

The time had finally come for Mary and Ossismi to leave this area where Yeshua's lifeless body still hung on the two wooden crossed boards.

Ossismi reached down and put two of his fingers into the puddle of blood that had come from Yeshua.

Ossismi then smeared the blood upon the bottom of the papyri that held the last recorded words ever spoken by a man who would later be worshipped throughout the world for many centuries, and by millions of people.

This man's name would later be changed to "Jesus."

Ossismi was true to his promises to Yeshua.

He was able to safely store all of the papyri with the written text of Yeshua into sealed pottery containers, and also store these important clay pots into a cave where Yeshua had instructed.

Strangely, the day that Ossismi stored these clay pots into this cave, an earth quake shook the mountains, and caused a massive landslide to occur.

A large boulder ended up sitting at the entrance to this cave to seal the entrance from possible future looters.

Ossismi then was able to transport Mary, who by then, was halfway through her pregnancy with Yeshua's child.

Even though Ossismi did not want to travel back to his homeland . . . Gaul . . . he did so any way, because of his promise to Yeshua before he died.

They traveled back to the ancient city of "Lutetia" . . . a city that would one day become the modern city of Paris.

Mary gave birth to a son whom she named "James."

Ossismi and Mary stayed together and raised James until he left home as a young man of twenty one, and went out to make a life for himself in ancient Europe.

Ossismi educated James with all of the knowledge that he held in his own brain.

Ossismi later died as an old man from unknown causes.

Mary disappeared into the invisible winds of time, to become a mystery in the future, for the people that were curious about her, and the life she lived.

The clay pots remained hidden in the cave until found by Dr. Darny.

CHAPTER THREE

D r. Darny and Suzie Howser traveled with the ancient clay pottery, very protective, comparable to a chaperone for a young woman at her first Prom dance.

They traveled for three days before they reached the National Museum of Egypt.

They left the rest of the students behind at the dig site to continue working, and documenting.

When they arrived at the museum, they were met by Egypt's head of national antiquities . . . Dr. Ismail Fortuk.

Dr. Fortuk was very excited by the findings of the ancient clay pots.

He had Dr. Darny, and Suzie, follow him along with a staff member, who brought the ancient unopened pots along behind them, on a pallet controlled by an electric pallet jack.

They all walked to a laboratory that was completely sterile from any foreign matter.

They all dressed into sterile lab suits, and rubber gloves before entering this laboratory.

The pots were placed on top of a stainless steel table underneath a large light and magnifying glass.

Dr. Fortuk silently studied the writings on the pots for several minutes before speaking: "I do not recognize these ancient writings."

"Do you have any theories Dr. Darny?"

Dr. Darny told Dr. Fortuk that he had studied these writings along with Suzie for the past few days, and did not have the slightest clue.

They all agreed that they would have to bring in a specialist in the field of ancient languages, and ancient writings.

The one candidate that they chose was one of only a few in the world with this special skill, and she was not to far away.

Her name was "Ribandella Ntangku."

She was a well known African professor who taught at a University in war torn Nigeria.

Dr. Fortuk called her that same afternoon to ask her if she might be interested in helping them figure out these ancient writings.

Professor Ntangku could not say yes to this request fast enough. She was totally excited, and very anxious to see these ancient writings on these pots.

She flew out to Egypt the very next day, and by mid afternoon she was standing in front of the ancient pots studying them intently.

She used her laptop to reference, and cross reference the many extinct ancient languages that were long ago forgotten.

After several hours of doing this, she was able to figure out that the text was actually spelled out in an ancient language called Aramaic.

It took several more hours before she was able to figure out that when you pronounced the ancient text the meanings were in a different ancient language.

This ancient language was an extinct French language, or commonly referred to as the language of Gaul.

It was called: "Transalpine Gaulish."

Professor Ntangku explained to everyone that this must have been done for a reason.

It was like a two layered code of languages that would only be deciphered by someone who knew both of these ancient languages.

Dr. Darny asked her to tell them what the writings said on the outside of these pots.

Professor Ntangku slowly figured out that the first five pots were similar to volumes in a book. They all said the same thing, except their numbers were different.

They all said: "The first writing of Yeshua."

"The second writing of Yeshua."

"The third writing of Yeshua."

"The fourth writing of Yeshua."

"The fifth writing of Yeshua."

The sixth pot was different because it was smaller than the others, and it did not have a handle on it.

The writing on this different pot said: "The final day's of Yeshua's life, and his promises for the future."

Right away, there was excitement in the air amongst the scholars.

They all knew that the name of Jesus did not ever exist in the ancient world as millions of people have always believed.

The reality is that there was not even a letter "J" in existence yet in any human language.

In fact, the letter "J" was still not in existence before the 14th century. All research indicates that the letter "J" became widely used in the 17th century.

If one were to look at a copy of the original "King James Bible" you would be able to see that there is no letter "J" in the entire text of the book.

James is spelled with an "I" . . . Iames.

Jesus is also spelled with the letter "I" . . . Iesous.

The name Jesus was originated in the 6th century by Jewish Masoretic priests, and they obviously did not use the letter "J".

These priests still used the letter "Y" and formed the name . . . "Yeshua".

This name "Yeshua" is more closely matched to the name of "Joshua".

But over time, the transliteration of the Hebrew name created by these priests was changed language by language.

Yeshua became Le-s-ous in the Greek language.

Le-s-ous became Le-so-us in the Latin language.

Finally, Le-so-us was transformed to Je-s-us in the English language.

Another known fact is that Pontius Pilate had these names inscribed on the cross above the head of Yeshua in Hebrew, Greek, and Latin.

The three professionals that now stood over these writings in fact knew that the name of Yeshua was the actual name of the person millions of people over the centuries have worshiped as a man called Jesus.

They knew that the actual fact was that Yeshua was the name given to the person known today as Jesus, by his parents when he was born.

They also knew that this was a common and very popular name to give to a son in those ancient times.

Dr. Fortuk decided that it was finally time to x-ray these ancient pots to see what was inside of them before they took off the sealed tops.

One at a time, the pots were carefully taken to a room to take x-rays.

This process took only an hour before they were all once again on the stainless steel table in the sterile laboratory.

The six x-rays were placed on a light table in the lab, and to everyone's excitement, it appeared that all of these ancient clay pots held more papyri's.

They already knew that this would probably be the case because of what the translated writings on the outside of these pots said.

Dr. Fortuk gave the go ahead to take the sealed tops off of the ancient clay pottery.

An eight hour hard drive video camera was put on the record mode for documenting this process.

Carefully, Dr. Darny took a small curved stainless steel tool, and carved away the waxy substance that was in the gap between the pottery tops, and the pots.

Chunks of this waxy substance fell to the tables surface as he slowly, and meticulously carved away.

After doing this for several minutes, the seal was finally separated, and the lid for the first ancient clay pot was ready to open.

Suzie Howser reached over and very carefully took the top off and gently laid it on the table beside the pot.

Dr. Fortuk, just as carefully, reached inside of the pot and retrieved the ancient, and very fragile papyri's.

He pulled a total of eight papyri's out of this first pot labeled: "The first writing of Yeshua."

Dr. Fortuk, very carefully separated the eight papyri's into individual sheet spread out across the table under the large magnifying glass.

These papyri's were absolutely immaculate, with no damage at all.

Everyone was shocked to see that there was not any degradation, it was as if they had been placed in the clay pot only yesterday.

Dr. Darny said out loud: "This is absolutely amazing!!"

All the people around him agreed with him excitedly.

Professor Ntangku started to look at the writing on the first papyri at the far left hand side of the table.

She read the first few lines silently to herself, and then finally looked up at everyone with a stunned look upon her face.

She walked away over to a chair nearby and sat down, still looking stunned.

Dr. Darny, Dr. Fortuk, and Suzie Howser came over to her and stood around her with concerned looks upon their faces.

Dr. Darny asked Professor Ntangku what was it that she had just read?

Professor Ntangku looked up at Dr. Darny and slowly answered: "It had the name of the writer . . . "Ossismi," he said that he was given permission by Yeshua, and Mary, to write about and document from here on after until his death, the life events of "Yeshua."

There was invisible electricity in the air surrounding the four astonished people.

Dr. Darny next spoke: "So, it appears that there is a possibility here, that the author of these writings . . . "Ossismi," might have been given permission to write the words, and document the events of "Jesus?"

And "Mary?"

"Mary who?"

"Mary Magdalene?"

"Oh my God!!"

Professor Ntangku answered back: "My initial thought is that what you just asked, might possibly be true!!"

"We need to carbon date these papyri's and clay pots as soon as possible Dr. Fortuk."

Dr. Fortuk agreed with the professor, and said that he would make the arrangements immediately.

He stepped out of the laboratory and went off to contact people with the expertise to do this.

Professor Ntangku went back to the papyri, and started to read more of the ancient text.

Every few minutes, she would raise her eyes from the papyri's text and explain what she had just read.

After doing this for several more hours, she was able to finish all eight papyri's from the first ancient pot.

Dr, Fortuk had returned, and sat mesmerized with Dr. Darny and Suzie Howzer, while the professor translated the ancient text from the papyri's.

It was agreed by all four people who had a chance to know what the ancient text said, that this more than likely was genuinely about Jesus.

The next day, two experts on carbon dating were given permission by Dr. Fortuk, to take very small samples from the ancient pots and papyri located within them.

All of the ancient pots seals were separated from their lids, and all of the papyri were taken out, and placed on the table near the pots where they had come from.

The smallest pot was of great interest to Dr. Fortuk, just because of it's difference to the others, and what it said on the outside on it's pottery surface.

"The final day's of Yeshua's life, and his promises for the future."

Professor Ntangku was asked to translate the ancient text from these papyri's next, instead of going in order with the other ancient papyri's from the other pots.

The other papyri's from those pots would be translated next, after this particular one of interest.

Amazingly, the carbon dating results were returned back to Dr. Fortuk within twenty four hours via the internet on a secured private account set-up for this project.

Dr. Fortuk wasted no time in passing along these results to Dr. Darny and the other's involved with the project.

The results were absolutely spectacular, in regards to the impact it made upon this now very important project.

The results showed that the papyri's, and the clay pottery were dated at between 26 AD. And 32 AD.

This information was a wonderful realization that gave stronger evidence that these ancient items were truly from the time when the much worshiped man called Jesus, walked the earth as a living, oxygen breathing, human being, over nineteen hundred years ago!!

As this new knowledge sunk into the brains of the four lucky professional's who were officially now slated to work on this fantastic project, Professor Ntangku started to translate the ancient text from the last ancient pot.

She thought to herself that this project would indeed be the project of a lifetime that she could only have dreamed might possibly someday occur.

She was pretty sure that the other professionals probably thought the same thing as she was at this proud moment in her life.

She took a very deep slow breathe of air and started to work on her new assigned job.

CHAPTER FOUR

Professor Ntangku slowly started to translate the ancient papyri's from this last pot.

Susie Howzer sat next to her and wrote the translations into English format on her laptop.

Dr. Darny, and Dr. Fortuk sat nearby listening to the professor as she read the translations aloud slowly, giving Suzie enough time to write the exact correct text.

They were all transfixed on what each word, and sentence said.

"For all of the people of this world, I will describe everything that I witness with my eyes, and everything that is said, for my dear friend and spiritual master . . . Yeshua, on what will be his last day to experience life as a living human being."

"My name is Ossismi."

"I truthfully write these words, as I bear witness, to all future events for Yeshua."

"Yeshua has told me that it is very important to start out these last writings by giving a physical description of how he looks to people as they see him with their eyes."

"Yeshua stands upon the ground measuring a height that is equal to subtracting the width of a man's hand from three and one half cubits."

"The color of his skin is a very dark ebony."

"The color of his hair is even darker than his skin."

"The texture of his hair is similar to that of a common sheep."

"His eyes are slightly lighter than his skin."

"His weight is 250 dextans, and add to that another 6 deunx."

This is the weight that he has averaged since I have known him, and started his personal writings."

"Today, his weight is much less, due to the large amount of blood that has flowed from his body from his wounds given to him by the Romans."

"His wounds start at the top of his head with an akanthine crown of thorns of the nubk bush."

"After Pontius Pilate pronounced the sentence upon Yeshua, Roman soldiers placed this crown of thorns on the top of his head."

"Yeshua had more wounds in many areas of his body from the scourging from the flagrum."

"Yeshua has suffered terribly from the pain of the iron spikes that were driven by the Romans into the bottom of his hands between where the hands meet the arm in the wrist area, and separate spikes were pounded through both sides of his feet to the sides of the plank that stands upright from the ground."

"The small sedile does not help very much to take away any burden of weight as Yeshua hangs from the crossed wooden planks."

"The final wound for Yeshua came from a piercing of a spear from a Roman soldier to the area of his lower ribs on the right side of his body."

"All of the blood from these wounds have trickled down and soaked the crossed planks, the sedile, and have caused a small pool to be created upon the ground measuring two cubits across."

"I stand here with Mary, below these crossed planks where Yeshua hangs in crucifixion, unable to touch him, without stepping into this pool of blood."

"This small hill where Yeshua's crucifixion is happening, is called by all of the people in this region "Gol Goatha.""

"This hill has been used for many crucifixions before this day."

"There are many skulls that lay on the ground across the top of the Gol Goatha" from these earlier crucifixions."

"The city walls of Jerusalem are only a stones throw away from where I stand with Mary Migdal of the village of Migdal Nunaiya."

"Mary Migdal carries Yeshua's child within her womb."

"Yeshua has asked her to name his son "James.""

"Yeshua has asked Mary to travel with me to "Lutetia" . . . the place where I lived before meeting Yeshua."

"I had promised myself to never return to Lutetia, but Yeshua has asked me to take Mary there to give birth to his son James."

"Yeshua wants me to take care of Mary, and James, and to give his son all of the knowledge that I possess, until he grows to be a man that will then make his own choices for his own life."

"Only because Yeshua has asked me to do this, is the only reason that I will devote the rest of my life to fulfill his personal request."

"I have many fears within my soul about returning to a place where I could be treated in the same way that Yeshua has at this place."

"Many followers of Yeshua have visited him during the time of his suffering to speak with him one last time before he dies."

"Many of these followers have been questioned by the Romans after they left this crucifixion site."

"Some of these followers were taken away after being questioned."

"The Romans have watched this area very closely since putting Yeshua upon the crossed planks."

"They know that Yeshua is loved by many people of the region, and I believe that they have fears that there could be an uprising after Yeshua dies."

"I fear that the Romans might take me and Mary Migdal away after Yeshua dies."

"I am sure that the Romans have noticed that me and Mary Migdal have been at Yeshua's crucifixion site from the very beginning of this sentence of death."

"Yeshua is barely alive now and has very few heart beats left before his soul departs his body."

"Yeshua does not hardly speak anymore, he only looks down at Mary Migdal with a smile upon his face."

"The sun is about to set upon the distant horizon, and it is my belief that Yeshua will be dead before the light of the sun disappears."

"All of a sudden Yeshua raises his head with great will for the effort, and speaks to me and Mary Migdal."

"These are his last words before he closes his eyes for the final time and breathes his last breath."

"I will return when the time is twenty years subtracted from twenty centuries into the future, it will be a time of reckoning, and judgment for all of the children of God."

"I will be the judge who will decide their fates when that time arrives."

"When I do return, It will be at a time when all of the children of God are close to perishing permanently from our world, I am now departing and will journey to the place of good souls . . . "Nevaehruo.""

"Farewell."

"Me and Mary Migdal bear witness to the last words of Yeshua, and watch in sorrow as he closes his eyes, and takes his last breathe."

"We both stand here on this sacred ground and wonder how life will really be like without this great man.

"Centuries will surely pass before my writings are found, and translated into other languages."

"Someday, as Yeshua said in my writings, people of this world will see him once again for his judgment and final decision of their fates."

"My writings are now complete for Yeshua, I will now leave this place of crucifixion with Mary Migdal, and start a new journey to fulfill the promises that I have made for Yeshua, Farewell Yeshua."

CHAPTER FIVE

The International Space Station drifts lazily in space looking down upon the Earth.

There are two astronauts from the United States who are departing this massive space structure for the very last time.

They will be departing from the space station via a special space capsule that was manufactured by the space agency of China.

The United States had decided two years before to scale down their space program.

The very first scale back was to discontinue putting astronauts on the International Space Station.

The next scale back was to retire the Space Shuttle fleet.

There would be no more traveling to space with a Space Shuttle, and no more experiments at the International Space Station.

In the future, if the United States wanted to put a satellite into an orbit around the Earth in space, it would have to be by cooperation of another country with access to space, or by paying another country money for their space services.

The two American astronauts who were now getting ready to depart the International Space Station would certainly be the last people from the U.S. to travel to space for quite a long time.

The senior of these two astronauts . . . "Vernon Montague" was disappointed by the decision of the U.S. Space agency to not have any people travel to the great endless abyss in the skies above his beloved planet Earth.

His personal opinion was that a grave mistake had been made, and that the U.S. would for sure fall way behind other countries that were now traveling to space for various reasons.

Vernon Montague had been a part of the U.S. space program for almost twenty seven years in one way or the other.

He was absolutely shocked the there would be no more Space Shuttles launched into space.

He had the honor of being on three Space Shuttle flights within the past eight years, and enjoyed those travels immensely.

He could understand backing away from the International Space Station, because it was common knowledge, that it was like an endless money pit for the U.S. budget allocations to the Space programs, with no real gains or accomplishments to show to date.

It seemed as if the only people that were making gains at the International Space Station were the other countries involved.

Vernon Montague had wanted to remain a part of the U.S. Space program for thirty years, and then retire.

But now with these new development had transpired, he made a decision to retire within the next few month after returning back to Earth.

The other astronaut . . . "John Crevelli" did not have much of an opinion about the U.S. decision to scale back it's space program.

He had only been a part of the U.S. space program for less then five years, and was more interested in continuing his military career.

He did have under his belt, one Space Shuttle assignment in the past year, but it was in reality, not such a big deal for him.

The reality was that he was actually more interested in building his personal profile, and making his resume shine as bright as the stars that now surrounded him as he awaited his departure from the International Space Station.

He was also starting to get a bit irritated with Vernon Montague, because of what he deemed as being constantly corrected for everything he did while in space.

He did not like how Vernon Montague would correct him like a child, and use the excuse of his vast experience to validate his actions.

It was true that John Crevelli had made a few errors on the current assignment at the International Space Station, and it was also true that these errors were noticed by the other members that were present from the other nations represented.

Vernon Montague made it a point to tell him that there was a slight embarrassment felt because the U.S. was supposed to be the top dog when it came to anything involved with assignments in space.

Other countries new to space, with the exception of the Russians, were looking to the U.S. astronauts to set the example for them to learn from.

The Chinese space capsule was already connected to the International Space Station, and both astronauts were already prepared for their departure.

Airlocks were now being unlocked, one at a time, to the Chinese space capsule.

The other astronauts from the other nations had finished saying their polite farewells to the two Americans, and now it was time to leave.

Vernon Montague led the way, climbing lazily through the first airlock, followed close behind by John Crevelli.

The two men went through three airlocks before they finally climbed inside of the Chinese space capsule.

The two astronauts secured themselves into their seats, and started their check-off list to break away from the International Space Station.

This last procedure only took less then fifteen minutes before they were ready to give the go ahead to the Russians to unlock the Chinese Space capsule.

Vernon Montague notified the Russians that they were ready to depart, and told John Crevelli to fire up the navigational jet boosters while he set the course that they would travel back to Earth.

After the Chinese Space capsule was unlocked from the International Space Station, Vernon Montague slowly backed the Chinese Space capsule away to a distance of three miles before starting their course back to Earth.

Within five minutes, the fuel for the jet booster was expired.

The capsule now shot like a bullet towards the re-entry point into the Earth's atmosphere.

As the capsule shook violently while getting back to the Earth's gravitation pull, both astronauts held on to their seats tightly.

These moments were always the most paranoid of feelings for any space travelers, as they came back from outer space back into the invisible bubble surrounding their planet.

All of a sudden, just as the Chinese Space capsule entered back into the Earth's atmosphere, there was a violent disruption that shook the outside of the capsule.

The panel in front of the two American astronauts started to throw sparks in many different directions.

Vernon Montague tried desperately to keep the Chinese Space capsule on course to the planned destination, but found out quickly that all navigational instruments were now out of commission, and inoperable.

They were now officially helpless as to what course they would now travel.

John Crevelli tried to communicate with the people of the Space agency down below on the Earth's surface, but to his utter horror, all transmissions were as silent as the outer space where they had just traveled from.

The two men were now helpless passengers within this Chinese built space capsule, awaiting their final unknown destination.

CHAPTER SIX

The President of the United States was immediately notified of the situation with the Chinese Space capsule that held their two American astronauts as helpless passengers.

As the capsule fell down from the skies towards an unknown landing area, the President sat with a technician who brought in a portable tracking monitor normally used for tracking terrestrial objects like meteors as they fell towards the Earth.

The technician was able to quickly locate the Chinese Space capsule and had it centered on the screen for the worried U.S. President.

Other high ranking people were gathered around the President and watched the tiny blip on the screen as it continued it's path towards the surface of the Earth.

Vernon Montague pressed the button on the panel at twenty miles above the Earth, to activate the parachute's for the capsule.

The parachutes did not engage.

The capsule continued it's rapid descent at a very high speed.

John Crevelli started to scream at Vernon Montague after he realized that the parachutes did not engage.

Vernon Montague did not say anything.

He just sat there in his seat and watched the GPS directional device that showed the capsule was now hundreds of miles off of their projected planned course.

The GPS showed the capsule was headed towards the Pacific ocean somewhere near the Philippine islands.

At this point in time, all the two American astronauts could do was wait for the impending impact of the capsule with what looked like the waters of the Pacific ocean.

John Crevelli started to openly hyper-ventilate with obvious open fear in every part of his heart and soul.

Vernon Montague remained silent, but also scared as hell.

Both astronauts felt light headed, and were on the verge of becoming unconscious because of the extreme "G" force from the speed that the capsule was traveling.

Moments later, both men closed their eyes and became oblivious to the world outside of the capsule.

The President of the U.S. asked the technician where the capsule was located on the GPS device.

The technician informed him that the capsule was on a course to impact the Earth in the Pacific ocean near the Philippine islands.

He also informed the President that the present speed of the capsule indicated that the parachutes for landing may not have engaged because the capsule was traveling much to fast, and it's velocity had not changed since entering the Earth's atmosphere.

The President hollered out loud: "What the hell are you saying!!"

The technician answered back: "Basically sir, it appears that the capsule is not going to slow down, and will impact the Pacific ocean at a very high rate of speed."

"I do not believe that the astronauts will be able to survive the impact."

The capsule was now traveling at an amazing speed of three thousand miles per hour, the two astronauts had just faded into unconsciousness from the "G" force.

All the President, and the people that surrounded him could do at this point was to watch the GPS screen helplessly and await the eventual impact of the space capsule.

The President was already resigned to the apparent fact that the American astronauts were doomed to experience their deaths in a matter of a few minutes somewhere in the Pacific ocean near the Philippine islands.

The President asked for a satellite communication contact with whoever was in charge of the U.S. Naval fleet in the Pacific ocean area near the Philippine islands.

He would make arrangements to recover the capsule and the astronauts after the impending and most probable destructible impact with the surface of the Pacific ocean.

Within a minute, a Rear Admiral from the U.S. Pacific Fleet was available to the President via satellite communication.

Rear Admiral "Mike" Downey was quickly filled in about what was happening in the skies miles above his head.

So now the Navy had ships on standby, awaiting orders from Rear Admiral Downey, to go to the site of impact, to recover whatever might be left over, after hitting the Pacific Ocean at such a high rate of speed.

Many people were doubtful that the bodies of the astronauts would be able to be found, let alone be recovered.

The capsule was now projected to hit the Pacific Ocean in about twelve minutes.

The capsule was now an extremely hot fireball of unrecognizable metal manufactured in China.

The difference between this Chinese capsule, and the capsule's built previously by the United States was that the metal density and weight was almost three times as much.

The Chinese insulated ceramic tiles surrounding the exterior shell of the space capsule were also almost three times thicker than tiles created by the American manufacturers for the U.S. Space agency.

A stream of smoke followed behind the falling capsule, and sonic booms were projected.

The space capsule quickly passed across the Pacific Ocean and the sonic booms could be heard by people in Japan, Guam, and the people of the Philippine islands.

A large amount of people from these island nations looked upwards to the skies after hearing this loud boom, and they all could see the trail of white smoke from the falling Chinese space capsule.

Moments later, the capsule impacted the Pacific Ocean at a conservative enough of an angle that actually minimized the force of the impact to the ocean water.

The capsule entered the abyss of the mighty ocean and started a quick downward descent towards the deepest part of the ocean on the entire planet.

This area of the globe was famous for being the location of the deepest trench of under water land that made the tallest mountain above the ocean . . . "Mount Everest" seem very small in comparison.

This trench is known as the . . . Mariana Trench.

The depth of this famous trench is 6.85 miles below the surface of the Pacific Ocean.

As the capsule sunk deeper within the depth's of the massive ocean, the astronauts remained alive and in an almost peaceful sleep, oblivious as to what was now happening to them.

Oddly enough, the reason that the capsule was actually sinking instead of floating back up to the surface, was because of a few factors.

First of all, there just happened to be a large area below this part of the ocean that had large pockets of rising methane gas from the ocean floor that had burst in recent years.

The effect of the rising methane gas caused objects to sink like a rock because of the difference of weight between the gas and the water.

Also, something unusual happened when an object sank within this rising stream of methane gas . . . the pounds per square inch (psi) remained the same as the pressure from the air above the surface of the ocean.

So, consequently, the Chinese capsule with the astronauts inside did not feel any pressure change at all.

Luckily for them, if the capsule was not within this stream of methane gas, they would all be crushed from the immense pressure down below as they sunk.

Downwards the capsule sank . . . one mile . . . two miles . . . three miles . . . four miles . . . five miles . . . six miles!! . . . and now that the capsule was descending the last mile before arriving at the bottom of the Mariana trench, another odd thing occurred, a large suction like a vacuum cleaner grabbed the capsule and sucked it towards a very large cavity near the peak of an underwater mountain.

The capsule was still being protected from the extreme pressure of the methane gas as this suction occurred.

The capsule slowed down slightly, and then entered inside of this massive cavity.

Now the capsule was taken away in an underwater river that was not completely filled with ocean water.

The capsule floated on top of this river.

The river filled about half of this massive cave and the other half . . . unbelievably . . . was filled with breathable air!!

This air was now, instead of the methane gas, the protector of the capsule from the extreme pressure of the Pacific Ocean.

The capsule traveled for several miles on the surface of the river, seemingly endless.

The capsule bounced off of the walls several times like an object flowing through a pipeline.

The impact of one of these brushes with the cave wall caused one of the astronauts to awaken.

This astronaut, Vernon Montague looked around and cleared his head a bit.

He then shook John Crevelli until he was also awake.

Both men could feel the capsule moving on the river, but did not realize where they actually were.

If they realized where they were at this moment in time, they might very well have had mental breakdowns, or even heart attacks.

The thought of being over six miles under the surface of the great Pacific Ocean would almost certainly cause them to freak-out unlike any other time in their entire lives.

As the capsule continued it's journey on this underwater river inside of a mountain of the Mariana Trench, Admiral Downey and several Navy ships were witness to the capsules impact and sinking under the Pacific Ocean's depth's.

Admiral Downey and the other Navy people waited for the capsule to rise back up to the surface of the ocean, but to their shock, after ten minutes, the capsule still had not appeared.

There was not even any debris of a capsule that should have been destroyed into several chunks of metal.

Everyone near the scene of impact was mystified.

Nobody had an explanation as to why the capsule had not risen back to the top of the ocean's surface.

The President of the United States waited for word from the Admiral about the status of the capsule carrying their two American astronauts.

Finally, Admiral Downey told the President that it did not look like the capsule would ever reappear, it was officially listed as lost . . . forever!!

Shortly thereafter, family and friends were notified of the sad news that the two men inside of the Chinese capsule would be listed as dead and forever missing.

Unknown to these family and friends was the actual fact that the two astronauts were indeed very much alive and not missing permanently . . . yet.

In the same time frame that everyone thought that these two men were dead and missing, Vernon Montague and John Crevelli were now finally awake and clear headed.

They had figured out that they were traveling on a river, but still did not realize the location of this river.

It was completely dark inside of this cave, so there was not anything for the two astronauts to view as they helplessly floated towards wherever this river was taking them.

It had the same feeling of a very long and tortuous carnival ride that one would want to get off of as soon as possible.

The capsule continued it's journey though this massive cave in the dark on this fast moving river, bouncing off of the walls here and there along the way.

Both men silently thought to themselves . . . Where in the hell are they going?

Will the capsule ever stop somewhere?

All they could do for now was to endure this wild ride, and hope that they would end up in a place where they would be able to leave the capsule and be safe enough to experience life once again.

CHAPTER SEVEN

As Professor Ntangku finished the last line of the translation . . . "Farewell Yeshua." tears of excitement welled-up inside of her eye sockets.

It was really hard for her to be a total professional at this moment, and hide how this affected her inner emotions.

Around the room, there could be seen, very similar reactions from her colleagues.

The room remained quiet for a few more minutes before anyone spoke.

Dr. Darny finally broke the silence within the room.

"Is this real proof that there was a man who actually wrote some personal eyewitness accounts of Jesus?"

"In the actual time of when Jesus was alive?"

Nobody answered his two questions.

So Dr. Darny continued to speak.

"Well . . . according to these writings, this appears to be the case."

"The carbon dating verifies that these writings come from the time period when Jesus was alive."

"The translations that we just listened too are absolutely amazing."

"I am very interested in the part of the writings that had a clue in a sort of mathematical format, that indicated when Jesus said he would return back to Earth."

"Did anyone try to figure that one out yet?"

Suzie Howser answered politely with this question.

"My initial calculations seem to indicate that the year is 2012."

"If you calculate the following . . . the year 32 AD when Jesus supposedly was crucified, and add 1980 years which is twenty years subtracted from twenty centuries, the math result is 2012."

Dr. Darny hollered out loud: "Oh my God!!"

"This is the year 2012!!"

"Isn't there a whole bunch of different theories going around the world, that some people are convinced that the end of the world is supposed to happen this year?"

"This is absolutely amazing!!"

"What do you think about this Dr. Fortuk?"

Dr. Fortuk shook his head slowly before speaking just as slow.

"Maybe this calculated year is just a coincidence."

"Or maybe this could be the most extraordinary discovery in the history of mankind."

"One thing that I do know for sure though is . . . we have to keep this a secret for the time being."

"If this discovery, and our initial findings were to get out into the media, we would be absolutely overwhelmed with people wanting to know more, and insist on further investigation."

"This could turn into a media circus that would not be comparable to anything ever witnessed."

"Until we have thoroughly looked at everything here, and have evidence that this is indeed all valid, I suggest that this remain a secret while we continue to investigate."

Dr. Darny and the others present, agreed with everything that Dr. Fortuk said.

All of the people within the laboratory made a mutual agreement to keep this discovery a secret until all of the papyri were translated, and then they would decide when to reveal this unbelievable find to the rest of the population on the planet.

It was also agreed that this would have to be done this year . . . 2012, because if it was indeed true that Jesus was going to return in 2012, then Earth's population would need to prepare themselves for this fantastic event before his arrival.

Suzie Howser quickly made a google check to find out when in 2012, was the date that everyone was saying would be the end of the world.

After only a few minutes, she was able to find out that December 21, 2012 was that date that everyone was keying on.

It was now only a week before June of 2012.

This left about six and a half month's before the date of December 21, 2012.

Of course, the majority of people on the planet were skeptical of the possibility of the world coming to an end on this chosen date.

The little bit of rumblings of this possible event occurring could be compared to the worldwide paranoia that happened at the turn of the century in the year 2000, also referred to as Y2K.

There was a number of people that actually went into extreme panic modes, and did outlandish things because of their beliefs of the world coming to an end.

One could only imagine what would happen when the data was released by these people inside of this laboratory from the desert's of Egypt.

If the data was released in the format that the information translated from the papyri was supposedly valid, then the world might once again go into a massive panic mode.

Maybe not the whole world, but certainly a percentage of the population would react in extreme ways, from the fear of the possibility of the released data possibly being true!!

Especially affected, would more than likely be the religious sects throughout the world.

There would be many skeptics in the religious world, but only until the date of December 21, 2012 came, would they know the truth.

CHAPTER EIGHT

The Chinese Space capsule bobbed, bounced, and floated through what seemed like to the astronauts, an endless tunnel system upon this river below the ocean floor.

It traveled at a speed of almost 30 knots per hour on the surface of this river.

The capsule traveled for nearly 45 hours with the astronauts sleeping and waking up many times during this time period.

It traveled a distance of a little over 1500 miles!!

At this time, the capsule all of a sudden started to increase the speed of travel to a pace of almost fifty knots.

This increase in speed was attributed to the fact that the capsule was coming upon a huge waterfall within the next half mile on this river!!

Both of the astronauts noticed this increase in speed.

Vernon Montague figured out what was happening because he had past experience's with kayaking at a few rivers around the world.

He told John Crevelli that he was pretty sure that the capsule was coming close to going over a waterfall.

Both men held on to their seats, and remained frozen while they waited for this scary event that was imminent within moments.

The capsule tilted backwards as it came closer to the edge of the top of the waterfall.

The feeling for the two men was very similar to that of a roller coaster ride at an amusement park.

Their stomach muscles tightened-up as the capsule started a freefall over the top of the massive waterfall.

John Crevelli winced in fear as the capsule fell.

The G-force was not as bad as what they would feel during a space launch mission when lifting-off, but it was still a prolonged uncomfortable feeling for their bodies to endure.

The capsule fell for an unbelievable mile and a half!!

Blood rushed to their heads, and they both felt as if their brains were going to explode from the pressure within their skull caps.

Finally, the capsule made impact with the surface of a massive lake at the bottom of this waterfall.

The capsule submerged completely underneath this lake for almost fifty yards before slowly floating back up to the surface of the lake.

The capsule popped up to the surface and violently bobbed from side to side for a few moments before coming to a floating vertical position.

Both of the astronauts survived this impact with the lake, and were still awake as the capsule started to float slowly across this massive lake, but still caught in the current of the river from above that was now moving more slowly, and still moving in a direction across the lake.

The two astronauts could now see out of the two windows of the capsule, because there was definitely large area's in the distance that projected light.

At first, this light was a dim light in the distance, but as the capsule continued to float in the current, this light became brighter.

The two men also noticed that the lake that they were floating on was inside of a massive cavern as far as their eyes could see in all directions.

They were both amazed at what they were seeing.

Neither man could speak because of this awesome sight.

It was the same reaction that was similar to what happens when people see the Grand Canyon for the very first time.

An absolutely unbelievable sight to behold for any human being.

The capsule slowly traveled closer to this light that was now becoming brighter by the moment.

The light now had what appeared to be movement within it.

Both men wondered silently, what could that movement possibly be?

It couldn't possibly be signs of some type of life . . . could it?

No way!!

But as the capsule continued to get closer to the area where this light was coming from, the movements within this light because more obvious.

It appeared now that there were many moving figures, and shapes like structures in many area's within this lighted area.

Vernon Montague spoke loudly all of a sudden, it shocked John Crevelli, who was still silent and transfixed on what he was seeing through the window of the capsule.

"Look at that movement in the light John!!"

"What in the Hell do you think of that?"

John Crevelli answered back in a lower tone of voice.

"Well Vernon, it appears that there might be some type of living entities over in that light."

"Maybe they are the space aliens from the UFO's that have been reported for so many years."

"Maybe this is an underworld alien base."

"Maybe I am still asleep and this is all just some weird dream."

Vernon Montague reached over and shook the younger astronaut firmly to make him realize that he was not dreaming, and that this was indeed something they were both witnessing while they were alive, and awake.

He once again spoke loudly.

"We are very much awake, and alive, and witnessing something utterly fantastic and unfathomable for both of us to believe could possibly be true."

"Do you understand what I am telling you John?"

"Maybe you are correct in your sarcastic theory."

"Could the movement over in that light be a civilization of beings that are secretly living here, and from another planet from another solar system?"

"As amazing as it sounds, it might in fact be the truth!!"

John Crevelli answered back, but this time there was no hint of sarcasm.

"If in fact it turns out that these are aliens from another planet, what is going to happen to us when they find out that we are here?"

"Are we going to become experiments for their curiosity?"

"I getting scared Vern!!"

Vernon Montague felt the same fear as John Crevelli, but did not show it to the younger man.

He did not want to cause the young astronaut to become more terrorized than he already was at the moment.

All the two men could do now was to helplessly wait and see where the capsule finally ended it's long arduous journey . . . somewhere within that lighted area in front of them.

CHAPTER NINE

The U.S. Naval fleet that had been on site when the capsule made impact with the Pacific ocean, and then sinking out of sight into it's great depth's, departed the area.

The order to depart, and continue their normal ordered operations was given by the President of the U.S. with much reluctance.

A few hundred miles away, in a small city, on an island that was a part of the nation of the Philippines, people went about their normal everyday activities for survival.

This small city was called . . . "Legazpi City."

Legazpi City is located in the province of "Albay" on the island of "Luzan."

Legazpi City was near a well known volcano called "Mount Mayon."

In the thick jungle, at the base of Mount Mayon, was a small group of Filipino men hard at work cutting down large mahogany wood tree's.

The leader of these hard working woodcutter's was a man called: "Enrique Batista Magsaysay."

For the first time, Enrique had brought along his oldest son: "Marcos Salvadore Magsaysay" to help in this hard work.

Marcos had for many month's, begged his father for the chance to help cut the wood this year in the jungles with his crew.

Enrique and his crew, including his son, had cut down thirty three large mahogany tree's for the day, and called it quits to finally rest so they could eat and sleep for the night.

Tomorrow would be a very long hard day to gather all of the cut tree's and prepare them to transport back to Legazpi City.

As all of the crew settled down by the camp fire and started to cook some food, Marcos told his father that he was going to go and do a little exploring in the jungle near the volcano.

Enrique gave his son permission to leave the camp for a bit of exploring, but told him not to be gone to long because he needed some rest for tomorrow.

Marcos wandered off from the camp with a broad smile upon his face because even though he had told his father that he wanted to help in the wood cutting, the real truth was that he wanted to explore the jungles near Mount Mayon volcano.

Marcos, since early childhood, had a great fascination for the famous mountain volcano.

Marcos walked very quickly through the dense jungle towards the base of Mount Mayon.

It took him less than twenty minutes to find an area where he thought would be the best direction to ascend the side of the great volcano.

He knew that he would not have enough time to climb even halfway up the side of this mountain, but he could at the very least, explore some of this area, and get a good general lay of the land for the future, when he could come back on his own, without his father's permission.

He had lied to his father month's ago about wanting to help with the family business of cutting mahogany tree's.

His real reason all along was to have the opportunity to explore Mount Mayon.

He knew that if he asked his father if he could simply go to Mount Mayon for the reason of exploring, his father would certainly deny his request.

So he lied . . . plain and simple to be able to have this chance.

Marcos felt bad about not being truthful to his father because he respected and loved him dearly.

But the strong drive within him to see Mount Mayon up close was almost like an addictive drug that he could not resist, no matter what his feelings were for his father.

Marcos found a small animal trail that seemed to zig zag back and forth up the base of the volcano.

This trail made it much easier for his movements, instead of fighting the thick jungle brush.

After traveling this animal trail for about ten minutes, the trail abruptly ended.

This seemed very odd to Marcos.

Why did this trail end like this so suddenly?

Marcos looked around back and forth, twenty to thirty yards on both sides of where the trail had once been.

Finally, he found a clue.

A fallen tree laid on where the trail veered upwards to the left, in a direct vertical direction towards the summit of the volcano.

The trail was no longer very visible because apparently, no more animals traveled upon it.

But Marcos was able to barely see signs of the trail.

He was able to see the trail enough to continue his ascent up the side of Mount Mayon.

It would not be dark for another two hours, so Marcos did not worry about making it back to camp before darkness finally came.

He would head back to camp at a very fast pace in about half an hour, just to be safe.

Marcos came to an area that revealed a small ledge about shoulder height.

He decided to climb up to this ledge and see where it might lead.

After he was atop this small ledge, he could see that it flattened out to a much larger area.

This intrigued him.

It also peaked his curiosity enough to distract him from keeping his bearings.

As he traveled along to this new area, he lost his bearings completely, and would certainly not be able to easily find his way back to this ledge to climb back down to the trail.

Marcos casually walked deeper into this area that once again started to climb gradually upward to the summit of the volcano.

Marcos realized after twenty minutes that he had made a mistake, and knew that he would not be able to make it back to camp before dark.

He knew that his Father would become worried about him not returning before dark as he had said when he left the camp.

The daylight quickly turned to a lighter shade of darkness, barely dusk.

So Marcos decided that he should find an area to sleep for the night and then return back to where his Father was in the morning.

Marcos walked another few hundred more yards before he came upon something unexpected.

Before his eyes, just ahead, only fifty feet away . . . a cave!!

Marcos knew instantly that this would be the place for him to stay for the night.

A cave!!

This cave was in reality what is called a volcano tube.

This tube was created at a time when the giant volcano erupted, and than erupted again at a later time.

For now, Marcos did not care what it was called technically, to him it was . . . a cave to explore!!

This excited Marcos, because he was sure that he was probably the very first person to ever see this cave.

No matter how much trouble he would surely get into once he reunited with his Father, Marcos now felt that his exploration up the side of this volcano was well worth it for him.

He now had a very legitimate reason to return in the future.

Marcos quickly went to the entrance of this cave, and did not hesitate to enter inside.

Marcos used his zippo lighter to quickly make a hand held torch so he could go deeper inside of the cave.

Marcos could see that this cave appeared to be massive in width and length.

He could only imagine how far back this cave would go.

He became even more excited from the thought that he was exploring a cave that surely no human had ever traveled before today.

He decided that he would explore only some of the cave for now, and then come back and set-up a campfire near the entrance to the cave for the night.

Meanwhile, back at the camp where Marcos's Father Enrique, and his fellow workers were, Marcos Father, as Marcos had predicted was already worried for his son.

It was not like Marcos to not do as he had said . . . return to camp before dark.

When Marcos's Father suggested that maybe they should go and look for his son, all of the workers agreed with one another, and convinced him that this would not be a good idea.

They were able to convince him that Marcos was more than likely safe, and realized that he could not make it back to his Father's camp in time before dark, and had probably set-up his own separate camp for the night.

They decided that it would be best to turn in for the night, get up early, leave one man behind at this camp in case Marcos returned, and go out and look for the young man.

Marcos's Father Enrique shared three emotions at the same time.

He was worried, upset, and mad about Marcos not returning back to camp before dark as he had said he would upon leaving.

For now, all he could do was close his eyes and fall into a slumber.

Some distance away, at a higher elevation, Marcos had already done the same thing . . . instead of being worried, he was happy.

CHAPTER TEN

The Chinese space capsule drifted closer to an area now that looked like it was completely lighted.

It was so lighted in fact, that it almost appeared to be actual daylight from the Sun.

The two astronauts knew that this was not the light from the Sun because of their present location.

Both of the astronauts had their eyes glued to the viewing port in the direction of the lighted area.

As the capsule drifted closer to the lighted area, a lot of movement could be easily seen along the shoreline.

Large structures could also be seen.

Moments later, to their astonishment, they could now positively see a large gathering of people!!

These people appeared to be humans like themselves.

The paranoid thinking of alien beings quickly disappeared from their thought process.

These people were all dressed in white gowns that flowed all of the way down to the ground.

The capsule all of a sudden came to an abrupt stop.

The weight of the capsule had now sunk into the shallow soft gravel twenty yards from the sandy beach where the large group of people were gathered.

The two astronauts looked in amazement at everything before them.

All of these people dressed in white gowns, and many large structures as far as their eyes could see.

It had all of the appearances of a large city.

Neither the astronauts, or any of the people on the shoreline made a move towards one another.

After several minutes of absolutely nothing but quiet staring at each other, the two astronauts decided to open the hatch of the capsule and get out.

Vernon Montague was the first astronaut to climb out of the capsule.

He used a portable rope ladder to climb down the side of the capsule until he was at the surface of the water.

He could see that the water was only a few feet deep, so he jumped down into the water and remained there next to the capsule to wait for John Crevelli to come out.

Moments later, the lone remaining astronaut appeared the top of the capsule.

John Crevelli quickly climbed down the rope ladder and joined his fellow astronaut in the shallow water next to the capsule.

The two astronauts stood there facing the crowd of people on the shoreline a short distance away.

Neither side spoke to each other.

The two astronauts could see the people in the white gowns turning around to face the opposite direction.

The majority of these people were now standing with their backs to the two astronauts.

Vernon Montague whispered to John Crevelli . . . "I think someone or something is approaching them from the other side."

John Crevelli nodded his head in silent agreement.

The crowd of people now started to spread apart from each other to create a clear path for someone or something to come through from the other side.

All eyes were now looking in that direction, including the two astronauts.

The two astronauts now had a feeling of nervous anticipation of what was apparently making it's way towards them.

Obviously, whatever was coming from the other side of the crowd of white gowned people, was coming because of the presence of the two astronauts and the capsule in the shallow water near the shoreline.

Finally . . . a man appeared and stood in front of the crowd of people.

This man was dark skinned, and appeared to be of African descent.

Vernon Montague whispered to John Crevelli . . . "Well, it looks like that black man over there in front of all those people is probably their leader or representative who will make the first contact with us."

Indeed, the more the two astronauts were able to focus on that man, it did look as if he was a black man as Vernon Montague had just suggested.

The black man stood there along the shoreline, almost casually, staring silently at the two astronauts from the outside world above.

Vernon Montague raised his right hand and made a friendly hand gesture in the form of a slow wave from side to side.

Moments later, the black man responded with a similar hand gesture and obvious smile back at Vernon Montague.

Vernon Montague turned to John Crevelli and said: "It appears that he is friendly, lets go over and meet these people."

Moments later, the two astronauts started to wade through the water towards the shoreline where all of these white clothed people stood silently watching.

As the two men got closer to these people, they could see the vast mixture of apparent ethnic groups.

There were Caucasians, Blacks, Asians, and many different brown skinned people that could be put into various possible ethnic groups.

The two astronauts slowly made their way towards the Black man who had waved at them moments earlier.

This black man took a few steps towards the approaching astronauts, and stopped a few feet from the water's edge.

He held out both of his arms in a way that indicated a friendly greeting.

Vernon Montague held out one hand and said to him "My name is."

The black man interrupted with: "Vernon Phillip Montague, and your friend is John Richard Crevelli."

Both of the astronauts stood there before all of these strangers dressed in white clothing in total shock.

They were totally speechless.

They both simultaneously wondered how this man knew their names, and even more surprised and amazed that he actually knew their middle names as well.

The black man smiled at their amazement and then spoke once again.

"My name is "Yeshua.""

"I am known by many other names, the most popular one that is still known worldwide is "Jesus.""

The two astronauts simultaneously opened their mouths wide in utter astonishment at this statement by this person before them.

They were stunned to the point that they could not even move a single muscle in their bodies.

They stood there for what seemed like an eternity, but in fact was only about a minute from a clock.

Finally, Vernon Montague spoke.

"Are you telling me and my friend here that you are the Jesus from the Bible?"

"The Jesus that over half of the people on this planet worship?"

"The man who was supposedly crucified upon a cross by the ancient Romans almost two thousand years ago?"

"I really find this hard to believe."

John Crevelli may not have said this same thing out loud, but he certainly was thinking in his head similar thoughts of non belief.

The man who announced his name as Yeshua to the two astronauts had a very broad smile upon his face.

His face looked so calm and peaceful.

Yeshua motioned the two astronauts towards him with a gentle movement of his right arm and turned sideways to start walking back in the other direction that he had just came from.

He spoke softly.

"Come with me and we will talk some more."

"I will answer all your questions, and explain to you everything about me and this place that you now find yourself to be with me and all these good people around me."

There was a slight hesitation for the two astronauts, but they finally moved forward towards Yeshua, and exited the water to dry land under their feet.

They walked silently behind Yeshua.

They were enveloped by the crowd of people dressed in white clothing behind them and all sides as they walked.

As they walked within this crowd of people behind Yeshua, they could hear some comments around them.

"Who are these men?"

"Where did they come from?"

"Why are they here?"

These were just a few of the inquiring questions that they could hear as they continued to walk.

The two astronauts could now see building structures in the distance.

These structures were all identical in color and shape.

The color was the same as the sand on the beach that they just left, a light tan color.

The shape of these buildings were completely round all of the way around from front to back.

The height of these structures were about twelve feet from the ground to the highest part of the curved roof.

There was a number of windows on these structures.

These structures appeared to be made of mud bricks, similar to adobe style bricks of the southwestern U.S. for many centuries.

Both men noticed that the ground that they walked upon was hard, and was very similar to the adobe bricks of the structures.

They had walked about half of a mile in distance before Yeshua came to a stop and turned to the two men.

They now stood a few feet from the only structure that was different from the others that they had seen while they walked to this location.

This structure was also dome shaped, but was at least twenty times larger in size when compared to the other surrounding structures.

There were no windows on this structure.

A large doorway with two doors was at the entrance to this building.

Oddly, there seemed to be an endless line of people entering into only one of these two doors.

Yeshua spoke: "Vernon . . . John . . . I welcome you to the "Beginning of Life building of Nevaehruo."

"Please enter inside with me, through this door, and we can relax, eat, and talk."

Yeshua turned back towards the doorway and entered inside through the door where nobody from this line of people were entering.

Both of the astronauts followed Yeshua inside of the "Beginning of Life building of Nevaehruo".

As the two men entered inside of this special building, they could see many candles that lit the interior.

The interior turned out to be only one very large room.

At the far right corner of this huge room was what appeared to be another doorway, but the curious thing about it that was instantly noticeable was that it had a bright glow to it.

This glow was so bright that it was almost blinding to the eyes.

What was also very intriguing to the two men about this glowing doorway was that there seemed to be a non-stop line of people entering into this glowing area.

The room was half filled with long tables with small stools on the floor for seating.

These tables were completely full with people eating lavish courses of food and drink.

As these people were completing their meals, they would get up from the stools and get into this seemingly endless line of people who were entering the glowing area.

Yeshua walked over to one of these tables and casually sat down upon one of these small stools.

He motioned the two astronauts to do the same.

The two men walked over to the other side of this table and sat down across from Yeshua.

Another odd thing that Vernon Montague noticed after he sat down and looked at a candle near him was that there was no wax running down the side of the candle.

The candle was basically burning and not decreasing in size as it burned.

Vernon looked over to John, who was still staring at the endless line of people entering into the glowing corner of the room, and told him to look at the candle.

John formed a quizzical look upon his face as he noticed the oddity about this candle, and all the other candles in the room that were identical.

John spoke to Yeshua: "How come these candles are not getting smaller?"

"Why is there not any wax rolling down their sides?"

Yeshua smiled after hearing these questions from John Crevelli.

He answered very simply: "They burn and give light as they do because I make it so."

Yeshua turned to the two astronauts and asked them if they were in need of some food and drink.

Both men nodded a yes silently back to Yeshua without speaking.

Yeshua smiled and spread out both of his arms before the two men seated in front of him and casually said in a soft voice: "Make it so."

Astonishingly . . . before the two men, food and drink started to materialize before them on the table on plates and in glasses.

Remarkably, the food and drinks were the exact favorites that the two men had enjoyed the most, throughout their lives.

This absolutely surprised the two men to the point that they momentarily lost their breathes and their mouths opened fully.

Vernon spoke finally: "All that I am seeing since we entered inside of this building is hard for me and my companion to believe."

"The candles."

"The food and drink."

"That endless line of people that are disappearing through that glowing area of this room."

"I am starting to believe that maybe you are the person called Jesus that is worshiped by millions of people on this planet."

"Could you please explain everything to me and John? . . . please?"

CHAPTER ELEVEN

Marcos awoke from his sleep inside of the cave. Likewise, his Father had also awoke with his men at his camp, and was getting ready to go look for his son.

Marcos decided that he would explore the cave a little before heading back to his Fathers work camp.

Marcos stepped out of the cave and quickly found a tree with a suitable branch to break-off to make a temporary torch for lighting as he walked farther inside the cave.

Marcos went back into the cave with the torch now lit.

His plan was to just explore the cave for about half of an hour, and leave the cave and go back to meet his Father at the work camp.

Marcos was sure that his Father would be very irate, and a punishment would surely follow.

Even though Marcos knew that his Father was upset at what he had done, he still had a strong feeling to continue to satisfy his curiosity about this newly found cave.

Minutes later, as Marcos started to descend down a path within the cave that was at a steep angle, and several hundred feet from the entrance to the cave, the entire cave started to shake violently.

Marcos stumbled forward and fell to the ground.

Marcos stood up back to his feet and continued to walk more cautiously further down the path in the cave.

All of a sudden, Marcos noticed some sparkling within the cave just up ahead, as the light of his torch reflected off of the walls.

Marcos walked directly over to see what was sparkling and took a closer look at the surface of the wall.

He could now see chunks of white rocks of many different sizes embedded throughout the wall for a long stretch that went beyond the light of the torch.

Marcos was no expert in rocks, but his first thought was that these may be diamonds!!

Marcos got really excited at this possibility.

Marcos reached down to his waist and took his knife from the sheath that held it.

Marcos then started to use the knife to dig out some of these white sparkly stones.

He dug out several stones from the wall, and put them in a satchel that was also attached to his waist near his knife sheath.

The more that Marcos looked at these stones, the more he was convinced that these might in fact really be diamonds.

After Marcos had the satchel filled with these stones from the caves wall, he departed the cave to return back to his Father at the campsite.

Marcos's Father and his men hiked in the direction that Marcos had traveled when he left the camp the day before.

They were all expert trackers, and had no trouble in following the path that Marcos had traveled up the semi-steep side of the mountain volcano.

At the same time, Marcos backtracked his path back to where he had climbed up to his present level.

Marcos soon discovered that he could not find the exact area where he had climbed up from below.

He was sure that he was somewhere near the area, but he just could not find the exact spot.

This frustrated him a little, but he also knew that his Father was probably looking for him at this very moment.

Suddenly, Marcos could hear a call from the distance.

This call was a call that he and his Father sometimes used to find each other in the dense jungle.

Marcos was delighted and relieved to hear his Father's call, and quickly answered back.

It sounded like his Father was probably within a hundred yards and getting closer with each call back to Marcos.

They made these special calls to each other several times in the next few minutes until Marcos could hear his Father calling his name nearby and down below him at the lower level that he had climbed from.

Marcos answered back to his Father and they started to talk to each other in their native tongue.

Marcos found out very quickly that his Father was irritated as he knew he would be.

Father and son were finally reunited, and once again standing on the same ground next to each other.

Marcos showed the contents of the satchel to his Father and his men.

They all agreed that the stones inside of the satchel were in all probability real diamonds as Marcos had suspected.

They all got very excited by this new development.

Of course they all questioned Marcos about where he had found these stones.

Marcos told them that he had discovered a cave up above at a different ground level, and that he could easily find the cave again if he came back in this area.

After much reassurance from Marcos, he was able to convince everyone that they could leave the area, and with a return trip in the future, they would be able to easily go straight to the cave where these stones were discovered.

As they traveled back to Legazpi City, and away from Mount Mayon, Marcos's Father toiled with many thoughts about these stones that could possibly be very valuable diamonds.

He would have to figure out where to bring the stones to verify if indeed they were actually diamonds.

He would have to do this in secrecy because of the possibility that the wrong people might decide to target him to get these stones.

Crime was prevalent here as in all other parts of the world.

So . . . for now, until he could figure out where to take these stones to be looked at by a professional, and do it safely without becoming a victim of a robbery, it was agreed by all, as they continued their walk back to their homes in Lagazpi City, that the stones would be placed in a safe place, and they would be the only people that had the knowledge of the stones existence.

After this agreement was made, they spent the rest of the day walking back to their homes and families with a secret that might possibly change their lives forever.

CHAPTER TWELVE

Trevor Johnson, a seismologist from the United States, was living and working in the National Seismology Center in Tokyo, Japan.

For the past seven hours, he had been monitoring on his computer, slight earthquake tremors in the area of Mount Mayon, an inactive volcano, on the island of Luzon, in the Philippine Islands area.

The tremors were not very large . . . 2.2 on the Richter scale, but the fact that the rumbling of the earth was happening underneath a dormant volcano caught his interest and undivided attention.

He already contacted the proper authorities and experts whose direct responsibilities were to monitor all volcanoes on the planet.

Another seismologist . . . Tioto Fujiaka, arrived a few minutes later and joined Trevor Johnson at his work station.

He immediately asked Trevor to update him about everything he had been monitoring in regards to this dormant volcano . . . Mount Mayon.

Trevor spoke slowly, but very precise in transferring all of the information that Tioto requested.

"Mount Mayon is showing small scale activity of earth tremors within it's base."

"It has tremors have stayed basically the same on the Richter scale since the tremors started.

"We have had eleven tremors since I started monitoring."

Tioto's eyes widened with this bit of information.

Tioto slid a chair over to the work station alongside Trevor, and started to look at all of the information on the monitor.

Tioto asked . . . "Have the population of people that are near the volcano been notified?"

Trevor answered . . . "Some of the authorities that I contacted have that responsibility to contact the people that live in the area that could be affected if there happens to be a volcanic eruption."

Tioto answered back . . . "When was the last time that is was recorded that Mount Mayon erupted?"

Trevor pointed to the screen underneath the history column.

It indicated that the last eruption was August 10, 2008

There had been a warning by the Philippine Institute of Volcanology and Seismology . . . (Phivolcs) in the early part of December 2010 that the volcano was showing signs of another possible eruption, but it eventually quieted down to a dormant stage.

It also read that Mount Mayon, with a height of 8,070 feet had erupted a total of 49 times in recorded history.

The worst eruption occurring in February 1, 1814.

Trevor then blandly said . . . "Everyone knows that a volcano that is getting ready to erupt is very similar to predicting when a baby is going to be born to the world."

"It is unpredictable, and just happens when it happens."

"That's not to say that there are plenty of warning signs before the actual eruption happens."

Tioto shook his head in a silent affirmation to that statement made from Trevor.

All the two men could do at this point in time was to simply wait and monitor the situation as it occurred.

This is what these two men were hired to do, no matter how long they would have to be there, they would see this volcanic event to the end, whether it erupted, or fell back into a dormant stage again like so many other times in the past.

The two men would work in shifts, relieving each other to accomplish this latest assignment.

CHAPTER THIRTEEN

Marcos and his Father were waiting for an important man to arrive in the area at any time.

This man had been contacted very discreetly to examine the white stones that Marcos had found in the cave at Mount Mayon.

This man traveled all the way from Manila to get a look at these stones.

When Enrique mentioned to him that he thought that these white stones could possibly be diamonds, and that they were found in a cave at a volcano, the man immediately said that he was interested in looking at these stones, and that he would make arrangements to travel to their location and meet them the next day.

He advised Enrique to not tell anyone else about these possibly precious stones or proposition anyone else to have a look at these stones.

This man was named . . . "John Marin."

John Marin reminded Enrique of two things . . . one: he was a very well known expert in the field of Gemology, and two: for security and safety reasons for all parties involved with this meeting tomorrow, this knowledge could possibly become dangerous for them because of greedy people that certainly surround them.

Enrique told John Marin that he was already aware of the possible dangers of this knowledge becoming known to the wrong people.

The less people that knew about these possibly precious stones, the safer he felt about being in possession of them.

Enrique also agreed that it would be best to let a known expert in the field of Gemology, discreetly examine these stones that very well could turn out to be diamonds.

Enrique and Marcos waited patiently down the street from the local outdoor market place.

They waited for almost an hour before a motorcycle pulled up with a passenger in the side car.

A man lifted himself gingerly out of the side car, stretched his back in all directions, wiped his brow, and started to look around the area.

This man was John Marin.

John Marin was bald, and very well built body that made that made his clothes look tight and clingy.

The many years that he had spent working out in the field, climbing mountains, and chipping samples of rock in many parts of the world, had kept him in tip top shape.

Enrique and Marcos approached this man that they were very certain was John Marin.

They both had polite smiles and outstretched hands for shaking as they walked towards him.

Enrique spoke aloud as they got closer . . . "John Marin?"

John Marin answered back quickly . . . "Yes I am, and you are Enrique? And this is your son Marcos?"

Enrique acknowledged this return question with a nod of his head up and down.

The three of them just as quickly shook hands and proceeded to walk away from the market place.

Enrique was in the lead as they walked, and walked in the direction of the local bank.

Enrique had made arrangements with a very good friend who happened to be the banks manager.

Enrique explained to John Marin that he had safely and discreetly put the stones inside of a safe deposit box at this bank.

He also noted that only he and Marcos were the only people that knew that these stones were hidden away in a safe deposit box at this bank.

Enrique's friend, the bank manager, only knew that Enrique was putting something thought to be of value in the safe deposit box.

He had not even asked Enrique what was being put inside of the safe deposit box for safe keeping.

It took the three of them only a few minutes to arrive at the front entrance to the bank.

The bank manager politely greeted them immediately upon entering inside of the bank.

The bank manager walked them directly to the back of the bank.

This area of the bank was where the safe deposit box room was located.

He took a ring of keys from his pants pocket, unlocked the door, and motioned them to enter inside.

Once they were inside, he closed the door behind them and locked the door.

He then walked over to another door and used another key on the key ring and unlocked the door.

He opened this door and once again motioned with his hands in a slow sweeping gesture to enter this room.

This room was the viewing room.

Once the three of them had entered the viewing room, the bank manager closed the viewing room door and left them alone and departed.

Enrique went back out of the room and entered back into the safe deposit room leaving his son and John Marin behind in the viewing room to await his return with the safe deposit box that held inside what he hoped would be diamonds.

Enrique took a key out of his pocket and looked at the number that was engraved on it's surface.

The number on the key read . . . # 297.

He then walked quickly over to the wall that contained all of the safe deposit boxes.

He stood there for a few moments and scanned them whole wall full of three different size boxes.

He finally was able to find the medium sized box that had the number # 297 that matched the key in his hand.

Enrique put the key inside of the lock mechanism on the box and turned the key counter clockwise.

There was an obvious clicking sound in the air as he done this.

It was the tumblers lining up to clear a path, to easily open the door to gain access, and then slide the safe deposit box out of the slot in the wall.

He opened the door and grabbed a handle that was on the end of the box, and pulled it out.

The box was a long box . . . sixteen inches long to be exact.

Enrique now shut the metal door and locked it back up.

He then carried the box over to where Marcos, and John Marin were standing, and entered inside of the viewing room.

Marcos shut the door behind his father as he entered inside, and then locked the door.

They all sat down at a nice rectangular mahogany table.

John Marin leaned forward in great anticipation as Enrique proceeded to unlock the safe deposit box.

After the lock was unlocked, Enrique lifted the top lid of the box and opened it.

Enrique reached inside very casually with a giant smile on his face. Marcos and John Marin also had wide eyes and big smiles on their faces as well.

Enrique started pulling the stones out of the box and put them one by one on to the surface of the table in front of his son but closer to John Marin.

John Marin reached into his pocket and pulled out two items.

The first item was a jewelers loop.

The second item was a magnifying glass the size of the palm of his hand.

John Marin felt excited as he reached over and lifted a stone off of the table.

He next brought the stone up close to his face and the jewelers loop and started his examination.

He looked ever so closely and very meticulously at the stone for a few minutes without saying a word.

His eye brows would raise upwards here and there, but no emotion was detectable as he slowly turned the stone in his hand.

He then exchanged the jewelers loop for the larger magnifying glass and once again started his slow precise process of what now seemed like a very serious examination.

Now it appeared that his eyes were very noticeably wider than before the examination began.

After a few more minutes of looking at this stone, he put it down on the table and picked-up another stone for examination.

He repeated the same procedures with the next stone, and then spent the next forty five minutes looking very carefully at all of the remaining stones from the table.

Enrique and Marcos made sure not to distract him and quietly left him alone to do his professional work.

Finally, John Marin put the last stone on the table and looked at Enrique and Marcos with very excited widened eyes that seemed to be on the verge of bursting from their sockets.

He spoke casually and controlled . . . "I am very certain, in fact I am 100% very certain that all of these stones in their raw form that lie on this table before us are amongst the highest and best quality diamonds that I have ever had the pleasure to examine."

"In all my years in my profession, I have never seen diamonds in their raw form as good as these before us."

"I also want to add to my statement that the size of these stones are immense."

"What I am trying to say is that the size of all of these stones are comparable to the sizes of the largest stones ever mined from the Earth."

"In fact . . . I am positive that four of these stones are the largest stones ever seen by a human eye."

"These diamonds make the DeBeers diamonds and all others throughout the world, look like cheap crystals."

"I never imagined that quality could actually be rated at a higher level then the standard that is currently in place."

"These diamonds will create a new standard to rate the quality of all future diamonds!!"

"These diamonds . . . after cutting from their raw form, will easily be worth millions of pesos."

"Congratulations . . . you are officially rich!!"

Enrique and Marcos sat there stunned in their seats as they heard this news from John Marin.

All of a sudden, Enrique snapped out of his daze and started to put the precious stones back inside of the safe deposit box.

He then got up from his chair and proceeded to leave the room with the valuable safe deposit box and return it back to where he had retrieved it in the other room.

He made double sure that the box was in fact really locked amongst all of the other boxes on the safe deposit box wall.

Enrique stared at the box for a few more moments before going back into the viewing room.

Enrique, with much respect paid John Marin his commission, and bid him a farewell and safe travel back home.

Enrique received a personal promise from John Marin that the stones existence, and also how valuable they were now assessed by a professional, would remain a secret for as long as Enrique wanted it to be.

Enrique trusted this promise from this prominent world known and highly respected professional.

He was not worried at all about the possibility of this secret becoming known to anyone, except the people whom he chose to know.

Enrique and Marcos left the bank in a state of supreme shock and utter delight.

Enrique turned to his son and said:"Well son, I guess we will have to travel back to that cave and mine some more of those stones."

"O.K.?"

This short simple statement and half request from his father pleased him very much.

Marcos shook his head up and down excitedly to affirm . . . Yes!! Yes!! and Yes!!

He could not wait to get back to the special cave at Mount Mayon.

Marcos felt very important, because knew that he was the only person on the planet that had the knowledge of the exact location of this cave.

Enrique told Marcos that they would first have to make arrangements to sell the diamonds in their raw form to buyers that would be interested.

He further explained to his son that once these diamonds were in fact actually sold, they would then next put the money in the bank for safe keeping.

After this was eventually done, they could make plans to go back to the cave, and hopefully find some more diamonds to mine.

He once again reminded his son how very important it was to keep all of this a complete secret as John Marin had explained to them before his departure.

Indeed . . . one way, or the other, their lives would be dramatically changed forever.

CHAPTER FOURTEEN

As Yeshua sat at the table inside the "Beginning of life building of Nevaehruo," He thought for a few moments about the request to explain everything to Vernon Montague and John Crevelli.

Everything?

It was simply too much to tell and certainly too much to realistically expect for them to believe . . . everything??

So Yeshua decided that he would tell them quite a lot, but hopefully just enough for their minds to process in a manner that they would indeed believe and comprehend.

So Yeshua turned to the two men and said: "I will explain to both of you as much information as I think you will be able to hopefully believe and comprehend."

"I will do this after you both have had a chance to eat all of the food that I have provided for your consumption."

"So relax and enjoy the food."

John Crevelli and Vernon Montague acknowledged this and began eating their most favorite meals.

They both ate for over an hour, and were amazed how the drinks inside of their glasses stayed near full even after gulping down several swallows of liquid.

Both men privately had many questions and thoughts racing through their brains as they gorged themselves.

Yeshua sat patiently across from them and waited for them to finish their meals.

Finally, both men, one at a time, within moments of each other, leaned back away from the table and silently indicated to Yeshua that they could not eat or drink anything more before them.

Upon seeing this, Yeshua bowed his head slightly and waved his right hand over the table where the food and drinks were located, and in a blink of an eye, everything vanished from sight from the surface of the table!!

The two men that sat across from Yeshua were frozen in place with utter astonishment as they witnessed this unbelievable feat before them.

Vernon Montague looked over to Yeshua very intently and once one on one eye contact was made, he said to Yeshua . . . "With much respect, before you start speaking to us, I have just one quick question for you to answer."

Yeshua nodded back at Vernon that indicated silent permission.

Vernon asked . . . "All the people of the Earth think that you are a white skinned man, like me and John here."

"Your skin is very dark."

"We call these people . . . "Black people."

"How is this so with you?"

Yeshua simply smiled at Vernon and replied rather quickly . . . "The sun shines most of the time very hot across the lands where I walked the Earth as a man."

"Have you ever seen a person with white skin who lives in that area of the world?"

"Over the centuries, man has changed the truth of how I appeared as a man while I was alive."

"The creation of a religion after I left made many convenient statements to fulfill their needs."

Silence took over the room after this statement from Yeshua.

Both men sat and waited for Yeshua to continue to speak to them.

Yeshua sat silently for another few moments, and then began to speak slowly and very precisely.

"Do you both see all of those people over there?"

"All of those people who are walking into that area of this room where the light shines almost to bright for your eyes?"

Both men silently and respectfully shook their heads up and down that indicated a yes.

Yeshua continued to speak.

"Both of you . . . John Crevelli, and Vernon Montague, have walked through that lighted doorway many times."

"Even my wife Mary, my child that she gave birth to, and all of the generations of heirs related to me have also walked through that lighted doorway many times as well."

This statement caught both astronauts by total surprise.

It was a stunning statement to say the least.

It was a shocking statement that very much confused them.

Suddenly, John Crevelli asked: "How is that possible?"

"I do not understand."

Once again Yeshua continued to talk, but now he has a slight smile upon his face as he spoke.

"That lighted doorway is called the: "spark of life doorway.""

"Both of you have been born through the "spark of life doorway" many times over the many centuries since I have last walked on the surface of this planet."

"I will also say that it is very possible that both of you may walk through the "Spark of life doorway" and be born more times in the future."

Vernon Montague asked politely: "Is that what is called . . . Reincarnation?"

Yeshua answered: "Over time, man is born, and reborn, after I have given my approval after judgment."

"After this approval, I eventually allow them to walk through the "Spark of life doorway" and be reborn as an entirely different human being to walk the planet."

"Men on Earth have made this a term called reincarnation."

"But I call this: "Rebirth of the soul.""

"If at any time, in any of their lives, they choose to follow the path of blatant evil, then I cease to allow them to ever experience the "Rebirth of the soul," ever again."

"Their souls would then perish forever and become grains of sand, or even smaller than the eyes can see, and become dust particles to float around endlessly throughout time."

"All of those people that are walking through the "Spark of life doorway" are each the chosen sperm that will fertilize an egg within a womb."

"After judgment of the life they lived upon the planet, each one has been given my approval to experience the "Rebirth of the soul" once again."

As expected, both men who sat across from Yeshua were listening with the utmost respect, so far they were having a very difficult time in believing and comprehending this information, and ultimately accepting it's validity.

Yeshua continued to speak: "Almost two thousand years ago, I decided to be born as a man upon the surface of this planet from a womb of a female human."

"I decided that I would have the experience of walking upon this planets surface."

"I tried with much patient effort to educate the people that I met, the peaceful and honest knowledge that exuded from my soul."

"It was knowledge that would make the people of the planet more peaceful and honest with each other."

"I felt very troubled by what I was witnessing of man's many evil deeds upon one another."

"I lived as a man, in living flesh, feeling pain, mentally and physically, for a little over thirty years, and then allowed for myself to be put to death by crucifixion by the race of people known then as Romans."

"I never had at any time, an intention of a religion becoming born after my death, because of my death."

"But it did indeed manifest itself to become something that is now practiced by a very large number of people on this planet Earth."

"I am not of this planet that is called Earth."

"I am indeed one of many son's of an entity that you would call God."

But this one and only God has created many planets that are inhabited by similar people such as yourselves."

He designated his many sons . . . myself included, to become caretakers of the peoples souls on these planets to be reborn."

"There is no Heaven and there is no Hell on this planet or at any other place . . . anywhere in the vast universe."

"For you people of Earth, there is only this planet, it's resources, and human souls who are born into human flesh and reborn over and over throughout time . . . with my approval."

"When the planet becomes to populated with people, and it's resources become depleted to the level of not being able to sustain life anymore, or the amount of humans who choose to practice the ways of evil rises to the point that hinders the lives of people who make a strong effort to practice complete honesty in their lives, and threatens their demise, I then will return to the surface of this planet and purge the evil people to become the grains of sand, or the dust that floats in the air."

"Whenever the planet finally gets to a point that all of it's resources have become used, and is not at a level to sustain life any longer, I then bring with me the good honest souls, and relocate to another suitable planet and start over again."

"I have been through this process many times throughout time."

"Earth is but one of many planets that I have traveled to and started the rebirth of man and the rebirth of the souls."

"When I start over at a new planet, I always start the rebirth of man in a very primitive manner."

"I allow man to evolve over time to become less primitive, and eventually to a point of advancement that would allow them to leave the surface of their planet and be able to look down upon it from the skies above."

"During this period of evolution, it is sometimes necessary to advance man's knowledge, mainly in mathematical form, by some of my brothers who travel the universe."

"These same brothers of mine will sometimes deliver souls to planets when there is a shortage."

"This shortage of souls has often occurred over time because the choice to go down the path of evil was made."

"My brother's make sure that there are plenty of good souls for this planet, and any other planet in the future."

"My hope is always that man will be honest with himself and other's around him."

"I sincerely hope that evil will ultimately be cast aside to never be able to manifest itself within a human body ever again."

"Mankind on this planet Earth is now getting near the point that I have just described to both of you."

"I am very disappointed, once again, with the many people on this planet who have chosen to practice evil, and have made the decisions that affect the people who make the effort to be good and honest."

"When I was crucified upon two crossed pieces of wood that the religious people worship as the cross almost two thousand years ago as a man in the flesh, I promised the people who were with me during this painful experience upon the flesh, and before I traveled to this place where you both now stand before me today, I promised these people that I would someday return back to the surface of this planet Earth and start purging the people who practice evil over the people who are good and honest."

Yeshua stopped talking for a few moments to watch the two men's reactions to what he had just said to them.

Both men's bodies were tremendously frozen, and they were totally speechless.

But finally, Vernon Montague was able to overcome his ability to speak and spurted out, as he had been holding his breath . . . "When are you going to return back to the surface of our planet Earth?"

Yeshua answered this question back at Vernon Montague very casually.

"I will return in the last month of this year."

"You call this month . . . December."

"At that time, I will make my judgments upon mankind."

"I will start purging many evil people who I have concluded deserve this punishment."

"There will be some people who have practiced evil that I will forgive."

"This forgiveness will have a stipulation of extreme honesty toward himself and his fellow man."

"This stipulation will also be the rule of life for all humans who I allow to remain on the surface of this planet Earth upon my departure back here at Nevaehruo."

"I will explain to all of the people of the Earth this stipulation for continued life when I return to the surface of the planet in the last month of this year that you call 2012."

"Tomorrow, I will show you both the path to return back to the surface of the Earth."

"Both of you do not belong here at Nevaehruo at this time."

"Both of you came here by accident, and tomorrow will be the time for both of you to leave Nevaehruo."

"Someday, both of you, as you have many times over the centuries, will return back here to Nevaehruo and wait again for me to send you back through the "rebirth of the soul doorway" to experience life once again."

"The exception to this would be that if you make a wrong decision and choose the path of evil within your soul, then you would become just another particle of dust in the wind, or a grain of sand on the ground."

After Yeshua completed this last statement to the two men, he rose to his feet and motioned for both of the men to also rise from the table to their feet.

Yeshua made a hand motion to a female in the room to come over to stand before him.

He gave instructions to her to take Vernon Montague, and John Crevelli to a place where they could get some much needed rest before their departure from Nevaehruo the next day.

There was no sun that shined in Nevaehruo, light emanated artificially from the powers of Yeshua.

Nevaehruo became a lighted area, or a pitch dark place as Yeshua made it with his powers.

Vernon Montague and John Crevelli followed the female that had received instructions from Yeshua, out of the large building and they were led to a much smaller dwelling for their comfort for the night.

As Vernon Montague, and John Crevelli settled down for the evening in this new dwelling for some rest, they both noticed that the light that had shown through the window as they came inside, was now pitch dark!!

Because of all the unusual and unexplainable things that they had already witnessed Yeshua do with his powers, both men were actually now unfazed by the light transforming instantly into total darkness.

They both easily figured out that this was certainly the work of Yeshua.

Vernon Montague began to casually talk about the events that both men had witnessed since arriving at this strange place called Nevaehruo.

He talked about what Yeshua had told them as well.

He spoke out loud, not necessarily speaking to John Crevelli, but just letting all of his words spill out of his mouth so that he could wonder about the validity of everything.

John Crevelli eventually started to act separately in a similar manner, verbally shooting the words throughout the air in a very animated and excited way.

Both men were actually in a tremendous state of shock with their brains.

They did not, or could not actually fathom the supposed facts of the moment.

Brain registration was extremely intense for both men.

The scope of all of the information that their brains were trying to process at the moment was simply too overwhelming for them to accept as the real genuine truth . . . or actual reality.

Both men wondered if they were actually at Nevaehruo by accident as Yeshua had told them, or if they were really here at this place because Yeshua had made it so.

Both men had deep suspicions that Yeshua had made them travel here through his powers.

Accidents did not seem to be something that occurred with Yeshua.

Another thought between the two men was that maybe they were not actually here at this place called Nevaehruo.

Maybe they were actually in a deep slumber and they were maybe really just dreaming all of this.

They honestly did not have the slightest clue as to what their actual reality really was at this moment in time.

Finally, after both men spent almost an hour "babbling" about all of this, their verbal venting expired to near silence once again.

Their brains were at a point of extreme exhaustion, and the two men mutually agreed that they should try and get some much needed rest while they had a chance.

Tomorrow they would begin a new journey from this place.

Would the space capsule be left behind?

Would they travel back as passengers of the space capsule?

Both men had the impression that they were going to travel on foot back to the surface of their beloved planet.

Both men had slight fears that they might not make it back to the surface alive.

All they could do for now was to hope that they would eventually make it back safely to their respective homes and loved ones.

Home seemed so very far away from this alien place called Nevaehruo.

It really did not matter what the distance was to get home safely, they just needed to get there.

Once they did finally get home, would they dare tell their stories of what they witnessed at Nevaehruo?

Would they tell of what they had heard from Yeshua, or what they had seen with their eyes?

Maybe the two men would decide to make an agreement between them to never speak about all of this, and simply make-up a false story.

How would people react if they did indeed tell about all of what they had heard and seen?

More than likely, as is the normal nature of human beings, any people that heard their real story would think that the two astronauts had lost their conscience minds, or were simply fabricating a false story.

There would also certainly be a percentage of people who would be inclined to believe, and pass on to other's, that a great government conspiracy and cover-up had occurred.

Many different possible scenarios remained for both men in the near and far future, to be played out, and the repercussions would certainly be felt by many people.

The most important question though was . . . were the people of the Earth actually ready for the return of the being that they had worshiped for almost two thousand years?

Were the people of the planet Earth actually ready to experience the return of who they call . . . Jesus?

Were they really ready to see Jesus return to Earth in the flesh, and speak to them?

Were they ready for him to pass judgment upon them?

Millions of people had spent their lives believing that someday he might return to Earth.

Were these lifetime beliefs of his eventual return 100% deep within their souls . . . real?

Would the people of Earth really believe that this being called Yeshua was actually the same . . . Jesus?

The ultimate test of their faith would certainly be tested if indeed Jesus were to actually return and stand before them.

Would there be an instant denial of the identity of this being claiming to be the Jesus who walked the Earth two thousand years ago if he appeared before the millions of people of the Earth?

As this supposed possibility approaches mankind in the present day, All humans of the planet Earth would most probably experience the same feeling as Vernon Montague and John Crevelli did at Nevaehruo.

December of 2012 was not to far away . . . The time for Yeshua to start making his judgments were fast approaching the people of Earth.

CHAPTER FIFTEEN

Almost two months had now passed since Professor Ntangku had initially translated parts of the papyri from the clay pots.

Doctor Fortuk, Darny, and Suzie Howzer were now all in complete agreement with Professor Ntangku that the proper time had finally arrived, and the timing was right to let the information out about the translations of the ancient papyri.

Professor Ntangku was now officially finished translating these ancient papyri, and there was a mutual agreement, no matter how controversial the information was, to officially let the people of the world know of all of the contents, and analysis from this team of experts.

All of the information that Professor Ntangku had revealed after almost centuries, was absolutely astonishing to the normal person, let alone a professional as herself.

She had most definitely lost a lot of sleep while working on this very important assignment.

So it was now up to Dr. Fortuk to arrange a press release at a press conference with live reporters from around the world to announce their findings to the populace of the planet.

Dr. Fortuk decided to have the press conference outside in front of the National Museum of Egypt building.

This press conference would be set-up where Dr. Fortuk, Professor Ntangku, Dr. Darny, and Suzie Howser could sit comfortably at a distance from what was expected to be a sea of reporters.

They would sit there as a team . . . together, under pressure, as all eyes of the world were watching, as the many reporters directed their inquiring questions at them to answer in a professional manner.

All four people of this very special team felt anxious and nervous about all that would be said at this free-for-all question and answer session with many reporters from many news media outlets throughout the world.

Dr. Fortuk had also already arranged for several important religious scholars that represented the whole spectrum of religions throughout the world, to be at this press conference as special guests.

These religious scholars would also be able to ask questions and give their personal inputs as well.

A special envoy from the Vatican was also invited, but they had a condition of waiting for the press conference to end, and then they could have their own personal private session with this team of experts involved with this project.

Dr. Fortuk did not have a problem with this condition because there would not be anything that was said the press conference that would not basically be the same in a private meeting afterwards.

There would not be any information held back at the press conference.

This had been pre-arranged by the team before the press conference had been arranged by Dr. Fortuk.

All information compiled by Professor Ntangku would be completely transparent for all inquiring minds to digest.

So if the representatives from the Vatican expected to learn of any new information that was not presented openly at the press conference . . . it simply would not be the case.

The questions from the Vatican would most probably be redundant or worded differently from the reporters that had assembled at the press conference but their content would basically mean the same thing.

The team had previously went out together to very lavish dinners to discuss anything that might be on their minds that might possibly had not been covered up to the present time.

Together, they all drank their favorite alcoholic beverages well into the night after they finished with their dinners.

It was somewhat of a celebration between them in anticipation of such an important moment in time.

All of the members of the team finally turned in for the night with only scant hours to try and catch some sleep.

It turned out that none of them hardly closed their eyes before it was time to get out of their beds, shower, and get ready for this all important news conference.

It was now 8:30 a.m. in the morning . . . Egypt time, and the members of the team were making their ways to the front of the National Museum of Egypt building.

They all walked together, surrounded by bodyguards from the Egyptian Army.

The news conference was scheduled to start at 9:30 a.m.

As they came closer to the area of where they would be seated, they all could see the entire front of the museum was inundated with news trucks, satellite dishes, and hundreds of reporters ready to start their salvos of questioning.

The team was led to the side of the museum building, and followed the wall around until they came upon two long tables.

These tables were set-up directly in front of the waiting crowd of media.

These two tables had microphones already sound checked and placed directly in front of each chair at each table.

Dr. Darny felt a cold chill starting to run throughout his body as he approached the chair where he would be sitting.

Suzie Howser had a fixed smile on her face, it looked similar to the phony smiles that celebrities are known for when they want to pacify their admirers.

In Suzie Howser's case though, this smile was not to pacify, but to hide the fact that all of a sudden she was extremely nervous to the point of almost a "stage fright" type of feeling.

She did not understand why she felt this way.

She had been a public speaker on many occasions during her time at various University functions.

Onward she walked, towards her assigned chair right next to Dr. Darny.

Dr. Fortuk looked out at the crowd of reporters with a stern and very serious expression upon his face.

He did walk very stiffly though, as if he could not bend his knees or his back.

His walking looked almost like that of a penguins gate as it waddled across an icy frontier.

His walk was also a sign of nervousness that was to hard for him to try and hide from the many onlookers that now were in front of him.

He was also feeling a little "hung-over" from the alcohol that he had consumed the night before.

Professor Ntangku was nonchalant as she casually walked towards her assigned chair.

Of all four of the team, she was the one who seemed to exude the most obvious confidence about her abilities to handle these large media crowds.

Secretly though, she was also a bit nervous as well.

She just had the ability to hide it better than the other members of the team.

This announcement today was the most important thing she had ever been a part of in her entire professional career.

This was her own silent . . . in her head . . . personal realization.

She also realized that the other members of the team were experiencing their same realizations of importance for their own careers because of the larger than life announcement to the populations of people throughout their planet.

An announcement that was almost twenty centuries in waiting.

It was almost a subject, and a belief by millions of people throughout the world, and over the many centuries that had passed in time, that Jesus Christ would someday make his return back in physical form.

It would be a return back to the planet where he had once been persecuted and crucified upon a roman cross of two wooden planks.

All of the reporters presently sitting or standing in the mostly media crowd had not even the slightest clue as to what these four professionals that sat before them were going to announce to them in a few moments.

Even the people that had traveled across the globe representing the Vatican did not even really know what this announcement was possibly about.

All that anyone, besides the team that was seated at a table up above them on the top steps of the museum knew was that this was being hyped as the most important announcement in the history of all mankind.

That was all that anyone knew.

Rumors and speculation were traveling about like a wild forest with no end in sight.

Some thought that the announcement was extraterrestrial in nature, and others suspected that a great calamity, like an asteroid was going to crash into their planet, and wipe-out all life on the planet.

Interestingly, not a single person out of all these curious onlookers even, had a thought in the direction of the possibility that this announcement was about the return of Jesus Christ and his actual return back to Earth to make a final judgment upon his many faithful, and doubtful subjects . . . possibly this year!!

There was almost a carnival atmosphere in the air as the team of professionals were finally all seated and about to start talking to the gathered crowd.

It was agreed upon by the members of the team that Dr. Fortuk would be the one to officially start the press conference with a brief statement.

After this brief statement, he would turn every ones attention over to Dr. Darny.

After Dr. Darny was finished explaining everything in detail that he had done in relation to this secretive important project that was about to be announced, he would then turn every ones attention to Professor Ntangku.

Professor Ntangku would then give a very thorough statement about all of her meticulous findings and translations.

Suzie Howser would also eventually help field questions about her personal role with this gathered team, and make an attempt answer any other questions that she thought she could give a legitimate answer too.

Really, the two most important figures today during this press conference would be Dr. Darny and Professor Ntangku.

So now, all eyes were pointed towards the direction of the team at these two tables.

Dr. Fortuk started tapping the microphone in front of him with the backside of his right hand.

The microphone made a loud thumping sound as he did this . . . it was almost annoying, but it got every ones attention.

Dr. Fortuk started to speak into his microphone slowly, in a steady voice that surprised him.

He thought his voice would be shaky and crackly because of the nervousness he was presently experiencing, but low and behold, he was sure and steady as he continues to speak . . .

"My name is Dr. Fortuk."

"I am the head of Antiquities for the National Museum of Egypt."

"I have the great pleasure today to be a part of an announcement to the many people of our world along with these three people seated alongside me at these two tables."

"Now let me introduce to all of you the other three people seated alongside me at these two tables today."

"Sitting next to me here is "Dr. Darny."

"He is very well known throughout the world in the field of Archeology."

"I am very sure that many of you already know all about his professional achievements, and vast background in his field of Archeology."

"It is mainly because of his initial efforts, that brought the other members of this very special team together to work on this shocking project."

"Sitting next to Dr. Darny is his assistant and colleague "Suzie Howser."

"She is someone who has worked behind the scenes with Dr. Darny, and has not received all of the credit that she truly deserves."

"She is here today because she deserves as much credit for her professional efforts as any of the others that make-up this special team."

"I am sure that one day, maybe starting after today, that she will become a very well known figure in the field of Archeology as that of her mentor who now sits beside her."

"Now . . . finally, sitting next to Suzie Howser, is another very well known figure in her field of Ancient languages."

"It gives me great pleasure in introducing to you Professor Ntangku."

She is in her own right, as large of a giant in her field of Ancient languages as Dr. Darny is in his field of Archeology."

After this statement, Dr. Darny and Professor Ntangku looked at each other with smiles and slowly bowed their heads in silent recognition.

Dr. Fortuk continued to speak to the crowd before him.

"For many years, Professor Ntangku has been able to give to our world, a large pool of information, that she has taken the time to painstakingly and very meticulously, translate many ancient and lost languages, thousands of years from the past, to ultimately be understood in our modern languages of today throughout our vast planet."

"She has given many of us the pleasure of understanding how ancient people lived their lives, many centuries before our present day."

"Now that I have introduced to all of you today these great professionals sitting alongside me, let me take a little time to explain how this team came to be united to cooperate and work together on this very special project."

"A little over two months ago, I was surprised to be contacted by Dr. Darny."

"He was very excited and wanted to tell me about a find that his assistant, Suzie Howser had made."

"This discovery by Suzie Howser occurred in an unknown cave in a region of Egypt that had been looked over by many people throughout the millennia."

"This cave had been undetected because there was a huge boulder that covered its entrance."

"Dr. Darny made a request to me to bring the items that had been discovered by Suzie Howser, to the National Museum of Egypt to be professionally analyzed."

"At the time, Dr. Darny and I, did not have any real true idea how important these items would eventually turn out to be."

"Of course, because of Dr. Darny's well respected reputation, I did not even hesitate in giving him permission to bring the items that he had in his possession, here to our great museum to study, and ultimately figure out what they might be."

"I have to admit, I became a bit excited by this conversation with Dr. Darny, and also a bit intrigued."

"I wondered . . . what might these items be?"

"I knew that they had to be ancient, because of Dr. Darny's field of expertise."

"So, I was very anxious for Dr. Darny and Suzie Howser to arrive to the museum."

"I started to immediately make arrangements to accommodate them upon their arrival."

"It did not take very long for Dr. Darny and Suzie Howser to arrive here at the museum with their precious and fragile items."

"Upon their arrival, it was already pre-arranged that the items they brought with them would be put in a sterile and very safe area of the museum."

"After our initial investigation was made of the first of these items, it was mutually decided that another professional expert would have to be requested to come and help in further study."

"What we found initially was way beyond our professional expertise."

"At this time, we decided that Professor Ntangku would certainly be the perfect person to help us, if she were to agree to do so."

"After talking to Professor Ntangku about the items that we had safely stored at the museum, and explained to her our lack of abilities to progress any further in a professional study, With much delight, Professor Ntangku quickly made the decision to travel here to the museum and help us continue our study of these ancient items."

"Once Professor Ntangku arrived here at the museum, and started to make her initial studies and translations, we were impacted so immensely, and unexpectantly, that it was quickly decided that we needed to stay together and form a professional team to study these special and very rare items."

"I can assure you all, that the impact of what we will announce to you today will be very similar to how the four people of this team felt that day earlier this year."

"I know that the build-up to this mysterious announcement must be a bit frustrating to all of you."

"I am also sure that your patience is almost at it's very end."

"So . . . without any further waiting for this momentous announcement, let me now turn your attention to the distinguished Dr. Darny."

"I am confident that Dr. Darny will unleash a tremendous shockwave of information that will totally stun you all!!"

Dr. Fortuk turned and faced Dr. Darny and respectfully announced to the crowd in almost a whisper . . . "Dr. Darny?"

As Dr. Fortuk said this to Dr. Darny, he looked at him with what looked like a slight mischievous broad smile upon his tanned face.

Dr. Darny began to speak to the anxiously awaiting crowd.

"Hello . . . as Dr. Fortuk just announced to all of you, my name is Dr. Darny."

"I sit here before all of you, as Dr. Fortuk just explained, with newly found information that has been scientifically tested, and let tell you that this is the real deal."

"Me and my assistant, Suzie Howser, this beautiful lady that you see sitting next to me, explored the inside of an ancient cave."

"We had no idea at the time, that what we would discover inside of this cave, would be so absolutely wonderful."

"But let me back-up a bit."

"There was a giant boulder that had to be moved, that blocked the entrance to this cave, before we could even attempt to enter inside it's interior."

"After getting some much needed help from some very wonderful hard working men to move this large boulder from this cave's entrance was completed, me and Suzie Howser started our exploration of it's interior."

"After some time, slowly inching our way within the depth's of this cave, we came upon a section of the cave where we found some ancient pots."

"Much to our satisfaction, these ancient pots were sealed!!"

"Of course we were very excited by this find, but we really did not have any idea how important these pots actually were."

"We did suspect at the time though, that potentially, these pots might indeed might contain ancient papyri with ancient text written on them."

"So anyway, after we were able to gather all of these ancient pots from where they had been stored in this cave for possibly, and we thought very probably, many centuries, we made arrangements to have them transported and relocated to where they still remain today."

"They are safely stored here at this wonderful museum . . . the great National Museum of Egypt."

"Once these pots were safely relocated here to this wonderful museum, we made a wonderful discovery."

"Inside of these pots were what we had suspected and hoped for . . . ancient papyri!!"

"These ancient papyri indeed had text written upon them.!!"

We all mutually made the quick decision to find someone qualified, who could help us translate this ancient text that was written upon these papyri."

"As Dr. Fortuk already told all of you, we were very lucky and also very honored to be able to have the distinguished Professor Ntangku agree to come here and help us to translate the ancient language that was written upon this papyri."

"Professor Ntangku was indeed, after examining the first few papyri, able to translate the ancient language that was written on the surface of this very ancient, and very fragile papyri."

"Once she was able to get an understanding as to what these writings actually were, she quickly decided that she wanted to join our team of experts, and translate all of the remaining papyri within these ancient pots."

"She decided that no matter how long it would take, she wanted to completely translate all of these rare papyri."

"Also, once Dr. Fortuk, myself, and Suzie Howser understood what was written upon these first few papyri, we also decided with much pleasure, to work together as a team, until all of these writings were completely translated."

"Within a few hours on the very first day in the lab, and recording what Professor Ntangku was translating, we were all absolutely stunned beyond our imaginations."

"So now, we all sit here today, together, with the special honor of being the first humans to know what is written upon these ancient papyri."

"These writings are almost two thousand years old!!"

"The name of the man who wrote the text upon these ancient papyri was named . . . Ossismi."

"This man who walked our planet twenty centuries ago who went by the name of Ossismi, was the personal writer, who traveled everywhere, and listened to, and then wrote a vast amount of words from the mouth of a man whose name is known throughout the world as . . . Jesus!!"

After Dr. Darny said this, there was a loud clamor throughout the crowd.

Dr. Darny continued to speak after the crowd quieted down a few octaves on the sound scale.

"The actual name of Jesus, as many of you may or may not know, did not actually exist two thousand years ago."

"The actual name of the man that is referred to as "Jesus," is actually "Yeshua.""

"All Theologian scholars already know this as common knowledge."

"But the common person, such as ourselves gathered here today, may not actually know this fact."

"So basically, all of these papyri are the writings of "Yeshua" from the time of his marriage to Mary Magdalene until the day when he was crucified by the Romans."

Again, there was a loud clamor throughout this crowd, and someone screamed out . . . "Jesus was not ever married!!"

Dr. Darny paused to let this information sink in and to have a chance to observe and listen to the reactions of the people of this gathered crowd.

As he had thought, there would be much excitement throughout these people gathered before him and the team sitting alongside him.

After about a minute of sporadic noise, the crowd suddenly became very quiet, almost in a stunned like trance.

At this particular moment in time, it was amazing to see this large crowd of media specialists not making any efforts to make even the slightest faint sound out of their mouths.

The quietness of this moment was similar to a soundproof room with nobody inside of it. Many people now had their mouths wide open in astonishment as they tried to make their brains understand the magnitude of importance of what Dr. Darny had just conveyed to them.

After almost two long moments of this type of silence, and looking back and forth at each other without uttering a single word, the crowd once again started to bustle with a frenzied excitement that could be compared to a heavy sell and trade session at the famous Wall Street Stock Exchange.

There were now many shouts coming from this large crowd of anxious media.

Of course, being the media, the shouts were questions upon questions similar to bullets exiting the barrel of an automatic machine gun.

Dr. Darny raised his hand and spoke into the microphone with polite pleads to the crowd to quiet down so he could continue to speak to them.

The crowd finally started to quiet down for Dr. Darny, not to the extreme silence of a few moments before, but enough for him to once again start speaking.

Dr. Darny started to speak into the microphone again.

"Our team did not gather here today only to make this announcement to all of you before us, but our intentions are to also share with you some of the actual writings of "Yeshua.""

"So . . . for that to happen, I need for you all to now listen to Professor Ntangku at this time."

"For now, I am finished speaking to all of you until the question and answer session."

"That will happen when Professor Ntangku finishes talking to you about the translations that she meticulously uncovered from these ancient papyri from within these pots that I have already mentioned to all of you."

"Please remain patient as Professor Ntangku speaks of her findings."

Dr. Darny now turned his head in the direction of Professor Ntangku and silently shook his head up and down to affirm that it was her turn to speak, and that she now had every ones attention Professor Ntangku pulled her microphone closer to herself and proceeded to speak to the crowd of media.

"My name, as you have already heard from Dr. Darny, is Professor Ribandella Ntangku."

"As you have already heard from Dr. Darny, and Dr. Fortuk, I joined this distinguished team to help translate the ancient text that was written on the ancient papyri that were found inside of the aforementioned pots that laid stored away in a cave for almost two thousand years."

"I know already that there is a percentage of non-believers in this crowd that sits here before me as I speak."

"What I mean by non-believers is not that you don't believe in "Jesus", or actually "Yeshua", but non-believers in the sense of the authenticity of these writings."

"You are probably doubting that what you have heard so far is not factual, but simply not true."

"Of course, me, and the other members of the team anticipated this reaction."

"But let me now tell all of you today, I can categorically, and scientifically prove beyond all doubt, and back-up with solid evidence that what I will share with you today is in fact . . . true!!"

Professor Ntangku said the word "true" at the end of this last sentence with loud confident emphasis.

"Later on, after this press conference is over, we can go into minute details of everything we as a team did to validate these writings as the genuine "real deal!!"

"I will sit here today before you and risk my whole professional career to have you believe that these writings are indeed legitimate and very real."

"So let me now, whether you choose to believe us or not, give to you some precise details of what I have translated from these ancient papyri."

"This man Ossismi?"

"He witnessed the marriage between two people named Yeshua and Mary Magdalene."

"This man Yeshua, who we have already mentioned is the man worshiped throughout the world as Jesus, asked Ossismi if he would be at his side and write the words from his mouth, and observations of his actions in every day life."

"Yeshua asked Ossismi if he would write all of his words with complete permission and no editing."

"He wanted to make sure that when Ossismi wrote of his everyday life that his wife Mary Magdalene was mentioned as well."

"Ossismi agreed with much honor, to be Yeshua's personal writer until the day came when either Yeshua requested he do so no longer, or when Ossismi decided he did not want to do it anymore."

"So after this agreement was made between these two men, they basically lived together almost as a family until the day when Yeshua actually died at the hands of the Romans."

Mary Magdalene was also in agreement with this arrangement between these two men of many centuries past."

"Ossismi . . . from that day on, wrote the exact words of Yeshua and wrote of what he observed in the every day life of the man whose name would later, gradually over the centuries, change to it's modern day version of "Jesus.""

"Of course he also wrote of what he observed of Yeshua's wife Mary Magdalene as well."

"Ossismi also wrote about his observations of Yeshua's followers as they became more and more obsessed with his words of apparent wisdom and even just being in his presence."

"Ossismi observed how Yeshua became widely known, loved and also hated."

"He observed and wrote about how Yeshua was to become the "Great Messiah"."

"This "Great Messiah was supposed to return to his people to help them solve their many problems, and guide them to better ways to experience their lives."

"Ossismi wrote all of this upon these ancient papyri with much love and passion and very careful not to exaggerate even the slightest of details."

"He often wrote of how proud he was and how completely accurate he was in these writings that he felt would eventually be very important to mankind in the distant future."

"Ossismi loved Yeshua to the point that he would have gladly volunteered to be crucified instead of Yeshua.

He made this statement in these writings because he felt that it was important that Yeshua should spend more time as a living being upon this Earth to continue his teachings to his fellow man."

"Ossismi was truly a very honorable man who could be trusted to write the whole truth and nothing otherwise."

Professor Ntangku continued to speak to the crowd of media for almost another solid hour before she finally ended in saying . . . "Remember, I have only given to you today, the highlights of these writings upon these ancient papyri."

In the following days after today, I will put the entire translations of all these ancient papyri online for all the people of the world to see and read at their own convenience."

After Professor Ntangku finished talking to this crowd of gathered media, Dr. Fortuk took over once again started to speak into the microphone.

"Now you have all had a chance to listen to Professor Ntangku and Dr. Darny speak."

"Now we will give you all a chance to ask questions of anyone of the team sitting here with me, including Suzie Howser who has yet to speak."

CHAPTER SIXTEEN

Vernon Montague awoke from his deep sleep and looked over to the other side of the room to see John Crevelli stirring slowly, but still in a deep slumber.

Vernon Montague laid there on his bed and thought about everything that had happened to him the past few days.

Because of the knowledge that he and John Crevelli now possessed, he had a new and very different outlook on life.

He had always been very thankful with himself and everyone around him, but now he had to make a tough decision of whether or not he would lie to everyone about his experiences with Yeshua, and of this strange foreign place located who knows where, far beneath within the belly of the Earth.

He thought of what choice John Crevelli would make in regards to this strange unbelievable experience.

Vernon Montague decided that he would take a big chance, and tell everyone the absolute truth and whatever the repercussions were because of his forthrightness, he was prepared to deal with them, no matter the consequences.

The darkness in the room started to slowly change to light and disappear altogether.

From across the room, John Crevelli rolled over, opened his eyes, and looked over at his fellow astronaut.

John Crevelli cleared his throat and spoke aloud . . . "Well Good morning Vern."

"How long have you been awake?"

Vern answered back . . . "Oh . . . only a few minutes, maybe five at the most."

Vernon Montague rolled over from his bed and stood-up tall and started doing some slow stretches throughout his tired body.

This was something that he always did every morning upon waking up.

John Crevelli also rolled out from his bed and stood up to his feet and also did a quick reflexive stretch.

He walked over to a table that was located in a corner of the room and sat down in one of a pair of chairs.

After Vernon Montague was finished doing his stretching, he also walked over to the table and sat down in the remaining chair next to John Crevelli.

Within a minute from when both men were seated at their chairs, the door to this dwelling slowly, without announcement, started to open up.

Once the door was wide open, Yeshua walked into the room and faced the two astronauts.

This surprised the two men because of the casualness of this entrance.

Yeshua greeted both men as if this was a normal daily occurrence for all of them.

Yeshua asked the two men if they were hungry or in need of something to drink.

Both men replied back to Yeshua that they were indeed hungry, and both requested some coffee.

Almost instantly, and exactly as they had witnessed the night before, food and drink materialized in front of them on the table.

This time around though, neither man acted surprised by this.

In ancient times, this would have been thought of as a "miracle," but this was just something that Yeshua could do with hardly any effort at all.

Both men had come to the conclusion that this being before them calling himself "Yeshua," was in fact the being that had been worshiped for many centuries by the name of "Jesus."

They were now sure that everything that Yeshua had told them up to this point and everything that they had witnessed with their eyes, was absolutely true.

They both began to drink their perfectly tasting coffee and once again ate their most favorite meals for the early morning.

This time, Yeshua did not silently sit and wait for the two astronauts to finish their meals before beginning to engage in conversation with them.

Yeshua began to speak aloud in a comforting tone of voice, very slowly and precisely.

"Today, Vernon, and you John, are both going to start your travels back to the surface of this plane called Earth."

"When you are both finished with your food and drinks, I will have both of you escorted part of the way out of Nevaehruo."

"You will both be given the instructions that you will need to be able to make it all the way back to the planets surface from where you came."

Yeshua continued to talk to both of the astronauts, reassuring them both that they would complete their journey back to the surface safe and unharmed.

He inquired of both men about what decisions they had made about, if at all, did they have intentions to tell everyone about what they had seen, and heard, since being in the presence of Yeshua.

Would they do this once they were back amongst living breathing people on the surface where they could once again see the clouds in the daytime, and the stars in the skies at night time?

Vernon told Yeshua that he very much intended to tell the absolute truth about everything he had seen and heard, regardless of the consequences.

John told Yeshua that he was basically going to do the same thing as Vernon.

He would also tell everyone about his experiences . . . truthfully, and whatever happened there after because of what he said, he was prepared to handle anything that might occur.

Both men waited a bit nervously at this point because they were not sure how Yeshua would react.

Would he rather that they keep silent?, or because they had told him of their intentions, would he change his mind and not let them leave this place so far away form their fellow man?

To their surprise Yeshua was very pleased about their truthfull decisions.

He realized how hard it was for both men to make these decisions and told them that he was pleased and felt slightly proud of them.

In fact, Yeshua encouraged them both to give as much detail as possible, and not leave a single moment of their experience expressed from their hearts.

He agreed that there would certainly be adverse reactions, and most probably a lot of negative responses from all of the doubters of what they said to be the truth.

Yeshua wanted the return of these two astronauts, and the stories that they would tell of their experiences, to be the first unofficial contact between himself, and the people on the surface of the planet since his departure many centuries in the past.

It was time to let the people of this planet called Earth, that he still indeed existed, and that he would be coming back to the surface as these two astronauts would also be soon doing.

Even though, the majority of the people who would listen to the two astronauts would not believe them, Yeshua still thought that at least a seed of the possibility of their stories being actually true, would be planted on the surface, whether believed or not, would soon grow to the point of some belief when he did in fact finally return on December 21, 2012.

When he did return, he would make sure to do it in a fashion that would leave no doubt at all that what they were witnessing was indeed . . . his actual return, in the flesh once again, to stand before mankind once again after almost twenty centuries.

On the day of his return to the surface of the Earth, he would make sure that this event would be so unbelievable, and not humanly or scientifically proven to be possible, that all of mankind who were witness to this event . . . his return . . . would absolutely have no choice but to believe that what they were seeing with their eyes was the person known to them as "Jesus."

At some point in time soon afterwards, it would be explained to them that his actual name was in fact "Yeshua."

The believers, worshipers, non-believers, and non-worshipers would all agree between them as they witnessed this event, that Jesus has actually returned, in the flesh, back to Earth.

Both Vernon Montague and John Crevelli finally finished their early morning meals, and waited for Yeshua to commence with his plans for them to depart from Nevaehruo, and start their return back to the surface.

Vernon asked Yeshua . . . "With the obvious powers that you possess, why can you not just simply return us back to the surface with a wave of your hand?"

Yeshua answered back.

"Since both of you are still flesh and blood and with beating hearts, and functioning souls within you, I can only guide you both in a physical way for your return journey back to your homes."

"All of these good souls here in Nevaehruo do not yet have a connection with a physical body until I allow them to pass through the "Spark of Life door."

"If I was to use my powers, as you call them, to just materialize both of you back to the surface, which I can actually do, you would both lose your memories of your experiences here, and everything that I have told you since your arrivals."

"It is my intention to make sure that your memories do in fact remain intact, so that you both will be able to relay to the people of the surface, that indeed, my return back to Earth is imminent."

"I want people to know that my return will no longer be just talk anymore, but in fact once and for all, after almost twenty centuries, as I had promised Mary Magdalene . . . my wife, and my friend and personal scribe Ossismi as I departed the flesh on a Roman cross, that I would return to give judgment, and speak to people once again as I am right now with both of you."

"Even now, as I speak, a chain of events have already been set in motion that will give people a clue as to when I will actually return back to the surface of this planet."

"There were writings of my daily life by my dear friend Ossismi before my departure from the flesh, that were recently found in a cave by people on the surface."

The discovery of these writings were supposed to be found, and coincide with the time frame of both of your arrivals back on the surface."

"As you both begin to speak of your experiences here with me, some people may come to the realization that yours stories, combined with the writings that were recently discovered, might give a true indication that I may indeed be returning back before them."

Vernon Montague and John Crevelli were a bit surprised by the news of these recently discovered writings and that it now appeared to them that they were a part of a plan to give the people of the Earth a forewarning of Yeshuas return.

They would be a part of what appeared to them to be a grand plan that was most probably prepared by Yeshua long ago when their souls lived in other bodies throughout the past centuries.

Yeshua rose to his feet and motioned the two astronauts to follow him outside of the dwelling.

Both men walked behind Yeshua out of the dwelling, and towards the outer edge of Nevaehruo to an entrance of a very small cave that blended in with the background.

Yeshua bid farewell to them, and told them that he would see them once again in the future.

Yeshua motioned the two men over to him and showed them, by pointing, a path that would lead them part of the way into the small cave, and then he gave them verbal instructions of how to take the proper path that would lead them all of the way to the top surface of the planet.

Yeshua reassured the two men that they would be successful in their journey back to the surface.

After saying this to the two astronauts, Yeshua very casually turned his back away from them and started to walk away.

Yeshua did not look back at the two men as he continued his walk back to the souls of Nevaehruo.

Both men silently wondered about when they would ever see Yeshua once again as he had just told them before he departed.

Would they see him as flesh and blood men, or would they see him as souls again in Nevaehruo?

This was a question that would only be answered as time progressed in their lives.

CHAPTER SEVENTEEN

Professor Ntangku, as she had promised, put all of the information that she had compiled since she joined the team, on the internet for all of mankind to see.

The team also, as pre-arranged and promised, met with representatives of the Vatican, and also with other religious people of other religions, to have a private meeting away from the media.

Professor Ntangku could only smile to herself as she reminisced this private meeting with no media present.

She closed her eyes and pictured that meeting in a slight daydream while she sat back in her comfortable lounge chair in her office.

The meeting started with a man from the Vatican called . . . "Father Stephano Kelossi."

He was all "fired-up" with an almost uncontrollable amount of energy, and waste any time with his questions.

He started by asking . . . "Do you, Professor Ntangku, believe in the Almighty God?"

Professor Ntangku answered back to him very casually . . . "That question is irrelevant, and much too personal for me to answer to you directly."

Father Kelossi started to shake both of his fists at the relaxed professor.

He began to speak once again, in obvious anger.

"O.K. I understand your response to my question, but I do not agree with your answer because of the possible importance of what you have told people at that media circus."

"So let me ask a few other questions . . . o.k.?"

"Whether or nor you believe on the Almighty God or not, and I am going to just assume that you do, would you possibly be influenced to believe that all of your research is indeed correct because you want everything you say to be true?"

"Did you come out with these supposed facts because you want to be known throughout the world as the person who gave mankind relevant information about "Jesus," the son of God?"

Professor Ntangku laughed aloud at these questions, and calmly . . . showing much respect, answered back to this Vatican Father Kelossi.

"All I did Father Kelossi, was to translate an ancient text into modern day English."

"That is what I do for a living, whether it brings to me fame or not."

"Without sounding to you conceded, I am already well known in my field throughout the world."

"I am certainly not a "Glory monger.""

"There definitely was not any type of personal influences involved while I did my job as I always do."

"All I really did was look at an ancient text that was written about two thousand years ago, and translate it into a modern day language so everyone who reads it would be able to easily understand the meanings."

"I never added or subtracted any of the translations from the ancient papyri found in those ancient clay pots."

"I translated every single ancient text, word by word, exactly correct, and without a doubt."

"Whether I want to be famous for just doing my assigned task within this select team of experts that was quickly formed, or not to be recognized for my professional efforts, is something that is far beyond my control."

"I imagine that because of the sheer magnitude of what these translations entail, that I have utilized my professional expertise will have such a profound effect on a large amount of the population of people of the world."

It is very probable that I will have my "15 minutes of fame," one way or the other."

Father Kelossi was silent as he digested this last statement from Professor Ntangku.

At this time, Dr. Darny, and Suzie Howser wanted to speak out loud, not to just Father Kelossi, but to all of the other religious people gathered at this pre-arranged meeting as well.

Dr. Darny spoke first . . . "We are all professionals in our respective fields of study."

"As was explained at the press conference, all we basically did was find some ancient clay pots inside of a well hidden cave that was hidden for nearly two thousand years."

"This cave had a huge boulder at it's entrance that required a large amount of man power to extract."

Thanks to the help of some very hard workers at this site, we were able to extract this boulder from it's resting spot and finally had the opportunity to enter inside to explore."

"Certainly, this boulder had been in front of this cave opening for as long as the clay pots were hidden inside."

"I can say to all of you today, that I am indeed a true believer in the almighty God, and that everything that I ever knew about "Jesus" was what I had read in the Bible, and taught to me by religious people such as yourselves."

"I was not influenced by my belief in God to somehow make the findings of the clay pots, or the translations of the ancient text on the papyri more than they actually were at the time of discovery."

"There is absolutely no exaggeration about anything in regards to the items discovered within this ancient cave."

Suzie Howser spoke-up . . . "I was there inside of this cave when all of these items were discovered."

"I was actually the first to lay eyes on those ancient clay pots."

"I was also present when the clay pots were unsealed and the ancient papyri were brought out to the world for the first time in almost two thousand years."

"What we have here is very genuine."

"It is as real as we are as people sitting here today!!"

"Everything has been meticulously made 100% transparent, every single step of the way."

"All precautions were taken to insure that this was done in a way where nobody could ever doubt the validity of the final analysis made by our team."

"These papyri are real."

"The text that was written on these ancient papyri was by a man called Ossismi."

"He walked this Earth over two thousand years ago during the same time period as the man called "Jesus."

"Through scientific testing, we know this as a scientific fact!!"

Father Kelossi interrupted Suzie Howser to speak.

"O.K., maybe what you just said . . . a man calling himself Ossismi wrote the ancient text upon those ancient papyri, but do you have evidence that this man Ossismi was not just some man from those ancient times who wrote an unbelievable story all on his own, and he was not actually at the side of "Jesus" as he did these writings?"

"How do you know that this man Ossimi was actually in the presence of Jesus?"

"I say to you . . . there is absolutely no evidence that I can see from your team, that these ancient writings were not just writings from a man who said that he was with Jesus as he wrote upon the papyri."

"I suggest that the actual fact is that he was alone, and what he wrote was fabricated."

"I say that all of what he wrote was from his imagination."

"He might have been a very good fictional writer today if he lived in our modern times."

All of a sudden, there was a loud outburst from everyone inside of the room.

It became uncontrolled verbal chaos.

Everyone in the room were talking at the same time and it seemed as if everyone wanted to speak louder than the other people around them to get their points of views heard.

At this particular point in time, the scene could be compared to a crowd of a cattle auction.

It appeared that all of these religious people had indeed been very skeptical before the press conference, and now it also appeared that they had the same opinions as Father Kelossi.

It looked like a 100% mutual consensus of non belief of the findings of the team.

Dr. Darny stood up to his feet and spoke louder than everyone in the room.

"People, I know that this is a very controversial subject for all of you gathered here today in this room."

I also know that most, if not all of you do not want to accept our findings as fact."

"It is also true that what Father Kelossi has just conveyed to us about the man called Ossismi who wrote the ancient text upon these papyri, could in fact be a true assessment."

"There is no real proof that this ancient man calling himself Ossismi was actually with Jesus when he wrote these ancient text upon the papyri found in those clay pots."

"But I can say that at the very least, these translations are indeed almost two thousand years old."

"I can also say that these papyri, and the clay pots have been scientifically tested and proven to be from the same time period as when "Yeshua," whom you all refer to as "Jesus," lived."

"The ancient language is also the exact language from that particular time period as well."

"Whether or not, any of you here today want to believe in the contents of this translated ancient text to be true or not, it is certainly your personal choices, your opinions are not important to me, and I am sure that the rest of the members of this team feel the same as I do."

"So now we have done our parts for all of the people of the world to see and analyze for themselves."

"All of the people of the world who will read these ancient text will all come to their own personal opinions, and beliefs as you all have here today."

"I guess that the only real way that we will ever have a definitive answer as to whether or not all of these translated ancient text is in fact true or not is pretty simple actually."

Father Kelossi asked instantly . . . "How is that Dr. Darny?"

Dr. Darny answered slowly and with a very broad smile upon his face as he spoke.

""The text basically said that "Yeshua" . . . or whom you call "Jesus" would indeed return to this planet we call Earth for all of mankind to witness in the last month of this very year!!"

"The actual month is supposedly . . . December."

"All we can really do at this time now is to wait and see if he does show-up in December of this year."

After this final statement from Dr. Darny, this private meeting quickly ended with all of the gathered people respectfully shaking hands with phony smiles upon their departures.

Professor Ntangku snapped out of her daydream, shook her head back and forth quickly, and started to concentrate on her next task at hand.

She would, until December of this year, answer all of the questions on a blog in regards to the writings of Ossismi.

Little did she know at this time was that when December actually did arrive in a few short months, her findings would turn out to be true.

The world would be more stunned and shocked then it ever has been in all of recorded history!!

CHAPTER EIGHTEEN

John Marin, the well respected man in the field of Gemology, went back home with a secret that was extraordinary.

What nobody really knew about John Marin was that he had fallen on hard times.

In fact, he was currently living in a state of desperation.

He pondered for much time, the secret of the amazing diamonds that he had recently held in his hands in the bank.

Thoughts that normally would not enter into the realm of his brain started to manifest and multiply.

Greed was now the driving force behind these thoughts.

John Marin knew of some people in the world of diamond sales that were always on the lookout for new diamond finds throughout the globe.

These people would certainly pay a very healthy "finders fee" to anyone that could give them the information about where to find a new discovery of diamonds.

John Marin felt a jolt of guilt as the overpowering feeling of greed fought with the honest integrity that was indeed his lifelong and proud reputation.

The combination of his desperate need for money to survive the way his lifestyle was accustomed too, and the fact that the information he had in his head was being overtaken by greed with a capital "G" was giving John Marin a tremendous soul searching headache.

This extreme soul searching was finally defeated by this greed after three days in total solitude.

Once John Marin made the decision to approach the people in the diamond industry that could give him a finders fee, and maybe more on a side deal, he started the process of contacting the people that could arrange a meeting with these people.

It took less then 24 hours to have a meeting set-up for the next day at his home.

These people would actually come to meet him in the comfort of his own home to make him feel as comfortable as possible, and minimize any pressure or thought of changing his mind about giving them the knowledge that they would no doubt, pay a handsome price for.

The next day seemed to come quicker then normal, maybe because of his anxiousness for the prospect of obtaining a large sum of money.

It was now only a matter of minute before these people were scheduled to arrive at his modest home.

John Marin paced the room like a caged tiger.

He felt a feeling of nervousness and excitement at the same time within his body.

There was also a little doubt mixed in with a slight paranoia floating on the edges of the other feelings.

Thoughts of the possibility of being killed after giving up the secret of these valuable diamonds loomed within his cranium as he continued to pace the room.

Finally, there came the sound of his antique chimes of his doorbell that echoed throughout his house.

John Marin quickly walked to his front door and peered through the peephole on the door.

As he looked through this tiny glass window, he could see two faces of Caucasian males dressed in finely tailored, very expensive, three piece suits.

One of the two men carried with him a briefcase.

These two men did not have even the slightest of what could be called a smile upon their faces.

They were very serious looking in nature.

The serious look on the faces of these two men actually made the nervousness that John Marin had been feeling . . . escalate to the point of almost changing his mind about going through with this meeting.

He had a fleeting thought to just not answer the door.

John Marin stood there for several more moments contemplating this thought as he continued to study these two men.

The man without the briefcase reached up and rand the doorbell once again.

After ringing the doorbell one more time, this man showed an obvious frown of impatience upon his face.

He glared over at the other man with the briefcase who stood shoulder to shoulder with him on the tiny porch.

Upon seeing this somewhat scary frown from this man, John Marin decided not to have these men wait any longer, and finally opened the door and let these two total strangers inside the confines of his home.

John Marin spoke aloud as he turned the doorknob on the door.

"I am opening the door!!"

John Marin pulled the door open wide all the way to give both men plenty of room to enter.

He greeted both of these strangers with a polite "hello," and extended his hand towards them to shake if they wanted.

Each man shook his hand very firmly and entered through the doorway into his home.

John Marin motioned for them to follow him into his study at the other end of the house, and up one level to a second story.

The two men were quiet as they followed John Marin.

Once they all arrived at the study, John Marin walked over to his desk at sat down.

The two men took seats in chairs across from him.

They both sat side by side . . . now expressionless, almost "zombie" like.

The man with the briefcase put the big leather case on top of the desk in front of John Marin.

John Marin asked both man very casually if they would like to have a drink.

Both men quickly declined with a shake of their heads back and forth very stiffly.

The man who had put the leather case onto the table reached over to the case and opened it up.

He lifted the lid of the case all the way back until it also rested on the table.

Inside of this case was a lot $100 dollar bills with the faces of the long dead men on the currency staring blankly ahead and instantly enticing John Marin.

There was silence in the study for a few more moments before the man who opened the case began to speak.

"So . . . John Marin, we have traveled all the way from London for this meeting."

"My name is Rex Ruppert, and my partner here is Spencer Ziegler."

"I am the "money man," and negotiator, and Spencer here is actually my body guard."

"You are probably wondering at this moment, how much money is inside of this case that sits before you on the table top."

"Am I correct?"

John Marin's eyes widened as he shook his head up and down silently to indicate . . . yes.

Yes indeed, he was very curious about how much money lay inside of this case only a mere foot away from him.

Rex Ruppert continued to speak.

"I am not going to tell you the amount of money that site before your greedy eyes."

"We will negotiate a deal, and I am confident that we have enough money in this case to come to an agreement."

"Now John Marin, you have indicated to my people that I represent, that you have held raw diamonds in your hands, owned by another party, and that you want to receive a finders fee in exchange for the information that we would need to pursue the place where these diamonds originally came from."

"Is this all correct?"

John Marin cleared his throat and answered this question from Rex Ruppert.

"I do know if you are aware of my credentials in the field of Gemology, but the fact is that I am renowned in this field."

"Yes indeed, I have recently held some of the most impressive diamonds in their raw form, that I am very sure, cannot be equaled, anywhere in the world."

"The clients who hired me to validate with my professional inspection, these spectacular raw diamonds made me promise them to keep he existence of these diamonds a total secret."

"I also promised them with mush reassurance that I would also keep their identities a secret as well."

"But, because of my current financial situation, I am forced to lower my integrity to a level of extreme greed."

"These people know of the exact location where I am sure that there are massive amounts of diamonds to mine."

"These diamonds, I can certainly assure both of you, are absolutely of the highest quality that I have ever laid my eyes upon in all of my years as a professional in the field of gemology."

"These people that possess these diamonds that I have held in my hands, and who also possess the knowledge of the location of where these diamonds were found, are of very simple means."

"I am sure that these people can easily be convinced, by money, to let you know where these diamonds were found, and where I am sure that there are others as well."

"Personally, I do not know where to find these diamonds, but without me breaking a promise I made to these people, and passing the information of their whereabouts to you, for the purpose of talking to them, you would never even come close to finding these precious stones."

"So . . . can we start negotiating some kind of deal?"

Rex Ruppert answered back immediately.

"If I give you money today in exchange for where these people can be found who possess the knowledge of where a possible diamond mine can be found, how do I know that you will not simply take the money and burn me and my friend here with false information, and maybe disappear?"

John Marin shrugged his shoulders and then coyly answered this question.

"If I was stupid enough to attempt to do something like that, I am smart enough to realize that I would not be able to hide from you and the people that you represent forever."

"Also, my career in the field of Gemology would for sure come to an abrupt end."

"I would have to hide in fear for the rest of my life, that is simply not something that I would ever want to do."

"I guess, because I do not have an actual diamond in my hand to show you that I am indeed telling you the truth, I can only hope that you will let me use my reputation as collateral."

"I could put up my house as physical collateral . . . in writing, with a lawyer making out legal documents, until you have personally met these people that I speak of."

Rex Ruppert thought this over for a moment, and then spoke very precisely.

"There will be no need for you to put your house up as collateral to prove that you can be trusted with the information that you are passing on to me."

"How about telling me how much money that you desire before you give to me the location of where I can find these people who know where these diamonds came from."

John Marin looked at the briefcase carefully.

He tried very hard to guess how much money might be inside it's four leather borders.

John Marin estimated that there was probably around $500,000 dollars inside.

So when John Marin said this calculated estimate out loud to Rex Ruppert . . . "Five Hundred thousand!!" Rex Ruppert stared into John Marins eyes very intently in silence before responding to that number thrown out into the air of the room.

Rex Ruppert laughed a little, and then replied back to John Marin with a very stern look upon his face.

Spencer Ziegler also laughed out loud as he sat there with his partner.

"We can sit here for hours and negotiate about the amount of money that you should or could be paid for the information that we traveled here to attain, but you know what I have decided to do?"

John Marin looked across from the table quizzically and shrugged his shoulders in silent curiosity, and waited for the answer to Rex Rupperts question.

Rex Ruppert answered finally.

"I am quickly going to agree that $500,000 dollars will be a good enough amount to give to you."

"Now if you try to increase this amount by even one single dollar, I would have to start lowering my offer considerably."

John Marin was caught completely by surprise by this sudden possible agreement.

He felt a deep sense of anxiety of the pressure of this moment in time.

Rex Ruppert and his partner, Spencer Ziegler, sat silently, staring at John Marin.

They both waited for an answer.

The walls of the room seemed to be inching from all directions towards John Marin.

John Marin started to get a feeling within himself that was very claustrophobic in nature.

All of a sudden he felt like a trapped animal that had no means of escape.

John Marin had a hard time trying to breathe a complete lung full of air.

He was not hyperventilating, but his breathing was definitely a laborious task.

Spencer Ziegler applied a bit of pressure to John Marin by saying . . . "We don't have all day to wait for you to give us an answer about accepting this deal."

John Marin spoke softly.

"I need to get a quick shot of whiskey to calm my nerves first."

"Are you both sure that you would not care for a shot of whiskey as well?"

Both men shook their heads side to side to indicate that they were not interested.

John Marin went over to the other side of the room and reached up on a shelf.

He moved two large books aside.

Behind these books was a decanter that contained some good old fashioned American made whiskey . . . "Jack Daniels."

John Marin grabbed a tall glass near the decanter and poured enough of the potent brew to fill half of the glass.

He then very casually, lifted the glass to his mouth and chugged down all of the whiskey in three quick gulps.

He exhaled heavily after doing this and then put the glass down and put the decanter back behind the books and slid them back to their places on the shelf.

John Marin looked over at these two men from across room and still felt a little nervousness linger through his body.

But the greediness that had crept into his soul was still in total control.

At this very moment, he decided that he was going to accept the offer of $500,000 dollars cash from Rex Ruppert, and Spencer Ziegler.

John Marin had officially crossed the line of integrity, and over to the dark side of blatant non-caring greed.

He did not care anymore about the safety of either Marcos or his father.

All he cared about now was getting that tax free half of a million dollars in his greedy little hands.

He also was anxious to have these two intimidating men leave his home forever.

John Marin walked over to the table and sat down.

He spoke now with a little more brave authority in his voice.

"Give me the money, and let me put it safely away in my safe, and then I will give to you both all of the information that you traveled here to get from me."

Rex Ruppert quickly answered back at John Marin.

"O.K.!!"

"Lets do it!!"

Rex Ruppert nodded at Spencer Ziegler and motioned with his huge hands to get the money out of the confines of the case, and give it to John Marin.

John Marin was practically holding all of the air inside of his lungs as his anticipation grew immensely.

Spencer Ziegler opened up the lid of the case full of American greenbacks and turned it towards John Marin and spoke.

"I do not know how you were able to figure out how much money was inside of this case, but you estimated the amount right on the dot . . . Five hundred thousand dollars!!"

John Marin looked at all of the one hundred dollar bills staring blankly . . . unflinchingly . . . back at him.

Spencer Ziegler next instructed John Marin to count the money.

"Count it all!!"

"It's all there!!"

John Marin took less then five minutes to take the wrapped one hundred dollar bills from the case and stack them on the table in front of him.

He created a pyramid of a famous American founding father in front of himself, and now had the largest smile upon his face that almost looked like his mouth was connected to the bottom of each of his ear lobes.

The amount in front of him was indeed, exactly $500,000 dollars!!

John Marin told the two men that he would be back in a few minutes after he put the money away safely within the interior of his personal safe.

Suddenly, Rex Ruppert pounded his large fist on top of the table surface and spoke in a very mean tone of voice.

"Let me tell you right now Mr. John Marin . . . "You will tell us what we want to know first!!"

"Then you can take this money on the table and put it safely away in your safe!!"

"That is how this deal is going to go down!!"

"Not any other way, otherwise, we will take this money and depart your home immediately!!"

Once again John Marin was completely startled by this aggressive demand from Rex Ruppert.

His body started to shake really bad, and he had an instant ill feeling.

He was now officially really hyperventilating, and the effects of the "Jack Daniels" whiskey did not help at all to calm his suddenly shattering nerves.

Rex Ruppert again pounded his fist on the table surface, but this time he stared silently into John Marins eyes.

This stare was one that would be seen from a dangerous homicidal maniac before committing a horrific crime against another human being.

John Marin felt very frightened now.

He was blinking his eyes very rapidly.

One more time, Rex Ruppert raised his fist up in the air and was about to pound it one more time down upon the table.

Upon seeing this physical gesture once again, John Marins voice blurted out loud.

"O.K . . . . O.K."

"No problem guys, no need to get all bent out of shape."

"I understand, it's a mutual trust thing."

"Even though we really do not know each other . . . it is definitely a trust thing."

"Let me tell you both verbally, and also write down in detail everything as I am telling you, so you do not have to hear me repeat myself."

At this moment, Rex Ruppert smiled.

He unclenched his fist, and put it back down onto his lap area.

Spencer Ziegler sat silently, but he also had a wry smile upon his face as well.

John Marin grabbed a pen and a tablet of lined paper from another table nearby.

He opened the tablet cover and began to speak very slowly and precisely.

"There is a young man, actually a boy, who goes by the name of "Marcos."

"His full name is . . . "Marcos Salvadore Magsaysay."

"The other person is his father."

"His father goes by the name of . . . "Enrique Batista Magsaysay."

"This young boy . . . Marcos, found a cave somewhere in their homeland."

"Their homeland is on an island of one of the vast chain of Philippine islands that stretches across the South Pacific ocean."

"The name of this island is . . . "Luzon."

"The province where the city is located, where they live is called . . . "Albay."

"The name of this small city is called . . . "Legazpi city."

"I am also very sure that the nearby volcano . . . "Mt. Mayon, is where this cave is most likely located."

"Only this boy Marcos knows of the exact location of this cave that has the most precious diamonds probably on the entire planet."

"Not even his own father Enrique knows of this exact location."

"I personally held these diamonds in my hands!!"

"Not only are these diamonds of the highest quality that any man might ever see with their eyes, or even imagine with no great exaggeration, but they are also are very large in size!!"

"I am not exaggerating when I say the diamonds are very large, I mean these stones that I held for several minutes at a time were absolutely HUGE!!"

"I am sure that if you travel to this Legazpi city, you will not have any trouble in finding these two people who might possibly give to you what you want in regards to what I have told you about these precious stones."

"Let me also tell you that these same precious diamonds that I held in my hands are located very securely in the confines of a bank in Legazpi city."

"These very same diamonds that I keep referring to are located within a safe deposit box at this bank."

Marcos father . . . Enrique, is in possession of the key that holds these diamonds inside of that safe deposit box."

John Marin stopped speaking.

He now watched for Rex Ruppert to say something in reply.

Silence now dominated the room.

This silence continued for several minutes as all three men pondered their next move.

Finally, Rex Ruppert spoke.

"So John Marin . . . is that really all of the information that you have for us?"

"Have you written all of the exact details on that paper tablet of yours for us?"

John Marin simply answered . . . "Yes I have."

Rex Ruppert spoke again.

"What if I told you now . . . John Marin, that we would need to actually meet this boy . . . Marcos and his father Enrique, and have them show us these diamonds that you speak so highly of, before we finished this deal and let you keep this money?"

"I mean, what if you are lying to me?"

"What happens if we leave this money with you and we travel to Legazpi city and find out that these people do not exist?"

"What if these supposed diamonds are a figment of your imagination?"

"By that time, you could be long gone with this money."

"Do you understand what I am now conveying to you?"

John Marin could not talk, he was very stunned by these questions from Rex Ruppert.

He continued to listen to this scary man called Rex Ruppert.

"So John Marin, I have a very simple plan."

"I am going to leave my friend Spencer here with you to stay until I have a chance to verify the information that you say is true."

"Once I have met this boy named Marcos, and his father Enrique, and also have seen the diamonds that are supposedly in a safe deposit box in the bank, I will contact Spencer, and you of course, and Spencer will then depart your home, and leave behind all of this money for you to keep."

"Do you have a problem with what I am saying to you now?"

Spencer Ziegler started to put the money back into the case.

He quickly, and very methodically dismantled the pyramid of stacked one hundred dollar bills.

He dad them back into the case in less then one minute.

Rex Ruppert raised his voice and almost hollered at John Marin. "Well?"

All John Marin could do was weakly shake his head to indicate that he would go along with this newest proposal.

Rex Ruppert lowered his voice and spoke more softly now.

"Furthermore, John Marin . . . if it happens to turn out that you lied to me and Spencer, and wasted our time, and almost ripped us off of this money, I promise you, Spencer will introduce you to his best friend."

After Rex Ruppert was finished saying this to John Marin, Spencer reached inside underneath his suit jacket shoulder area into a hidden gun harness and revealed a very large pistol . . . he had an even larger smile upon his face as he did this.

John Marin slumped in his chair.

CHAPTER NINETEEN

Enrique spent the past few days trying to find the right people in the diamond industry that would possibly interested in purchasing the raw precious diamonds hidden away in the safe deposit box at the bank.

It turned out to be way more difficult than he had imagined it would be.

Also, the few leads that he did get, wanted money up front before they would help him garner this information.

Unknown to Enrique, was the fact that there already was an interested party that wanted to meet him to see the diamonds that Marcos had found at the cave at Mt. Mayon.

But selling these diamonds to this person was not necessarily a guarantee by any means.

This person . . . Rex Ruppert, already knew of Enrique and his son Marcos.

He was in fact, already traveling to Legazpi City to find Enrique and his son Marcos to talk to them about the diamonds that they had in their possession.

Unfortunately, Enrique was not aware of this.

It would only be a matter of just a few more hours before Rex Ruppert was to arrive in this small Philippine city near the great Mt. Mayon.

Enrique woke his son Marcos from his comfortable slumber and told him that they would be going to the market place to stock up on food for the next week.

This was a weekly ritual that the two of them shared that was not always an enjoyable task, but obviously very necessary.

Marcos had a pet monkey that would sometimes tag along with him when he left their small dwelling.

This monkey had the playful name of "Kevvy".

Today Kevvy decided that he did not want to go with Marcos and his father.

He wanted to just kick back and relax, just have a lazy monkey kind of day.

Marcos did not force him to go.

He just left him alone after Kevvy screeched at him.

So Enrique and Marcos departed their home and started their short journey to the market place.

Meanwhile, a ferry boat was only half of an hour away from tying-up to the pier at the local boat landing.

The ferry boat tied up at the Legazpi City port once a day.

It would spend the night, and then return back to one of the other neighboring islands.

It was on a continuos cycle of travel within the many islands.

Rex Ruppert was on this ferry boat, and he was very anxious to arrive in Legazpi City.

Rex Ruppert carries a disassembled hand gun on his body inside a single nylon carry bag that draped his shoulder.

The gun parts were mixed in with computer wires and other assorted electronic parts to avoid detection by any security that may check the bag.

These parts on his body were all plastic parts that were easily capable of avoiding any scanning from any metal detection devices that might check him.

Rex Ruppert had successfully traveled the world with this gun in this manner for many years.

He had never even come close to being caught.

The Sun was blazing hot as usual.

The air had the normal humidity lingering throughout the valley where Legazpi City sat like a cat waiting for a mouse to come out of it's hiding place.

A half of an hour later, the heaving lines for the ferry boat were cast to line tenders on the pier.

The ferry boat quickly tied up it's mooring lines to the giants cleats like it had a thousand or so times in the past.

Rex Ruppert just as quickly, disembarked the ferry boat to dry land off the pier.

As Rex Ruppert was now touching his feet to dry land once again, Enrique and Marcos were about half finished with their shopping at the market place.

They were not in any particular hurry because they did not have any other plans for the rest of the day.

So they continued to barter the vendors at the market place for the best deals of the day as Rex Ruppert started to make his way into the heart of Legazpi City on a hunt for them.

Rex Ruppert had a plan to con Enrique and Marcos.

The con would be enough to see the supposed diamonds in the supposed safe deposit box at the bank.

After verification that these diamonds did in fact exist, the next step in the con would be to convince Enrique that he was indeed interested in purchasing the diamonds from him and his son.

He would also at that point use any means necessary to also find out where these diamonds actually came from.

The plan was actually a very simple one . . . find the location of where these supposedly most precious diamonds in the world could be found, and hopefully, later, they could be mined by the people that he represented.

Rex Ruppert was not really interested in purchasing any raw diamonds from anyone.

He was only in fact, really interested in finding out where these raw diamonds originated from so he and the people that he represented could hopefully have access to many more.

Rex Ruppert was in fact a very dangerous man at this moment as he pondered his plan in his head.

He had a very cruel and sadistic feeling that fluttered at the highest point of evil and greed.

He walked over to an outdoor bar and bought a bottle of beer.

He did not dare drink any local water because of the fear of getting sick.

While he was at this outdoor bar, a few native girls approached him and asked him if one of them could sit with him and then buy a drink for them.

Rex Ruppert thought that he could possibly get some cheap information from one of these girls about maybe where he could find Enrique and Marcos, so he told all three girls that they could sit with him and he would buy all of them a drink.

The girls giggled at him, and quickly sat down.

They motioned for someone to bring a drink for each of them.

They would next try to convince him, if he desired, pay a "bar fine," and take one of them to a hotel room for a quick session of sex, locally referred to as a "short time."

Rex Ruppert was already aware of this little cat and mouse game that was played by many females around the world in various countries to try and wrestle him of his money by bribing him with their bodies for sex.

He played along with their little game.

"I am a bit lonely for some female company."

"Maybe I can have a "short time" with one of you ladies?"

All three girls squealed in delight at this proposal and proceeded to try and convince him that one of them would be the best choice for the "Short time."

One girl rubbed his thigh under the table, another girl licked her lips in a sensual manner, and the other girl grabbed his right hand and placed it on her thigh area.

He removed his hand from her thigh quickly.

He spoke at the three girls in a low firm voice.

"How about all three of you girls take me for a short time?"

The three girls looked at each other and giggled once again.

One of the girls replied . . . "I have to go get our "Mama san if you want to do as you say."

Rex Ruppert nodded his head in agreement.

A few minutes later, an older lady walked over to the table where Rex Ruppert sat with the girls.

This lady . . . basically a bar pimp . . . sat down next to Rex Ruppert and greeted him.

"Hello mister."

"Are you interested in one of my girls, or all three as one of my girls told me?"

Rex Ruppert quickly replied.

"I am a very lonely man who would really like to have all three girls for company for the rest of the day and over night if that is at all possible."

"I will pay for them whatever your price is."

The Mama san looked him over, up and down and smiled at Rex Ruppert silently.

She spoke once again.

"You no hurt my girls?"

"Nothing kinky?"

Rex Ruppert replied back firmly.

"I would never in the world ever think of harming any of these beautiful young ladies."

All three girls giggled at this in unison.

Mama san shook her head up and down in a gesture that affirmed that it would be alright for Rex Ruppert to take all three girls for the rest of the day and all night.

A cash deal was quickly agreed upon, and all three girls left with Rex Ruppert to go to a hotel room nearby a few blocks away near the market place.

Rex Ruppert and the three girls entered the hotel room on the third floor at the end of the hall.

Once inside of the room, Rex Ruppert made sure the shades to the window were drawn, and the door to the room was locked securely behind them.

He motioned the three girls over to the bed.

They all three conformed to this request right away.

They also started to take their clothes off as they nestled on the lumpy bed.

Rex Ruppert told them to stop taking their clothes off.

The girls acted very surprised by this request.

They all had confused looks upon their faces.

Rex Ruppert pulled a chair over near the bed where the three girls continued to sit . . . confused.

Rex Ruppert spoke softly to the three girls.

"Now ladies, do not act all surprised that I do not want to engage in sex right away with any of you."

"We have plenty of time for all of that."

"We have all night . . . right?"

All three girls giggled and shook their heads that indicated that yes, they understood.

Rex told the girls that for right now, he wanted to talk to them about something very important.

He told them that he would pay them extra money if they could answer some questions for him.

All three girls agreed with much delight.

Rex Ruppert started to ask the questions that he hoped would lead him to the people that knew the location of the diamonds.

These two people . . . Enrique and Marcos Magsaysay.

"I am looking for two people."

"These people are a father and son."

Their names are . . . "Enrique and Marcos Magsaysay."

All three girls looked at each other with coy smiles.

One of the girls spoke.

"We know these two people, we want money first, before we give you the information where to find them."

Rex Ruppert smiled with very obvious pleasure.

He spoke once again.

"O.K. girls, let me give you some money and then you can tell me where to find these two people."

Rex Ruppert reached inside of his alligator skinned wallet and pulled out U.S. American currency.

He asked the girls if they would prefer American money, or their national money called the peso.

They all agreed, without much hesitation, that they would prefer the U.S. American dollars.

Rex Ruppert pulled out of the wallet, three one hundred dollar bills and flashed them to the girls.

The girls reached out to grab the money like a pack of wolves vying for a piece of raw meat.

Rex Ruppert pulled the money back towards him quickly.

He spoke once again.

"Not to fast ladies."

"This money will be yours, once you give me the location where I can find the two people that I mentioned . . . Enrique and Marcos Magsaysay."

One of the girls blurted out loud.

"O.K.!!"

"They live in the Santiago Barrio."

The other two girls agreed out loud that this was in fact a true statement.

Rex Ruppert asked the obvious question upon hearing this new information.

"Where is this Santiago Barrio?"

"Where in this Santiago Barrio do they live?"

All three girls held out their hands at the same exact time, almost like a practiced routine.

Rex was going to get angry and more firm with them because he already told them he would not give them the money until he had the information, but he decided to relent, and just give them the money to get this information . . . right now!!

"O.K. ladies . . . here is the money for you."

All three girls grabbed at the money like the desperate people that they were.

Once the girls had the money safely in their hands, one girl spoke very softly.

"Enrique and Marcos Magsaysay go to my church, and I have known them my entire life."

"You are not going to harm them are you?"

"If so, then I will return your money to you, and I am sure that my friends here will do the same."

Rex Ruppert said aloud to the girl that spoke, in a tone of voice that was borderline mean.

"I am only looking for these two people because I want to talk to them."

"What I want to talk to them about is very important, and they will surely be very happy after I talk to them."

"I promise you that I have no intentions whatsoever to harm them in any way."

"I have very good news for them."

"They might be getting a lot of money if all goes well."

The one girl finally sighed and relented the information that would lead Rex Ruppert to where he would be able to find the two people that he sought.

"These two Magsaysay's live just around the corner from where I live."

"I can show you their exact place where they live if you would like me too."

Rex Ruppert shook his head that indicated that no . . . he would not want that at all.

He told the girl to just give him the address, and he would hire a ride to take him there.

The girl gave him the exact address.

Once Rex Ruppert received the address from the girl, he turned to the three girls and told them to stay here in the hotel room until he returned from his visit from the Magsaysay's.

He reminded them that he had paid the Mama san money for them to be with him over night.

The three girls giggled once again and stretched out upon the rickety old, often used bed.

Rex Ruppert got up from his chair and departed the hotel room to go and find the location of where the girl had told him that he would be able to find Enrique and Marcos Magsaysay.

He felt an extreme rush of adrenaline shoot throughout his body at the thought that he was getting very close to completing want he had set out to do since leaving his partner behind with John Marin.

If all turned out well, and indeed the existence of the diamonds was really true, then he would contact his partner, Spencer Ziegler and give him further instructions how to deal with John Marin.

Rex Ruppert walked out of the hotel and waved over to him a driver of a motorcycle taxi.

The driver pulled up to him and skidded to a halt and asked him where he would like to go.

Rex Ruppert gave the address to the driver, he looked at the address and nodded, and off they sped, to this destination.

They weaved in and out of the congested traffic, not even hardly slowing down.

It seemed as if this driver could have easily gotten into a wreck several times in the few minutes that it actually took to get to the requested destination.

Finally, the motorcycle came to a halt, and the driver stuck out his hand to be paid.

Rex Ruppert quickly paid the man.

Rex Ruppert looked at the place where the two people that he sought supposedly lived.

It was an old brick structure with two alleyways on either side, and many people on both sides and in front of it.

He walked casually over to the front of this structure.

He asked a woman near the doorway if this was the place where the Magsaysay's lived.

The woman told him that this was indeed the place where the Magsaysay's lived.

Rex Ruppert smiled, and thanked the woman and walked closer to this doorway.

Once he got to this doorway, he knocked on the door very loudly to make sure that someone who might be inside would for sure here the knock.

After waiting a solid minute, without anyone answering, he once again knock very loud on the door.

After another long minute, there was still no answer to his knock on the door.

So now Rex Ruppert decided that he would go around the back of the dwelling and see if he could enter inside without anyone noticing him.

There was a small door on the backside of the dwelling that looked as if a five year old child could easily knock it down with a very small push.

Rex Ruppert looked around both ways to see if anyone was noticing him as he came closer to this wimpy door.

He could not see anyone that was watching him as he came right up to the door.

Again he looked around to make sure no one was watching him.

Again, he noticed nobody looking at him.

So now, in one smooth swift motion, he grabbed the door handle and pushed open the door.

He entered inside and closed the door behind him.

Right away, out of nowhere, Rex Ruppert was attacked.

The attacker was a small monkey.

He was on Rex Ruppert's back, on top of his shoulders, and starting to bite on the neck area, and scratching with sharp claws everywhere that he clung onto.

This surprised Rex Ruppert immensely.

He grabbed this little violent primate from his shoulders and threw his across the room where he bounced off of a table near the far wall.

This little monkey screeched loudly as he hit the floor.

Rex Ruppert was not aware of the fact that this monkey lived here in this dwelling and his name was "Kevvy."

Kevvy, was hurt badly by this, but was able to scurry away to another room nearby.

Rex Ruppert followed Kevvy.

Blood dripped from his neck and shoulders because of the scratches and bites that Kevvy had left.

Rex Ruppert felt the anger of someone who wanted to commit murder.

His intended victim weighing a scant six and a half pounds.

Poor Kevvy, he did not have a chance against someone like Rex Ruppert.

It was only a matter of time before Kevvy would be going to monkey heaven.

Rex Ruppert entered the room where he saw the little primate scamper to and looked around as he blocked the doorway.

Kevvy was hiding in the closet inside of a bamboo basket.

Kevvy squealed slightly, but it was just enough for Rex Ruppert to hear and make his advance on the poor little primate.

As Rex Ruppert now stood in front of the closet, blocking any escape, he reached down and grabbed Kevvy by his exposed tail and flung Kevvy across the room very hard.

Kevvy once again bounced off of a wall, and came down hard to the floor with a dull thud.

This time, Kevvy did not move, his neck was broken.

Rex Ruppert walked over to Kevvy to make sure that he was not acting like he was dead.

He picked Kevvy up from the floor and hung him upside down and swung him back and forth like a pendulum.

Kevvy was as limp as a strip of well cooked pasta noodle.

There was no doubt that his monkey spirit had departed the furry little body that once played throughout this dwelling.

Rex Ruppert carried his dead victim into the other room where he had entered the dwelling and flung Kevvy over to the floor near a ratan chair.

Rex Ruppert next started to look throughout the dwelling for anything that he could find that indicated anything about diamonds.

He completely tore the entire dwelling apart, all three rooms plus a storage space near the back door.

He found absolutely nothing that made any kind of connection to diamonds.

Finally, Rex Ruppert pulled the ratan chair over to the doorway entrance to the dwelling and took a seat.

It was time to play the waiting game.

He would now wait for the father and son who lived in this dwelling to return home.

He had his gun out and laying upon his lap.

An evil smile stretched across his face as he gazed in the direction of the poor little monkey that he had killed.

Evil thoughts raced through his brain as he made a plan on how he would deal with Enrique and Marcos once they finally returned to their home sweet home.

He also had other evil thoughts about how his partner who still remained with John Marin, would deal with the gemologist.

He chuckled slightly about that particular situation.

It was not really a matter of . . . if . . . John Marin was going to be eliminated in due time, but . . . when . . . would be the right time for Spencer Ziegler to carry out what he always considered an enjoyable task.

His main enjoyment in life, torture and ultimately murdering a sniveling victim.

Unfortunately for the unaware John Marin, he would not get any money as he had greedily hoped.

Oh no . . . he was going to eventually become a horrible victim of murder at the hands of Spencer Ziegler.

He would meet the same fate as poor Kevvy had at the hands of Rex Ruppert.

Meanwhile, unknown to Rex Ruppert, Enrique and Marcos were only a matter of a few minutes away from returning home to their dwelling.

The two unsuspecting Filipinos's were definitely in for quite a surprise.

The second hand silently circled on Rex Ruppert's Rolex watch as he continued his wait.

CHAPTER TWENTY

Vernon Montague and John Crevelli walked through a small cave and saw three separate pathways before them.

As instructed by Yeshua, they walked down the center path of the three path's.

He told them to always stay on the center path, no matter if it went down or up, stay in the center.

Yeshua told them that staying on the center path was the only way of eventually exiting the vast network of caves that lie before them.

They stopped a few times to rest and to eat and drink before continuing their arduous journey back to the surface of their planet . . . Earth.

They actually did not do much talking along the way, they just concentrated on moving along at a sustainable pace.

If they would have had pedometer's upon their shoe's, they would be able to see that they had traveled a distance of seven miles since they departed Nevaehruo and Yeshua.

They trusted the instructions that Yeshua had given to them in regards to how to successfully make it to the surface.

All of a sudden, the ground around them started to shake tremendously.

Both men stumbled forward.

Neither of them fell to the ground.

They maintained their balance, and stood together for a few moments.

They waited for the trembling ground to stop it's violent motion under their feet.

After almost thirty seconds of intense ground movement, the shaking dissipated back to a complete calmness.

Both men looked at each other, still remaining silent, and then started back to walking down the center pathway.

They walked for several more hours before they finally stopped to eat once more and to get some sleep.

They were exhausted to the point that their bodies felt like they had run an Olympic marathon at an all out sprint as if it were actually a hundred yard dash.

It only took only a few minutes for each man to fall into a deep slumber, and dreams of finally making it home to their friends and loved ones.

After the two men were asleep for about an hour, suddenly there was a loud fluttering noise.

Both men awoke from their sleep to pay attention to this loud noise that seemed to get louder by the second.

About ten seconds later, they were finally able to see what the loud noise was.

Bats!!

The two men had been using handheld chemical tube lights, commonly called "chem lights" for lighting the pathway for them as they traveled.

Each man had a portable backpack with essentials, and the "chem lights" were one of them.

Even though the illumination from the "chem lights" was not that good, just well enough to see the pathway, they were easily able to determine that what was now flying through the cave system where they were located was definitely bats.

There were so many bats that the two men could only hunker down low to the ground and feel the wings of these many bats pass by them.

There must have been millions of these bats, because it took almost fifteen minutes for all of these bats to finally pass by them on their own journey.

After the bats had finally disappeared somewhere ahead in the cave system, the two men agreed that they had enough strength to continue their journey for a little while longer.

They also agreed, and concluded that it was a good sign to see these bats, because they both knew that bats had to depart the cave system in order to go outside and search for food.

This conclusion excited them and made them think that maybe this cave system would finally come to an end very soon.

They traveled for almost two more miles of a real treacherous area of this cave system and finally made it to an easily manageable track once again.

They could go no more at this point, and decided once again to try and get some sleep before continuing their journey.

They were asleep in mere moments once they laid down upon the ground.

CHAPTER TWENTY ONE

Trevor Johnson and Tioto Fujiaka were still monitoring the seismic activities of Mount Mayon on the island of Luzon in the Philippine islands area of the Pacific Ocean.

They had already witnessed many tremors from this area since they started officially monitoring for a possible volcanic eruption from the famous Mount Mayon.

The people that lived in the area of Mount Mayon did not really think much of the tremors because they had felt many tremors throughout their daily lives.

What they actually did not know though, was that even though the tremors beneath their feet felt like normal movement, the reality was that Trevor and Tioto were indeed documenting that the tremors were actually becoming more powerful and coming more often as time went by.

Soon, there would be official representatives sent to the island of Luzon to warn of a possible eruption of the giant mountain that was located on their island home.

It was also very possible that these representatives might be accompanied by some Philippine National military types to help start an evacuation of the island.

The tremors were not yet often enough, or powerful enough to warrant such action, but on a scale of one to ten, it was almost halfway there.

This invisible scale would have to be at least a seven or an eight before such action could take place.

Trevor and Tioto would be the people responsible for passing on official word to the proper authorities of what they would believe to be an imminent eruption of Mount Mayon.

Before this type of important information could be passed on by Trevor and Tioto to the authorities responsible for alerting the Philippine government, they would have to be absolutely sure of what they were witnessing, and show valid proof of what they had recorded up to the moment.

The two men worked in overlapping shifts so they could get proper sleep between them.

Each shift was eleven hours with an overlap of an hour so information could be passed along, and they could analyze the data together.

Both men agreed that there was most probably going to be an eruption of the sleeping giant volcano, Mount Mayon, at some point in the very near future.

For both men, this would be the biggest thing that they had experienced since entering this field of study.

For Tioto, he had been around earthquakes and volcanic eruptions throughout his childhood as he grew-up in the Pacific area where this was quite common.

For Trevor, on the other hand, he had never experienced anything of the sort.

He grew-up in an area of the United States where the biggest event from mother nature might be a large amount of rainfall followed by some mud slides.

Nevertheless, here he was halfway around the world, on the verge of being a witness the a tremendous event from mother nature.

Earthquakes, and volcanic eruptions.

How exciting for him to be lucky enough to have this opportunity to safely experience such events.

Unlike the residents of the island of Luzon, who would eventually have to be evacuated to a safe zone.

All these two young men could do for now was to just continue doing their assigned jobs, and keep monitoring and gathering pertinent information about Mount Mayon until it was time to officially notify the proper authorities.

CHAPTER TWENTY TWO

Enrique and Marcos walked around the corner and came to the door of their dwelling.

Enrique fiddled with the key in the lock of the door for a moment before turning the door knob to the door with one hand while the other arm was occupied with a bag of food from the market place where they just came from.

They did not have any idea that on the other side of this door was a man with bad intentions for both of them.

Rex Ruppert stood ready with his gun now drawn directly at the door and waiting for the two people to enter to a big surprise.

Rex Ruppert had put his "silencer" on his gun just a few minutes before so as to not draw any attention in case he had to fire off a round or two.

The door opened slowly.

In walked Enrique with his head down, not yet noticing what was in front of him.

At the same time that Marcos stepped inside of the room behind his father, Enrique looked up to see Rex Ruppert pointing a gun at him and his son.

Rex Ruppert told both of them in a calm voice to sit down.

Marcos was shocked beyond belief, as was his son.

Enrique sat down first, still holding the bags of items that he had bought at the market place.

Marcos was still standing up, frozen in his tracks, unable to command his body to do as this man with the gun had just told him and his father to do.

Enrique, realizing that his son was not obeying the order from this man, and fearing that his son might have harm come to him, verbally snapped at Marcos . . . "Sit down Marcos!!"

Marcos was finally able to sit down near his father.

Just as Marcos sat down, he noticed on the floor nearby, the lifeless body of his dear friend Kevvy.

It was very obvious to anyone who were to see this small primate on the floor, that he was very dead.

As this realization came to register with Marcos, a feeling of extreme anger and fear materialized at the same time.

He felt like attacking this man who had obviously did this to poor Kevvy, but the fear of joining his small furry friend held him back from doing this.

Instead, he was able to scream out at Rex Ruppert . . . "Why did you do this to my Kevvy!!"

Rex Ruppert laughed at Marcos in a low tone of voice, and did not answer the question from the saddened boy right away.

Instead, he pointed the gun at Kevvy, and shot a silent bullet into the lifeless, unmoving monkey.

The bullet was so silent that one would not have known that a shot was fired from the gun unless they had watched the gun be pointed at the body and fired, and then observe the body from the impact of the fired bullet, slide several inches along the floor.

This made both Marcos and his now petrified father jump both at the same time.

Again there was sadistic chuckle from Rex Ruppert directed at both of the frightened people before him.

Enrique, with a trembling voice, asked Rex Ruppert why he was in his house.

He told Rex Ruppert that there must be some sort of mistake.

Because he and his son were not rich people, and had nothing valuable to take.

He pleaded with Rex Ruppert to please just leave his home and he promised that he would not go to any authorities about what was now happening.

After letting Enrique snivel for a few minutes, Rex Ruppert pointed the gun at Marcos with a huge smile upon his face as he wavered the gun slowly up and down.

Enrique screamed in a low voice ... "Please do not harm my son!! ... please!!"

Rex Ruppert now pointed the gun over in the direction of Enrique and tilted his head sideways in almost a confused way.

Rex Ruppert's smile turned into an ugly frown.

He spoke slowly with a lot of aggression beneath the words as they came out of his mouth.

"Actually ... you do have something of value that I have come here to get from you!!"

"You may look like a poor man, but the reality is that you are on the verge of becoming a very wealthy person."

"How do I know this?"

"Does the name of "John Marin" sound familiar to you?"

"Let me warn you right now ... if you give me an answer that turns out to be a lie, I will shoot a bullet into your sons knee."

"Well ... ?"

Enrique answered back to Rex Ruppert.

"It is true."

"I do know the man named John Marin."

Rex Ruppert once again smiled broadly, because now he really did know for sure that the possibility of the story about the diamonds that John Marin had told him and his partner Spencer Ziegler was most probably in fact very true.

An exciting rush of adrenaline passed throughout his body as he came to this realization about the diamonds.

He gathered himself and once again started to speak to Enrique who was now looking sadly over towards his son.

"Look at me!!"

Enrique quickly complied, and gave Rex Ruppert his total attention.

"John Marin told me about some very large diamonds that your son found, and now they are supposedly stored in a safe deposit box at a bank."

"Is this true?"

Enrique answered back feebly.

"Yes . . . it is true."

"There are a number of large diamonds that my son found in a cave at the large volcano on this island, and they are now being stored in a safe deposit box at the only bank in the area where we live."

Rex Ruppert looked silently over at Enrique, listening to this very good news.

He spoke again, but now in a normal voice.

"Look, I really do not want to hurt you or your son, I just want for you to give me the diamonds at the bank, and then tell me the location of where this cave is located where your son found the diamonds."

"I will even give to you a few of the diamonds for you to keep so that you can improve the quality of your lives."

"Of course, if you were to tell the authorities about any of what we are talking about, I would have to make sure that you and your son end up the same as that monkey over there on the floor."

"Even if I were to be arrested, I guarantee you, there are people that would make sure that both of you would become very dead."

"If you want to take that chance, and gamble with your life and that of your sons, then that will ultimately be your choice that you will make."

"I did not come here to kill you or your son, or even that damn monkey over there on the floor."

"He attacked me, and so I did what I had to do."

"All I want is for you to go to the bank and retrieve those diamonds and bring them back here to me."

"I will wait here with your son while you do that."

"After I get these diamonds, then you will tell me where this cave is at the volcano."

Enrique spoke.

"I will go get the diamonds for you, please do not harm my son."

"I promise that I will not tell anybody about you being here at my home."

"As far as being able to tell you exactly where this cave is located, we cannot tell you, we would have to show you."

Rex Ruppert thought about that for only a few moments before he answered back.

"I do not have a problem with being shown exactly where this cave is located."

"Actually that would be much better than being told, because I could then get a GPS location stored away.

GPS was a foreign word to Enrique, and so he did not ask what that term meant.

Enrique spoke once again.

"I need to leave as soon as possible because the bank will be closing shortly."

Rex Ruppert was totally all for that, and agreed that Enrique should leave right away and go to the bank to get the precious diamonds from the safe deposit box.

Once again he warned Enrique with the reminder that he was sitting here in his home with a gun pointed at his son.

Enrique shook his head to confirm that he understood this statement from Rex Ruppert.

Enrique stood up slowly.

Rex Ruppert waved the gun in the direction of the door and spoke one more time.

"Hurry-up . . . get those diamonds back to me quickly!!"

Enrique walked cautiously over to the door and opened it.

He looked back at his son as he walked out through the door into the open air.

The door closed softly behind him.

Rex Ruppert stood up and waved the gun at Marcos.

Marcos was now trembling almost uncontrollably.

Rex Ruppert spoke to him gently now.

"It will be alright boy, I will not hurt you unless you try to do something stupid."

"Of course the same goes for your father as well."

"Why don't you take that food and put it away, and hey . . . maybe you can make something for me to eat while we wait for your loving father."

Marcos gathered his strength and came to a standing position, still not able to say a word to this scary man before him.

But silent thought were indeed rushing very fast throughout his brain about everything that was now going on.

His father, himself, the diamonds, Kevvy, traveling once again back to the cave at the mountain volcano, and the possibility that he and his father would also be killed by this man, like his dear little friend Kevvy who he wanted to pick up and hold . . . but obviously could not at this moment.

Marcos slowly walked towards the area of the dwelling where he and his father normally prepared the food.

Rex Ruppert was close behind him, towering above him with the gun still pointed at him.

CHAPTER TWENTY THREE

Enrique quickly walked towards the bank where the diamonds were stored safely.

He was very terrified about his current situation.

The thought of that man with the gun being with his son back at his home was enough to almost make him faint from extreme stress.

He arrived within five minutes at the bank.

As he entered the bank, he immediately spotted his friend the bank manager and motioned for him to come over to him.

By the expression on Enrique's face, the bank manager could detect some level of stress.

He asked Enrique if he was alright.

Enrique assured him that he was alright, and asked him to take him to the safe deposit box room.

The bank manager turned and started to walk towards the safe deposit box room and repeated his question to Enrique if he was alright.

Enrique did not answer this time, he just kept walking towards the door to the room that held the precious diamonds.

Enrique thanked the bank manager after he opened the door and told him to have a nice day.

Enrique closed the door behind him and walked over to safe deposit box #297.

He slid the box out of it's slot and quickly opened it up to reveal the precious diamonds, all of them just sitting there, oblivious to the world of the air breathing flesh beings who call themselves human.

Enrique picked up one of the huge diamonds and rolled it around in his hands admiring it.

His hands shook like a drug starved "junkie" anxious for a fix of their addictive medicine.

For a fleeting moment, he had thoughts of keeping these diamonds, but snapped out of that thought as he reminded himself of the dire situation for him and his son.

But . . . there was a thought greed induced . . . that made him stop for another moment and think about.

This dangerous man with the gun did not know how many diamonds were in this box . . . did he?

Then he realized once again that John Marin had told this man with the gun all about the diamonds.

Surely he knew how many because John Marin had personally looked at all of these diamonds.

Maybe he could innocently test this man to figure out if he did indeed know how many diamonds were in this safe deposit box.

Even though this man had said that he would give to him a few of these diamonds in exchange for giving him the diamonds from this box and then show him where the cave was that other diamonds might also be found.

He did not trust this dangerous man with the gun.

So Enrique hatched a simple plan to figure out whether this man did indeed have the knowledge of how many diamonds Marcos had found in that cave at the great mountain volcano.

He would stash all of the diamonds on separate areas of his body, and when he started to give the diamonds to the dangerous man, he would give them to him slowly, one at a time to see how satisfied he was.

He would carefully watch the man.

He would see if he acted satisfied and content after each diamond was given to him.

Surely this man would eventually ask if that was all of the diamonds.

If he actually did ask that particular question, then Enrique would know that this man did not actually know how many diamonds there actually were.

If the man did not ask this particular question, and instead asked where are the rest of the diamonds? . . . then he would act all innocent and apologetic and give the man the rest of the diamonds hidden throughout his body.

So Enrique started to hide all of the diamonds at various spots throughout his body . . . one by one . . . very carefully.

As he walked out of the bank, and waved goodbye to his friend, he had a temptation to tell him what was going on, but obviously could not do so because he did not want to take any chances where he and his sons life was concerned.

He could feel the many large lumps of precious rocks against his skin as he walked down the street.

He also felt slightly paranoid that all of the people that he passed as he walked were staring at him.

Onward he walked anyway.

Walking as fast as he possibly could without looking too suspicious to the many people around him in these rough streets.

Within a few minutes, he approached the entrance to his tiny home where the dangerous man with the gun was inside with his son Marcos.

As Enrique came up to the doorway, he breathed very deeply into his lungs and started to focus himself for the task before him on the other side of the door.

Enrique turned the hand of the door knob very slowly and as he entered, he announced that he was back by himself.

Quickly, he closed the door behind him, and to his surprise, there was not anyone in the room.

He felt extreme anxiety at that moment.

This anxiety disappeared when he heard the dangerous man say something to his son Marcos in the other room where the food was always prepared.

Enrique walked into the other room and with much relief, he could see that his son Marcos was safe and not harmed.

Rex Ruppert looked over at Enrique and point the gun at him with a huge smile upon his face.

He asked Enrique if he had the diamonds with him.

Enrique told him that he did indeed have the diamonds with him, and once again made sure that the man knew that he had come back alone.

This pleased Rex Ruppert very much.

He suggested to Enrique that he should sit down and relax . . . eat a little food, and to put all of the diamonds that he had, onto the table in front of him.

Enrique did not hesitate to follow this mans instructions because once again, he could detect the extreme danger that he and his son were in.

Enrique asked Marcos if he was alright.

Marcos told him that he was indeed alright.

Marcos was preparing some food for all of them to eat, acting as if nothing in the world was wrong.

Rex Ruppert waved the gun at Enrique once again and told him to start putting the diamonds onto the table.

Enrique slowly took the first diamond out of his pocket and placed it onto the table top near a bowl of rice.

Rex Ruppert's eyes swelled to the point of almost bursting out of their eye sockets.

He had never in his life seen a raw diamond as large as the one in front of him on the table.

He was so shocked and surprised that he hollered out in total amazement.

"Oh my God!!"

"Look at the size of that son of a bitch!!"

He reached over and picked it up off of the table.

He was now officially entranced with this stone that he held in his huge hands.

He blurted out at Enrique.

"Are you sure that this is a genuine raw diamond?"

Enrique answered this question back, with no hint of fright this time with his voice.

"John Marin is a world renowned expert in the field of Gemology, and he assured me and my son Marcos that these stones were indeed very real and of the highest quality that he had ever seen as a professional in his field."

Marcos remained silent, looking at the invisible greed, evidently flowing out of all of the pores of this man with the gun, who sat only a few feet away from him.

Marcos could also detect that his father seemed to be very confident and acting slightly crafty.

This is something that only a son could notice.

Thank goodness for Enrique that Rex Ruppert was not able to sense this as well.

Finally, after several moments of admiring this first raw diamond, Rex Ruppert put it down on the table and told Enrique to put the rest out onto the table.

Enrique slowly and silently shook his head up and down and took out another raw diamond from his body, and once again placed it onto the table next to the first diamond.

Amazingly, this diamond was actually a little larger than the first diamond that had so mesmerized Rex Ruppert.

Once again, Rex Ruppert made a verbal sound of extreme astonishment about this next diamond on the table.

Once again, he also picked this diamond up and held it firmly in his hands.

He put this diamond only a few inches from his eyes and looked at it very carefully.

He exhaled rather loudly after a few moments and looked over at Enrique and motioned with his head to continue putting more diamonds onto the table.

This time Enrique quickly put all of the rest of the diamonds on the table with the exception of two.

Now was the time to find out whether this dangerous man with the gun actually knew exactly how many diamonds there were found from the cave.

Enrique sat there silently, acting as if he had put all of the diamonds onto the table.

He looked over at Rex Ruppert and tried not to show any signs of paranoia that might indicate to this very dangerous man that he was trying to pull a fast one on him.

Rex Ruppert looked at the rest of the diamonds sitting there all together on the table.

It did not look like he was counting them, the extreme greed that was taking over his body was making him blind . . . not with his eyes, but with his inner soul.

Rex Ruppert picked up another diamond that was the largest now on the table.

He was so amazed that his voice box became paralyzed.

He absolutely could not say anything at this moment.

He was sure that he now held in his hands, the largest diamond that any human had ever held in their hands.

Rex Ruppert reached into the inside of his jacket and pulled out a soft leather satchel and started to put all of the diamonds inside of it.

As he got to the last diamond, he looked over at Enrique for a moment.

This moment in time lasted much to long for the comfort of Enrique.

Enrique was about to flinch and act as if he made a mistake and forgot that he had two more diamonds upon his body, and reluctantly give these to this man as well.

But . . . to his surprise and amazement, he handed over a single stone to Enrique and announced that he was giving this stone to Enrique as he said he would.

He put the satchel away underneath his jacket, and proceeded to start eating with one hand while the other hand still held the large intimidating gun.

CHAPTER TWENTY FOUR

Vernon Montague and John Crevelli awoke from their slumber within the cave system.

All was eerily silent in all directions.

Both men stood up to their feet and started their regular wake-up routines.

Mostly stretching and getting their bearings.

They went into their backpacks and retrieved some food that was packed inside . . . thanks to Yeshua.

Of course, they had their favorite items of food, under these conditions.

What the two men found was pretty awesome to both of them was that the water container would not ever run out of water.

Thanks again to Yeshua.

The two men ate heartily and filled up with water as well before restarting their arduous journey back to the surface of the planet.

Within half of an hour, they were once again traveling upwards within the cave system.

Meanwhile back in Legazpi City, Rex Ruppert, Enrique, and his son Marcos completed their meals.

Enrique was still happily surprised that he had two large diamonds hidden upon his body, and to top it all off, Rex Ruppert had given him another diamond that he thought was the last diamond from the safe deposit box at the bank.

So now, Enrique had three diamonds, and even though he still felt the extreme danger from this strange man with a gun, he felt sure that if he and his son cooperated, they would come out of all of this ordeal unharmed and still be able to make enough money from these three diamonds to be set-up for the rest of their lives.

So now he and Marcos waited for Rex Ruppert to give them further instructions.

They did not have to wait very long.

Rex Ruppert barked out what sounded like an order with an aggressive overtone.

They both paid complete attention to him, almost in a trancelike state.

"Tomorrow we will travel to where the location is that your son found these wonderful diamonds!!"

"Do you both understand this?"

Both Enrique and Marcos nodded yes in mutual silence.

Rex lowered his voice now and started to speak a bit more less intimidating.

"Where exactly, or should I ask, where, in your best judgment, is the location where we will be traveling to?"

Rex Ruppert, with wide eyes, looked directly at Marcos when he asked this question?

Marcos swallowed some saliva down his throat, looking as if he had a small egg within.

He felt very nervous at this exact moment . . . as the big scary man with the gun stared at him, awaiting an answer from him.

Enrique nodded silently to his son telling him to go ahead and tell this man what he wanted to know.

Marcos breathed deep for just a moment, and exhaled a lung full of air, and then followed that with an obvious sigh.

He began to speak to Rex Ruppert.

"I found these diamonds inside of a cave high up on the great volcano behind our city."

"It is called Mt. Mayon."

Rex Ruppert next asked how far, and how long would it take to travel to this cave on the mountain volcano.

Marcos gave an answer back to that question and waited for the next question, now answering almost in a robotic way.

Rex Ruppert shrugged his huge shoulders, and nodded his head in affirmation.

He now told Enrique that they should pack some food, drink, and supplies for their travel in the morning.

He told them that they would be leaving very early before the sun rose.

He also explained to both Enrique and Marcos that it would be necessary to tie both of them up with ropes for the night so that they would not be able to escape, and that he . . . Rex Ruppert, would be able to get some sleep.

All of the food, drink, and supplies were packed within what seemed like just a few minutes.

After this was done, Rex Ruppert ordered Enrique to retrieve some rope so he could start tying them up for the night.

He now pointed the gun at Marcos, and told Enrique to hurry-up and find the rope.

Enrique was able to find some manila twine in only a few minutes.

He gave this twine over to Rex Ruppert, and then sat back down beside his son.

Rex Ruppert pointed the gun now at Enrique, and ordered him to tie-up Marcos very tightly.

He told Enrique that he would check afterwards to make sure that the knots were very tight and secure.

He also warned Enrique that if he thought that the knots were not secure, that he would have to physically harm him.

Enrique followed these instructions exactly like Rex Ruppert demanded.

After he tied up his son very securely with the twine, Rex Ruppert, as he said he would do, checked the knots himself.

After doing this, he was satisfied that the knots were in fact very tight, and he felt confident that there was no chance that Marcos would be able to escape the bonds.

He then hit Enrique in the back of the head and dazed him to the point that there was absolutely no struggle at all when he took some twine in hand . . . laying the big gun down next to him as he did this, and tied up Enrique very tight to his satisfaction.

Next, he found some pieces of clothes on a shelf and stuffed them inside of the mouths of Enrique and Marcos.

He then wrapped some tape around these same clothes to make sure they did not come out of their mouths.

Lastly, he secured the door of the dwelling so that nobody would be able to enter without kicking it in.

If that were to happen, he would hear that noise, and be able to get his gun in his hand quick enough to start shooting if it was necessary.

Finally, he felt comfortable enough to relax and actually get some type of sleep for the night.

As Enrique laid upon the ground, he once again felt a slight joy. Even though he was in this awkward, and uncomfortable position, he was once again happy that Rex Ruppert had not checked his body when he started to tie him up.

He felt terrified that the diamonds that he had stashed on his body would be found, and then he would probably be seriously harmed, or maybe even killed.

He just kept telling himself that after all of this was all over with, he and his son would be able to live a happy life.

He looked over at his son Marcos and could see the fear on his face as he helplessly lay there only a few feet away.

Enrique motioned with his head, and closed his eyes for a few seconds, to try to convey to his son that he now must try to go to sleep.

Marcos was able to understand this gesture, and shook his head slowly, and closed his eyes for the night.

Rex Ruppert fell asleep within a few minutes, oblivious to the world, not caring about anything except finding that location tomorrow at the volcano, and see for himself if it was really true that there were indeed more precious diamonds to be found.

It was true that he did represent someone who was very large in the diamond industry.

It was also true that if it turned out that there was really a cave with more of these type of diamonds, he would be rewarded immensely for his efforts.

Maybe this could actually be his last job in this ruthless, cold blooded business . . . probably not . . . this was only a fleeting thought . . . he enjoyed this line of work to much.

His sadistic personality had to have a fix like a junkie and his needed drug.

He liked to hurt people, and make good money while doing so.

He was now officially in his own sadistic dream world . . . snoring away almost loud enough that it was difficult for Enrique and Marcos to get to sleep.

CHAPTER TWENTY FIVE

Unknown to the two astronauts was that they were only really a few hours away from reaching the surface of the Earth.

They were not exhausted from their hiking through this cave system, surprisingly, they both actually had plenty of energy.

The temperature of the cave system was getting a little warmer the further they traveled.

It was not unbearable, but very noticeable to both men.

They talked about how close they must be getting to the surface of their beloved home world.

Onward they hiked, hoping to see with their eyes, real sunlight sometime very soon.

They talked about the real possibility that they might be thought of as dead by now by the outside world.

All their loved ones were probably heartbroken by now.

All of their friends must surely feel that they will never again experience interaction with their astronaut pals.

The military probably already signed them off as dead as well, and might even have had military funerals for them without their actual bodies to bury.

The whole world in fact might, through the mass media, already think that they are dead, and will never be seen again.

They are probably old news by now, not even talked about anymore by anyone except their loved ones.

As the two astronauts rounded a corner of the cave system, they both started to see that the walls were sparkling in many patches in large areas.

Both men walked up to the walls and studied what was making these shimmers of light.

Vernon Montague pulled out his Swiss army knife and opened a blade.

He leaned over and started to pick at an area on the wall with the blade.

The wall was powdery in texture, but whatever the light colored objects were, they were very hard.

He scraped around the edges of one particular object until he had a noticeable border completely around it.

He dug deeper into the groove.

The wall gave away a lot at a time.

After digging for about three minutes, he was able to feel with the knife blade, the backside of this hard object, which he now figured out was some kind of a stone.

He now changed the blade on the knife, and pulled out another one shaped like a small spike.

Vernon Montague looked over at John Crevelli and shrugged his shoulders as he placed this small spike shaped blade behind the stone.

He pushed back and forth in a rocking motion, loosening the stone more and more.

Finally . . . the stone gave way from the wall, and popped out and fell down to the ground at their feet.

John Crevelli bent over and picked up the stone.

Vernon Montague shined a light on the stone up close.

John's eyes widened a little.

He blurted out . . . "Is this a diamond?"

The stone was the size of an ordinary plumb.

Vernon Montague took the stone from the other astronauts hands and looked at it while he twirled it around slowly, letting the light bounce off of it's edges.

Vernon Montague spoke in a normal tone with no excitement at all.

"I honestly think, and of course I am not an expert, but I really think that this indeed is a real diamond, in raw form."

"This is probably amongst the very largest diamonds in the world if it is actually a diamond."

Both men went silent for almost a full minute before they started to speak again.

John Crevelli started to speak in an excited tone of voice.

"Wow!!"

"If this is a diamond, and look around Vern, these must all be diamonds!!"

"We could take as many of these back home with us and be rich beyond our wildest dreams!!"

"Hell . . . we could both retire, and be set for life to do whatever we well pleased."

"I don't know about you, but I am going to take as many of these as I can with me, just in case it turns out that these are indeed real diamonds."

"Lets take a little break, and carve some of these stones out of the wall."

Vernon Montague answered . . . still with no excitement in his voice.

"I agree with you John, if these are in fact diamonds, we could live a very different life than we are used to."

"But . . . you know, there might be all kinds of problems we could face in trying to keep these supposed diamonds for ourselves."

"We don't even know which country we are going to end up in."

"Whatever country we ultimately end up in will surely try to claim the stones as theirs because the stones came from their country."

John Crevelli was oblivious to what his fellow astronaut was saying to him.

He started to carve diamonds out of the walls around him in almost a frenzy.

After each stone was taken from the wall, he would quickly look at it, make a short excited sound of obvious greed, and then place it down on the ground, forming a small pile of untold riches.

Vernon Montague shrugged his shoulders, and then he also started to carve-out the precious stones from the cave walls as well.

He did not really show too much excitement as he collected the stones.

He just went about in a workmanlike manner.

All of a sudden, John Crevelli screamed in extreme excitement, sounding almost like a little girl.

"Look at the size of this damn rock!!"

In his hands, he held what was most probably the very largest diamond ever discovered by a man since the dawn of time.

This particular diamond was a little larger then a regulation size softball.

Both men stood looking at the huge stone for several minutes.

Finally, they both agreed that they had gathered enough stones from the cave, and it was time once again to resume their journey back to the surface where they could once again see the Sun and sky.

CHAPTER TWENTY SIX

The morning light of the Sun arrived, and created streaks of light throughout the dwelling where Enrique, Marcos, and Rex Ruppert still laid sleeping.

A partial part of one of these beams of sunshine started to rest upon the face of Rex Ruppert.

As it crossed the right side of his face and passed over his right eye, he became sensitive to it through his eyelid and awoke.

He quickly looked over in the direction of the two people on the floor and could see that they were still tied up, and asleep.

He hollered over at them to wake up.

Both Enrique and his son woke up instantly.

Enrique felt a very uncomfortable cramp in his right upper thigh that he could not do anything about to relieve the pain.

Rex Ruppert got up and walked over to Enrique and bent down in front of him.

He was only a few inches from his face.

He spoke in a menacing tone of voice.

"I am going to untie you and your son, and take the gags out of your mouths."

"Are you going to do anything stupid and cause me to have to injure one of you?"

Enrique shook his head to indicate that he would not do anything once he was untied from these tight knots that dug into his skin.

Rex Ruppert untied Enrique, and then instructed him to do the same for his son.

Enrique massaged the area of his leg to loosen the cramp that gave him pain since he awoke.

He asked his son if he was alright.

Marcos indicated to his Father that he was alright, under the circumstances they were in.

Enrique started to speak in their native tongue to try and tell his son something without Rex Ruppert understanding what was said.

But Rex Ruppert quickly noticed this, and smacked Enrique across the face with the back of his hand.

He told both Enrique and Marcos that they would only speak in English whenever they talked in his presence.

He also warned them that if he caught them speaking again in their native language, that they would most definitely have regrets after doing so.

He told them, without going into any details, that he would hurt them in a very painful way if he heard them saying anything that was not in the English language.

Enrique apologized for talking in his native tongue, and promised that he and his son would only talk in the English language from now on.

Rex Ruppert ordered Marcos to fix them some food really quick so that they could start their journey to the volcano.

Marcos did as he was told.

The three of them ate the food and then gathered up all the provisions that they would need for their journey to the great volcano . . . Mount Mayon.

Rex Ruppert showed both man and boy that he had his gun underneath his baggy jacket, and would not hesitate to use it upon either of them if they made any false moves.

He also warned them that other people around them would also be shot as well if they tried to warn them of what was going on.

He wanted them to act very ordinary, and carry about in a normal manner so as to not draw any undue attention to them.

They left the dwelling very casually.

Nobody around them seemed to even notice them as they walked down the street.

A few people called out to Enrique and Marcos, and they were met by ordinary, casual head nods.

They traveled on foot in a northward direction on an invisible map.

Enrique and Marcos both knew this route by heart.

It did not take long before they were at the outskirts of their small city, and then into the thick jungle that went on for as far as ones eyes could see.

They came to a small creek and filled up a few of their canteens with natures liquid . . . water.

Onward they traveled, deep within this jungle of extremely thick vegetation.

The sounds of this jungle threw at their ears a variety of noises that were unnerving for the normal person not from these parts.

The sounds were mostly from monkeys and birds as they themselves traveled throughout the many trees and vines that engulfed all living things.

They traveled in total silence . . . onward.

CHAPTER TWENTY SEVEN

Roger Tusk was leaning back in his chair behind his desk, looking at a computer screen, reading all of the translations of the ancient papyri that a Professor Ntangku had recently put online for anyone to read.

Roger Tusk was well known in political circles as someone who liked to "stir the pot."

He was not a politician, or a lobbyist.

He was basically a freelance media specialist who was famous for cornering famous people with questions that put them on the spot.

The questions were usually very controversial in nature.

There had been many elections in the past that had been determined because a candidate had answered a particular question in a way that was not favorable to the electorate.

Thus causing that candidate to lose their election to whomever they were running against.

These translations that were put online by Professor Ntangku for all of the world to see, were just the type of information that Roger Tusk could take and ask some very controversial questions to various important people.

Many names immediately came to him in his head.

He could definitely have a "field day" with an assorted group of people, ranging from world leaders, politicians running for different offices, and a variety of other famous people.

Basically, the one quick question that popped into his head was about this person called "Yeshua" or supposedly "Jesus."

This person named Yeshua, or Jesus, was supposedly going to come back to the planet Earth in his physical form on December 21, 2012.

Roger Tusk took this information as just a bunch of nonsense.

He thought that this was absolutely just another example of an over zealous professor that was trying to make a name for herself with these findings.

Roger Tusk did not doubt what the actual translations said on these ancient papyri.

He doubted that what was said on these old writings would ever actually ever happen.

Jesus coming back?

The actual return of the most worshiped person in the history of religion?

Nonsense!!

He laughed inside of his brain as these thoughts raced through his head.

But . . . that does not mean that he could not take this information and create an immense amount of controversy.

In fact, he thought that this might be the greatest bit of information that he would ever find, and be able to use it to cause the greatest amount of turmoil in his entire career.

He thought . . . what if I were to just take the simple question . . . "Do you believe that Jesus will come back to Earth on December 21, 2012?"

He could already picture the faces of some of the people that he already thought of asking this simple question.

Talk about putting someone on the spot.

There had always, throughout the many centuries since Jesus died on the cross, been the talk of his return back to mankind someday.

There had, come and gone, many actual "cults" that believed this to be so true that they would preach it to their dying days.

Many of the worlds different religions were heavily based upon this one particular belief.

Also, many of the main world leaders were in fact members of these various religions that believed that one day . . . Jesus would return back to Earth for "Judgment day."

So now . . . supposedly . . . Jesus was to return on December 21, 2012 of this very year, not to much time from now.

Roger Tusk thought . . . Wow!!

He was really going to have a lot of fun with this one particular question.

He started to make a list of targeted individuals.

The Presidential race for the United States was already almost here for voters to make their choices for who would lead their country for the next four years.

The current President . . . "President Trobama" would certainly be his first targeted person with this question.

The man that he was running against . . . "Matt Cromney" would certainly be his next choice to ask the question.

Coincidentally, Roger Tusk had already been asked to be on a panel to ask questions of the two candidates, in a little over three weeks, for an important Presidential debate, that would most certainly be viewed by millions of people that were possible voters in the Presidential election that was "just around the corner."

Roger Tusk had accepted the offer just yesterday.

What perfect timing!!

CHAPTER TWENTY EIGHT

After many hours of nonstop hiking through this vast cave system, Vernon Montague, and his fellow astronaut, John Crevelli, were nearing the entrance to the cave to the outside world.

Of course, they were not aware that they were getting so close to the entrance.

They would probably be at the caves entrance within the next hour or more if they did not stop.

Meanwhile, outside the cave, down below in the thick jungle, Enrique, Marcos, and the man they feared with a gun pointed at them ... Rex Ruppert, were trudging their way to the area where they would climb to the plateau where the cave was located.

They were only a few hundred yards from this location for their climb to the cave.

But the jungle was so thick of vegetation that it would probably take about half of an hour to get there.

Rex Ruppert was getting tired, and anxious at the same time.

He asked Enrique how much farther, and how long before they would get to the cave.

He started to threaten them that they better not be trying to trick him or deceive him in finding the location to the cave.

They both reassured him that they were being honest with him, and that they were getting very close to the cave.

They all stopped for a quick water break.

This took less then a minute, and then they were once again on their way to the cave on the volcano.

Both groups of people, two inside of the cave, and three outside of the cave, were now very close to coming to the same location where the excitement level was different for all five individuals.

The two astronauts would certainly be very excited to see the outside world once again.

Enrique and his son Marcos would probably have a feeling of doubt as to whether they would actually walk away from this cave alive or not.

They feared that this man with the gun would kill them after finding out the location of this cave.

Rex Ruppert was filled with an extreme amount of greed and anticipation.

Once he found this cave, and verified that there were indeed more of these precious diamonds within it's interior, he would have an orgasm of happiness that he had never felt in his entire life.

He also had already decided, without much thought, that he would kill both Enrique and Marcos, no matter if there was a cave of diamonds or not.

They were potential witnesses that could put him in jail for what he was now doing to them.

Marcos stopped all of a sudden.

He spoke without being asked.

"Over that way."

He was now pointing towards a small clearing where he had climbed down from the side of the mountain when he left the cave with the diamonds that Rex Ruppert now held on his body.

Enrique asked Marcos if he was sure about that area for them to make their climb.

Marcos answered back, almost in an irritating tone, that it was for sure the area to make the climb to the cave above.

When the three of them had taken their water break, Rex Ruppert had taken out his compact GPS device to start getting a reading of their location.

He would make sure that he documented the exact location of this cave with this GPS device so that information could be transferred to the people he worked for.

In about twenty five minutes, they arrived at the clearing to where they would start their climb up to the cave.

Rex Ruppert had Enrique climb to the plateau first.

He then had Marcos start his climb while he was directly behind him on the ascent.

He was only inches away as they made their climb.

He did this so that Marcos could not get away, and he could keep control.

If he were to lose control of Marcos, while Enrique was already at the top of the plateau, then they could both make an escape, and potentially get away from him.

The climb was a little more difficult than if he were to climb completely alone, but this was the only way to maintain the control that he had over these two people.

Finally, he and Marcos made it to the top of the plateau and stood beside Enrique.

Rex Ruppert looked around and could see over in the distance . . . a cave!!

His heart started to beat at a rapid pace, it almost felt like it would leap out of his chest.

A feeling of despair, and extreme paranoia instantly started to form in Enrique, and his son Marcos.

The thought of death was a very real feeling.

There was not even a faint microscopic feeling of any type of happy feeling at all within their bodies at this moment in their lives.

Marcos felt faint.

He stumbled forward a few feet in front of his frightened father.

He bent over, and lowered his head, almost blacking out.

Enrique held his son securely, preventing him from falling over to the ground.

Rex Ruppert verbally snapped at them very loudly, and told them to stand up.

Enrique, instinctively, turned his head towards Rex Ruppert and glared at him with obvious hatred.

Rex Ruppert raised the gun and pointed it directly at Enrique and gave the "look of death" upon his face.

Enrique instantly stopped glaring at Rex Ruppert, and pulled his son upward to a standing position.

Enrique apologized repeatedly to Rex Ruppert, over and over . . . pleading for his life.

Rex Ruppert did not fire the gun.

He just waved it towards the direction of the cave.

The two men, and young boy walked over towards the entrance to the cave not to far away.

It only took about thirty seconds for them to walk over to the entrance to the cave.

Every step towards the caves entrance made the excitement inside of Rex Ruppert intensify immensely.

It was quite the opposite for Enrique and Marcos.

With every step towards the cave, both father and son had feelings that their lives were about to come to an end.

They both looked at each other with love and fright mixed into one single silent emotion.

Enrique had quick flashbacks of happier times with his son.

If only he could figure out a way to help his son escape from harm from this scary man with the gun.

He now was feeling like he would definitely risk his life at a given moment to try and at least give his son a chance to escape harm from this evil man.

They now stood just outside of the caves entrance.

Rex Ruppert spoke.

"Well?"

"Is this the cave?"

"Is this where you found those diamonds?"

Marcos answered back to him that it was indeed the cave where he found the diamonds.

Rex Ruppert took his GPS device back out of his pocket, and clicked save in a file.

The exact area on the globe was now officially marked on the GPS for other people to later come back to this location.

He put the GPS back into his pocket.

He now turned his attention back to the two frightened people.

He took out a flashlight from another pocket and handed it to Enrique.

He instructed Enrique to enter the cave, and motioned Marcos to follow his father inside of the cave.

Rex Ruppert followed them with the gun pointed at them.

As the beam of the flashlight bounced off of the caves interior walls, their eyes were greeted with many bright sparkles . . . everywhere!!

Rex Ruppert was absolutely stunned.

It took him almost a full minute . . . all silent, to snap out of his daze and regain his composure.

He walked over to the wall and touched one of the sparkling stones that was embedded into the sediment.

He noticed right away that the sediment was not very hard.

He took from his waistband a knife from a sheath.

He started to dig into the sediment around this particular stone to see how easily it would come out of the wall.

To his utter delight, he had the stone carved out of the wall in a matter of a few minutes.

Enrique and Marcos stood near by watching this evil man greedily carve away at the caves wall.

Rex Ruppert stopped after he dislodged this one stone and handed the knife over to Enrique.

This surprised Enrique.

He was very tempted to attack Rex Ruppert with the knife to try and give his son a chance to escape.

But Rex Ruppert was totally on top of that possibility.

He pointed the gun at Marcos, and ordered Enrique to start carving some diamonds out of the wall.

He warned Enrique that if he made a move that made him nervous, he would immediately shoot and kill Marcos.

Enrique started to dig away at the wall.

One by one, he carved out some diamonds from the wall, and started a pile on the ground nearby.

After about an hour of doing this, Rex Ruppert was satisfied with the pile of diamonds on the ground.

He ordered Enrique to stop after the next diamond was out of the wall.

He told Enrique to drop the knife down to the ground and to step back away from it.

Rex Ruppert bent down quickly, and put the knife back into it's sheath.

He had Marcos put all of the diamonds into a belly pack, and handed it over to him to put on his waist.

After securing the belly pack full of diamonds onto the girth of his waist, Rex Ruppert told both Enrique and Marcos to exit the cave to the outside.

Enrique now felt very scared, because he thought that this was going to be the time that this evil man would try to kill him and his beloved son Marcos.

As they came back outside of the cave, Rex Ruppert had them both stop.

He spoke in an evil tone of voice.

"You are both probably thinking that I am now going to take this gun and kill both of you."

"That is not correct."

"I am not going to kill both of you."

"I am only going to kill one of you."

"I will need for one of you to guide me back to the city so I can leave this island."

"Now . . . which one is going to be my guide?"

"I will let you both make that decision."

Enrique pleaded with Rex Ruppert.

He told him that he and his son would not tell anyone about what had happened.

Rex Ruppert laughed at this heartily.

He answered this weak plea.

"Of course you are going to say that . . . you little idiot!!"

"Do you think that I am some kind of a dumb ass?"

"I guess that I will make the decision as to who will guide me out of this damn jungle, because you want to disrespect my intelligence like that!!"

"You will be my guide kid!!"

Rex Ruppert pointed the gun at Enrique with a large smile upon his evil face.

Back within the cave, the two astronauts came around a corner, and could happily see some light from the outside world.

They both had large smiles on their faces as they came closer to the caves entrance.

Just as they got up to the entrance to the cave, they became witnesses to the horror that was developing outside not to far away from them.

Both astronauts backed away quickly once they seen that there was a large man outside of the cave brandishing a large caliber pistol aimed at two people in front of him.

One was a man and the other was a young boy.

They looked like they might be some type of island people.

Rex Ruppert did not see the astronauts inside of the cave.

The two astronauts stood by helplessly, silent witnesses to what would probably turn out to be a ruthless cold blooded murder.

They backed away a few more feet, just to make sure this man did not see them.

But they did not back away to far, where they could not see the whole horrific event take place.

They both felt so badly for the two helpless people outside of this cave . . . only a matter of yards away.

Suddenly, Enrique lunged at Rex Ruppert and hollered at Marcos in the same moment to run.

Marcos did not look back as he did as his father told him.

Even though he knew that his father was now going to be dead in a matter of seconds, he did not look back.

He ran for his life!!

Marcos ran toward the area where they had climbed to the plateau from the jungle down below.

Enrique struggled with the arm of Rex Ruppert that held the gun.

He tried feebly to dislodge the gun from the hand of this large evil man.

His efforts were predictably not good enough.

This struggle only lasted about twenty seconds.

But . . . this twenty seconds was enough time for Marcos to get to the edge of the plateau and dive to his stomach onto the hard ground.

He rolled a few times and was able to slide half of his body over the edge and hang on with his elbows.

Now he was able to look back in horror and see his fathers struggle for his life.

Rex Ruppert threw Enrique down to the ground and quickly fired the pistol three times at him.

The pistol still had the silencer attached, so there was only a faint sound of compressed air that could be heard.

Rex Ruppert looked at Enrique for a second, kicked him in the side once . . . it appeared that Enrique was dead.

He quickly turned and started running towards the edge of the plateau where Marcos still was for only a few more seconds.

Tears swelled up in his eyes as he witnessed the shooting of his father.

He saw Rex Ruppert running towards him, and so he started to climb down the side of the plateau very fast.

He was able to make it down to the ground into the thick jungle only seconds before Rex Ruppert arrived at the spot of where he started climbing down from above.

Rex Ruppert leaned over the edge of the plateau and saw a quick glimpse of Marcos as he started to blend into the thick vegetation of the jungle.

Rex Ruppert hollered at him to come back.

Of course Marcos ignored this request, and started running through the jungle as fast as he could.

Rex Ruppert started to shoot his gun in the direction of where he last seen Marcos.

Bullets hit many of the branches of the tree's in the area where Marcos was only moments before.

Luckily, none of the bullets hit Marcos as he ran for his life.

He was sure that this dangerous man who was shooting at him would most certainly chase him to try and catch him.

Then . . . what would happen?

Certainly nothing good was his initial thought to this question.

Onward he ran.

Rex Ruppert bent over and started to climb down the side of the plateau, and then he remembered the diamonds that were still back near the cave.

He openly swore out loud to nobody in particular, and raced over to the diamonds, and retrieved them.

Once he got the diamonds, he sprinted back to the edge of the plateau, and climbed down very quickly.

He fell to the ground from about five feet still to climb down, and twisted his ankle slightly, but not enough to affect his running very much.

There was an extreme amount of adrenaline pumping throughout his body as he started his chase to try and catch Marcos.

Marcos had the advantage of knowing exactly where he was at in the jungle.

Rex Ruppert was instantly lost as he started to run though the thick jungle.

Marcos was already a good three hundred yards ahead of Rex Ruppert at this point.

He kept running.

Back at the cave, the two astronauts watched everything happen without being seen.

Once they seen that the man with the gun was gone from the plateau, they ran out of the cave over to Enrique.

Vernon Montague reached down and felt for a pulse.

Amazingly, there was still a faint sign of a heartbeat.

Enrique was quickly rolled over and covered up, and his feet were raised above his heart to slow the onset of shock.

Three red wet spots on his shirt showed where the bullets had entered the body of Enrique.

Both astronauts quickly made a makeshift stretcher similar to what Native American Indians used to move their people when they were injured and could not walk.

They tied the long sleeves of their shirts to two five foot long poles they got from breaking branches off of a nearby tree.

They quickly moved Enrique over to the edge of the plateau.

They needed to get him to a doctor as quickly as possible.

They really had no time to celebrate the fact that they were once again on the surface of the planet.

All they could think about right now was to try and save this mans life.

They tied a rope that they had to one end of the stretcher.

John Crevelli climbed down the side of the plateau to the ground below to the jungle.

Vernon Montague lowered Enrique down as gently as possible to John Crevelli.

Finally Vernon Montague climbed down below to the jungle.

They had no idea where they were as they started to make their way through the jungle.

They could see the broken branches where Marcos and Rex Ruppert had ran through.

They decided to change direction away from this path in the hopes that they did not run into the man with the gun who had just shot the man that they held on the stretcher.

It was slow going, but they trudged on, knowing how important is was to get Enrique some help as quickly as possible.

He was bleeding very badly, and it did not look like he would survive the inflicted bullet wounds.

They tore up another shirt and put direct pressure on these wounds and tied them off to slow the bleeding.

Enrique's eyes were closed, and his breathing was very shallow as he laid on the stretcher.

He was totally oblivious to the world right now.

Death was very nearby and was trying to rest his life force from his flesh and bones.

Death was winning this battle as the seconds ticked away.

Elsewhere in this same jungle, Marcos was actually extending his lead on Rex Ruppert.

He had not stopped running since he came down from the plateau where he thought his father lay dead.

He did not know that as he raced for his life from Rex Ruppert, There were two astronauts racing just as well in an effort to safe his father's life.

The sounds of the jungle continued as always . . . birds chirping, monkeys screeching, they were also caught up in their own life and death struggles to survive in this dangerous jungle.

CHAPTER TWENTY NINE

Spencer Ziegler sat across the room from John Marin comfortably in a lounge chair.

Since Rex Ruppert had left, he had to carefully watch John Marin to make sure that he did not try to escape, or do anything to get out of his situation.

So . . . Spencer Ziegler basically kept both of them in the room and tied John Marin up at night so he could get some sleep.

During the daytime, he had John Marin handcuffed to a pole in the study where they now sat.

Spencer Ziegler was very intoxicated.

He had drank a lot of the liquor that John Marin had stashed in various places.

Spencer Ziegler was waiting for Rex Ruppert to contact him via laptop.

It was already agreed beforehand that John Marin would be executed once Rex Ruppert called back with the information about the supposed diamonds.

There was only one reason why John Marin was kept alive.

Just in case more information was needed from him about the diamonds.

Spencer Ziegler did not know what the current situation was with Rex Ruppert.

He certainly did not know that at that very moment, he was running through a jungle chasing a young boy with his gun.

He also did not know that there were indeed real diamonds from a cave.

He did not know that Rex Ruppert had actually gone to this cave and found even more diamonds.

Rex Ruppert had only marked the GPS coordinates.

He had not transferred the GPS information yet to his employer, or had a chance to contact his partner Spencer Ziegler.

It was very apparent to Rex Ruppert that he had to catch Marcos before he made it back to the authorities.

He could possibly be stuck on this island and in hiding if Marcos was able to tell the authorities what he had done to him and his father up on the volcano.

After running for a solid hour, Rex Ruppert finally stopped from exhaustion.

He came to the conclusion that he was definitely lost, and probably not going to catch that young boy.

So, he had to make other plans, right now.

He found a clearing a short distance away where a part of a small hilltop had been washed away.

He reached in his pack and took out his laptop.

He had the best state of the art laptop that could bounce off of various satellites around the globe.

He logged in.

He now contacted Spencer Ziegler.

Spencer Ziegler was surprised to hear his laptop alarm him of an incoming message.

It gave off an alarm that sounded like a fire engine going to a fire.

John Marin was also startled to hear this alarm go off on the laptop.

Spencer Ziegler smiled when he heard this sound.

John Marin frowned at that same moment.

He opened up his laptop, and went online to check the incoming message.

It was from his partner Rex Ruppert.

He quickly did the special cryptic code to make a secure line between them.

Both laptops between both men had camera's.

Rex Ruppert's face popped on the screen in front of Spencer Ziegler.

There was a very wild look on Rex Ruppert face.

He looked angry and exhausted.

Spencer spoke first.

"What's the matter Rex?"

"You look tired and angry."

Rex Ruppert answered back.

"It's a long story Spencer."

"But let me tell you, there are diamonds!!"

Rex Ruppert reached into his waist pack and took out a few of the diamonds.

He put them up to the screen.

He spoke again to his partner.

"Look at these diamonds Spencer!!"

"Look how large they are."

"I'll bet that I probably have a few million dollars worth of diamonds on me right now."

"There is a cave up on this volcano."

"I have the GPS coordinates registered."

"I have not sent them off to our employer yet."

"I am definitely in trouble now though."

Spencer Ziegler asked what type of trouble his partner was in.

Rex Ruppert explained to him that he had shot Enrique up on the volcano near the cave where the diamonds came from.

He told Spencer Ziegler that he was now lost somewhere in this jungle, trying to catch the son of the man who he shot.

He explained how the boy had witnessed everything, and was surely on his way to contact the authorities.

Here he was, lost in a jungle with all these diamonds on him, and on the verge of being a hunted man for shooting Enrique up on the volcano.

Spencer asked Rex Ruppert what he was going to do.

Rex Ruppert explained to him that he was going to try to avoid being captured, and that he wanted Spencer Ziegler to kill John Marin, and then contact their employer and explain what the current situation was with Rex Ruppert.

Rex Ruppert told Spencer Ziegler to make sure that their employer understood that there was indeed a cave with a bounty of diamonds within.

He also wanted Spencer Ziegler to pass on to their employer and make sure they understood that he had the GPS coordinates, and would not give them up unless they were able to help him get off of the island safely.

He told Spencer Ziegler to quickly kill John Marin, and then go to London England and wait for him at his girlfriends bar.

Spencer Ziegler understood what his partner wanted him to do, and assured him that he would do everything, as instructed, as quick as possible.

Spencer Ziegler signed off on his laptop.

Rex Ruppert signed off as well, and continued his journey, now more carefully, because he was not the hunter anymore, he was soon to be the hunted.

He hoped that he would eventually be rescued by some people sent by his employer.

Spencer Ziegler turned to John Marin and told him that he had bad news for him.

He told him that his partner had instructed him to kill him.

John Marin said aloud . . . with sarcasm and fear mixed together . . . "I heard everything from across the room, my hearing is still functioning properly."

Just as he said that to Spencer Ziegler, the doorbell rang.

Spencer Ziegler turned quickly towards the door.

He asked John Marin who it might be.

John Marin said that it was probably a friend of his that stops by every once in awhile.

Spencer Ziegler got up and walked over to the door and looked through the peephole.

He could see on the other side a stocky man in a large oversized jacket.

The man on the other side of the door hollered to John Marin . . . "Open up John!!"

"I know that you are here."

"I really need to see you."

"I'm not going to leave until you open the door John."

This man rang the door bell once again, but this time he did it repeatedly like a machine gun being fired on automatic.

This irritated Spencer Ziegler immensely.

He decided that he had to let John Marin see this guy and make him leave.

Then he could finish eliminating John Marin, and carry on with the instructions that Rex Ruppert had given him.

Spencer Ziegler ran over to John Marin and freed him from his bonds.

He warned John Marin that he would shoot and kill him and his friend if he tried anything suspicious.

He told John Marin to let his friend come into the house.

He told John Marin that he would be hidden behind an entertainment center with his gun loaded and ready to shoot.

He wanted John Marin to assure this guy that everything is alright, and that he wanted him to leave because he had to take care of some business.

John Marin agreed with no hesitation because he thought that he should already be a dead man if the doorbell had not rang when it did.

John Marin hollered back at his friend on the other side of the door as he himself walked towards it to open it.

"I'm coming Arnie!!"

"Just give me a second!!"

His friend . . . Arnold Sandvick, answered back.

"Well . . . hurry your ass up friend!!"

Spencer Ziegler positioned himself about fifteen feet away, hidden behind the entertainment center as he had said.

John Marin looked at him.

Spencer Ziegler shook his head up and down, signaling him to proceed, and open the door.

John Marin opened the door, and without hesitation, bolted out of the door, and hollered at his friend to run for his life!!

Spencer Ziegler was caught totally off guard by this, and by the time that he was able to react, John Marin, and his friend Arnold Sandvick were already down the driveway and turning down the road out of sight from the front porch of the house.

Spencer Ziegler quickly realized that he could not give chase in daylight brandishing a firearm.

He would surely be noticed right away, and especially if he was chasing John Marin, who was probably hollering his head off that a man was chasing him with a gun.

So . . . Spencer Ziegler had to resort to a new plan.

Get the hell out of here without getting caught by the authorities that John Marin was surely getting by now.

He put his gun away, and grabbed all of his belongings, and left John Marin's place as casually as possible so as to not draw any attention upon him.

He walked down back alleys away from any main streets.

He eventually made his way to an area that had transportation for hire, and quickly left the area.

He made his way to another city a short time later, and rented a hotel room.

Once inside of the hotel room, Spencer Ziegler contacted the employer that he and Rex Ruppert worked for.

These people were involved in the diamond industry.

They were a part of a large cooperation of business people whose main objective was to track down places on the globe where diamonds might be located, and then set up mines, and hire people to mine the precious gems to get ready for the lucrative market.

Spencer Ziegler made contact with these people in a short period of time.

He told them about Rex Rupperts current situation over in the Philippine islands.

He explained to these people that Rex Ruppert did indeed make his way to a cave that had a large bounty of precious raw diamonds.

He told them that he had seen on video, these diamonds that Rex Ruppert had on him as he hid in the jungle.

He made sure that they also understood that he seen with his own eyes on the video, that these diamonds were very large . . . unusually large.

Lastly, he told them that Rex Ruppert had marked the location of this cave with his GPS device, and that he would need to be rescued if they wanted to ever get a hold of this GPS location.

Basically, a leveraged type of blackmail to save his life in that far away jungle near the volcano that had a cave full of diamonds.

Spencer Ziegler was instructed to stay where he was at, and wait for other people to arrive to try and help rescue Rex Ruppert.

What they did not tell Spencer Ziegler was that they were first going to try to bribe the local authorities where Rex Ruppert was, and hopefully arrange a safe exchange of Rex Rupperts safe passage from their island for an amount of money that they would most assuredly not turn down.

They were definitely not pleased about the situation, and had plans to eventually eliminate Spencer Ziegler, and Rex Ruppert after all of this mess was cleaned up.

But for now, the most important thing was to get that GPS location from Rex Ruppert.

Spencer Ziegler finished his conversation with these employers, and waited for further instructions.

Thousands of miles away, Rex Ruppert was still hiding in the jungle of the great volcano, and could only hope that sometime soon . . . very soon, that he would be rescued by some people that would be sent by his employers.

He felt very confident that his partner, Spencer Ziegler, had contacted his employers, and passed on the information about the diamonds, the GPS location to the cave that he possessed, and most importantly, his dire situation in this jungle.

At about this same time, Marcos was finally entering his hometown . . . exhausted to the point of feeling like he would die if he ran anymore.

He was now walking at a slow steady pace towards the local constables office where he would be able to tell them about everything that had just happened to him and his poor father Enrique.

He was having "flashbacks" of the horrible events that he had recently experienced.

The main one was of his father Enrique being shot dead up near the cave at the great volcano.

It took Marcos about ten minutes before he finally made his way to the Constables office.

Outside of this office stood two local police officers smoking cigarettes.

He recognized both of them.

They were both friends of his father.

One was named Marion, and the other was Francisco.

Marcos had known these two men for as long as he had a memory, from the time he was an infant to the present.

He screamed out at both of them in a very frightened voice.

They both instantly recognized Marcos, and immediately came to his aid.

Both men ran a few more yards and stood in front of Marcos.

Marcos hugged Marion. Marion put his hand gently on top of the heads of Marcos, and rubbed his scalp.

He just as gently, asked Marcos what was wrong.

Francisco grabbed Marion's arm and guided him towards the entrance to the station.

He suggested to Marion that it would probably be best to listen to what Marcos has to say, at a little more private setting inside of the station.

Marion agreed with his friend, and walked Marcos into the station for more privacy.

As they entered inside of the Constables station, right away, their boss, Constable Javier St. George noticed them from across the room.

He could see that Marcos was distressed.

He motioned his men to have Marcos sit down in a chair across from his desk.

They complied quickly . . . but still gently with the young boy.

After Marcos was comfortable in the chair, Constable St. George asked Marcos to tell him and his men what was wrong, and what had happened to make him so upset.

He was offered a glass of cold pineapple juice as these questions were asked of him.

Marcos took a sip of the juice before talking.

His eyes were full of tears and ready to flow down his face.

He spoke in a whining scared voice.

"There is a bad man with a gun who has shot my dear father, and I believe that he is now dead."

"I witnessed this with my eyes, and I am not making up a lie sir."

Marcos started to cry uncontrollably after saying this.

The Constable did not say anything for a few moments.

He then exhaled loud enough to sound like a person who had a feeling of defeat.

He spoke to Marcos in a calming voice.

"Do you know who this man with the gun is?"

"Where is this man? and where is your father?"

"Talk to me Marcos, tell me everything that you know so that I can help you."

Marion and Francisco were stunned by what Marcos had just said to them.

They could only hope that this was not really true.

Enrique was a very good friend of all three of these law enforcement people.

They waited in silence, not wanting to push Marcos to answer right away.

Marcos wiped some of his tears from his face.

He stopped his verbal whining, and shook his head slowly to indicate that yes, he was ready to tell the complete story.

"There was a man with a gun at our home when we arrived back from the market yesterday."

"He killed my monkey friend . . . Kevvy."

"Kevvy is still laying dead on the floor of my home."

Sniveling started once again for Marcos, but stopped after a few moments.

He continued to talk.

"This man with the gun is a very large and mean person."

"He tied up me and my father overnight, and had us leave early this morning to travel to the great volcano."

"He forced me and my father to take him to the diamond cave at the volcano."

All three men looked at each other quizzically after hearing this statement from Marcos.

They did not know of any cave with diamonds at the volcano that towered over their humble city.

Marcos continued to speak, as he realized that he would not be interrupted, and that these men wanted, and needed to know everything as quick as possible.

"I guided this man up to a cave on the great volcano where there are many diamonds inside on the walls."

"He had my father dig some of these diamonds out of the wall for him."

"After my father scraped the walls, and dug out some diamonds for this man, this man took us back out of the cave and he shot my father, I think it was three times."

"My father struggled with this large man as I made my escape from the plateau where the cave is located."

"As I was climbing down from this plateau, I turned to see that mean man shoot my father with a large gun that did not hardly make any sound at all."

"That is why I am not sure how many shots were fired at my father, but I think it was three times sir."

"I climbed down to the ground of the jungle, and started to run as fast as I could to save my own life."

"I wanted to get back here as fast as I could so that I could tell somebody what had happened."

"Look!!"

Marcos bent over slightly, and reached inside of his pocket.

"My father gave this to me to hold while he was digging on the cave walls."

Marcos pulled out of his pocket a large diamond, and handed it over to the Constable.

The Constable held the large diamond in his hands for several seconds.

He was just as amazed at what he was looking at as everyone had been who knew and had also seen these precious stones from the cave on the volcano.

He blinked in shock several times as he remained silent.

His men were just as quiet as he was.

There was definitely one thing to realize at this point, Marcos was very obviously telling the absolute truth!!

It was now time to go to this cave, and find the boys father, and it was also time to start a manhunt for this dangerous man with the gun that Marcos speaks . . . Rex Ruppert!!

The Constable gave instructions to his men to get others to help in this search for Enrique, and his supposed killer.

He asked Marcos if he could lead them to the cave where his father could still maybe laying on the ground mortally wounded.

Marcos said that he could.

It took only an hour to get enough people to help the Constable do what he wanted.

Half of the people would search with his men, for the dangerous man with the gun in the jungle.

The other half would go with him to the cave to find Enrique.

All of the men were given weapons for their own personal protection for this assignment from the Constable.

Word traveled fast about what was happening, and by the time the Constable and his men left towards the jungle, several hundred people were already spreading this information, not really knowing all the details that were given within the Constables station by the young boy.

CHAPTER THIRTY

Vernon Montague and John Crevelli kept walking through the thick jungle with the terribly injured . . . near death Enrique.

They had no idea if they were getting any closer to civilization, or further away.

They traveled for hours, and finally came upon a small creek of water that was so small that you could step across it in two normal steps.

They crossed this tiny creek, and walked for about thirty yards and all of a sudden Vernon Montague said to stop.

He suggested to John Crevelli that maybe they should go back to the small creek and follow the direction that it flowed.

Maybe . . . just maybe, this creek might flow into a larger river, or even there might be people somewhere near this creek at some point.

They decided that there probably was a good chance of finding some people somewhere near this creek . . . eventually.

Hopefully, "eventually" would come quick, because Enrique did not look like he would survive much longer.

He was totally unresponsive to anything.

If he would only wake up for even a few moments, they might possibly get some kind of information from him, like his name, or just anything.

They wondered who the young boy was who had escaped in the jungle.

They thought that he was probably related to this wounded man, maybe even his son.

But, since this wounded man that they were carrying was not able to talk to them, they would not know at the answers to these questions anytime soon.

They also wondered about that man who had shot this poor wounded man, who was he?

Why did he shoot this man?

They had a mutual fear that they could possibly run into this man while they were in this jungle, and become victims of the gun the same as this man that they continued to carry.

They noticed, after traveling for another hour, that this small creek was actually growing in size.

You could no longer step across it in two steps.

This creek appeared to also be getting deeper as well.

It was now about fifteen feet wide, and probably two feet deep by there estimates.

This was very encouraging to the two astronauts, because it looked like what they had thought about this creek eventually leading to some people at some point had a pretty good chance of actually happening.

Even though they were extremely tired from the walking, and carrying of this wounded man through this thick jungle, they continued without stopping.

They both were very anxious now.

They felt very confident that they would soon be in contact with some people . . . they could feel it in their bones.

They hoped that it would be soon enough to save this mans life.

Suddenly . . . as they went down a slight incline and around a turn, they could hear sounds!!

The sounds were human related!!

Not necessarily human voices, human caused.

They started to move faster towards this sound.

The closer they got, the more they realized that they were on the verge of being reunited with civilization once again.

Adrenaline pumped through their veins rapidly.

They now had no feeling of being tired at all.

They now had enough renewed strength and energy to make it back to humanity . . . safe and alive!!

There was a large amount of joy within their hearts as they made their ways towards this sound of humanity.

They both could now hear sounds that appeared to be motorcycles and cars!!

As they came to another incline, this one much steeper than the last one that they went down, they stopped in their tracks.

Before them they could now see a small city.

This small city was Legazpi city.

Home of where this wounded man came from.

They carefully started to go down this steep incline, one small slow step at a time.

They traveled almost one hundred yards before they made it down to flat land again.

They were now only about two hundred yards from the outskirts of Legazpi city.

They quickened their pace with Enrique, almost at a half jog.

They cared more at this moment of getting him medical attention than anything personal about themselves.

Finally, they came into the very outskirts of this small city, and started to see people again.

Simultaneously, a large number of people from Legazpi city gazed upon the two astronauts as they carried Enrique on their makeshift stretcher.

Several people instantly ran over to them.

There were several of these people that could speak the English language as well as their own.

Without yet having to speak a word, it was obvious to these people that Enrique was in dire need of immediate medical attention.

They quickly took Enrique from the two astronauts, and told them that they would take over from here.

Several of these people indicated that they in fact knew this wound man.

They told the two astronauts that his name was Enrique, and that he was in fact a resident of this city.

They also told the two men . . . Vernon Montague, and John Crevelli, that they were in the city of Lagazpi.

They gave other information as well, the name of the island, the name of the volcano that towered over the small city, and the proud fact that they were a part of the Philippine nation.

So now, the two astronauts knew where they were.

The Philippine islands!!

Enrique was quickly taken away to a local medical facility in the hopes of saving his life.

Now all attention fell upon the two strange white men who stood among these local people of Legazpi city.

They started asking them questions.

Who were they?

Where did they come from?

How did they come upon Enrique?

They knew that Enrique had a son named Marcos, and a few of them actually had already seen Marcos earlier over at the Constables station.

A few of these people left the area where the two astronauts stood, and ran over to the Constables station to get a Police officer to come to talk to these two strangers.

Vernon Montague told these people that he wanted to talk to an official of the city, such as a Mayor, of head of the Police.

These people really did not need to know all, or any details of what they were now asking.

His priority now was to contact someone who could help him and his fellow astronaut contact representatives of the United States of America.

He was told that the Mayor would be contacted as soon as possible, and that now at this very moment, law enforcement people were being contacted.

They offered to guide the two astronauts to the Constables station.

Vernon Montague thanked them for their offer, and asked them to proceed.

So they started to walk towards to Constables station.

A small crowd surrounded the two astronauts as they walked.

As they walked, this crowd of people grew in size.

By the time that they had arrived at the constables station, the crowd numbered in the hundreds.

Chatter and rumors about these two strangers was already starting to intensify as every second ticked away.

A number of these people were already looking at these two strangers as possibly being bad people.

Once they arrived at the Constables station, they were all surprised to see that the door to the station was locked.

There was not any law enforcement people anywhere.

Where were all of the Police officers?

They did not know that the majority of Police officers, along with the Constable himself, were already deep in the nearby jungle searching for another stranger . . . Rex Ruppert, and Enrique.

Luckily, the mayor of the city was found, and he invited the two astronauts to join him at his home not to far away.

The mayor lead the way as they walked.

The astronauts, and the mayor made it to the mayors house in a few scant minutes.

There were bodyguards outside of his home, which was normal.

They stood guard, and made sure that none of the crowd was able to enter inside of the mayor's compound to his home.

Once inside his home, the mayor was very hospitable to the two astronauts.

He offered them a cold drink of anything they wanted as they sat down comfortably.

They all agreed on some nice cold beer.

The beer tasted so good to Vernon Montague, and John crevelli, that they gulped down the beer in a fast minute.

The mayor looked at them in surprise when they did this with the beers.

Without asking, the mayor handed over another two beers to the two astronauts.

This time, they took their times on the beers.

The mayor started to ask the same questions as the crowd of local people had a short time earlier.

This time, Vernon Montague was ready to answer some of the inquiries.

First he told the mayor that he and John Crevelli were United States citizens.

Next he told the mayor that the two of them were astronauts whose space capsule had been lost in the ocean that surrounds their island.

The mayor was also surprised to hear this bit of information.

After hearing this, his first thought was that these two men were actually crazy men escaped from some mental institution.

He also thought that maybe they were bad criminals on the run from other authorities.

Vernon Montague could see the doubt in the mayors face as he spoke.

He assured the mayor that he was indeed telling the absolute truth about what he was saying.

He told the mayor that all he had to do to verify what he was saying was to contact a representative of the United States, maybe an embassy official.

He assured the mayor that once he contacted the proper United States official, it would quickly become apparent that everything that he was now telling the mayor would in fact be understood as the 100% truth.

The mayor relaxed a little, sensing now that this man might very well be really telling the truth.

The mayor silently thought of who he should contact to verify what this man was saying.

He motioned for a young man who stood across the room, to come over to him.

He told him to go and get a friend of his.

This friend was someone who would be able to quickly contact the American Embassy, and notify them that these two people were here with the mayor of Lagazpi city, claiming to be two American astronauts lost at sea from a recent mission.

This young man quickly left the room on his own person mission for the mayor.

Next, the mayor asked about what they knew about the wounded man that they had carried to Legazpi city from the jungle.

He asked for all the details . . . politely.

He still did not fully trust these two strangers.

For all he knew, they could be fabricating everything, but for the moment, he would give them the benefit of not doubting what he was now being told.

All the mayor could do for now was to find out as much as he could from these two men who were obviously not from Legazpi city, and most probably not even from the Philippine islands.

After he was through talking to these two supposed astronauts, he would make arrangements for them to stay somewhere safe without being bothered by anyone until he found out what the truth was about them.

They talked for well over two hours before they came to a point of there was basically nothing else to say.

The young man came back and relayed to the mayor that he had contacted his friend.

So now the mayor made a few phone calls, and finally found a safe haven for these two men to go and wait for his friend to meet them as soon as he could.

The two astronauts followed the young boy and two bodyguards out of the back of the mayors compound and were taken to another compound about a mile away from the mayors home.

They had told the mayor everything, with the exception of the "Yeshua" adventure from the bowels of the Earth.

They knew that if they were to tell him about Yeshua, then he would for sure think that they were lying about everything else that they were telling him.

The most important thing for them now was to get back home to the United States of America!!

They settled down in this new compound, and waited for this friend of the mayor to arrive.

Within two hours, one of the mayor's bodyguards knocked on their door.

He told them that the mayors friend was there to see them.

Vernon Montague let the man inside of their room.

Once the man was inside the room with the two astronauts, he explained to them that he had spent some time before coming to them, to talk with the mayor about their conversations that they held with the mayor.

He wanted to know beforehand why he was being asked to talk with them.

He admitted right away to them that he had serious doubts about what they had told the mayor.

He also told them that if it turned out that they were lying about what they were saying, there was a good chance that they would both be arrested and taken away to the local jail until the real truth was revealed.

This would be done for the safety of the people of Legazpi city.

Both astronauts were adamant that they were indeed really telling the truth.

The told this man that they already knew that they would not have to be taken to a jail.

They urged him to please contact the proper people and tell them what information he had about them.

They assured him that once he did this, he would find out in short order that they were indeed the two lost astronauts that had most probably been reported about around the world by all the news media outlets.

He was even asked by them if he himself not heard about a space capsule being lost at see recently.

He told them that he actually had heard recently about a space capsule that had crashed into the Pacific Ocean.

He also told them that the two astronauts had been reported as lost and presumed to be dead because the space capsule had not surfaced after crashing into the ocean.

There had been an extensive search, and the capsule had not ever been found.

Not even remnants of the capsule.

The two men were firm in what they were saying, and challenged him as an honest citizen, to at the very least, follow through with their request, and find out one way or the other.

They told him that there would certainly be a large media circus shortly after it was found out that they were alive.

He was also warned that their small city would be inundated with a large amount of media reporters who would be anxious to gather information for their media employers.

Finally, this man was convinced enough that he should make the proper contacts, and find out the truth.

He bid the two astronauts farewell, and told them that if all that they said was true, then may God bless them, and hopefully they would make it home safely.

They thanked him for this comment, and he left.

Now all they could do was . . . wait.

The comment that this man had made about God blessing them was an interesting statement to make to them, if that man had only knew about their experience with Yeshua, he might have said something different.

The anxious wait for these two men officially began as soon as the door shut behind the mayors friend.

They had not even got that mans name when he was here.

CHAPTER THIRTY ONE

The American Ambassador for the United States at the embassy of the nation of the Philippines stood on a balcony looking out at the bustling city around him below.

A messenger came to the balcony and told the Ambassador that he had an urgent message from the city of Legazpi.

He stood there wondering what the message might be.

He had not heard about anything from the media . . . television or the radio today.

Maybe it was something good like a capture of a terrorist, or the killing of a terrorist.

That would be good news.

Terrorism had plagued his country for over a decade now, and the people of his country were getting tired of their evil antics.

He told the messenger to give him the sealed paperwork that contained the message from the small city of Legazpi.

He took the message paperwork from the messenger, and asked him politely to leave so that he could have some privacy as he read this message from a neighboring island, amongst all the other islands in the vast Philippine island chain.

He broke the seal from the paperwork.

He started to read the text from the message.

His eyes widened as he read the message.

What he was reading almost took his breath away.

Apparently, the mayor of Legazpi city had two men requesting to have contact with someone that represented the United States.

That would qualify him for sure.

He continued to read.

These two men were claiming to be the two U.S. astronauts who had disappeared this year when their space capsule had crashed and sank into the depths of the vast Pacific Ocean, never to resurface or be found.

This was interesting news for the Ambassador.

If it turned out to be true, he would be at the forefront initially in the media.

He liked being in the media.

After reading the entire message from the mayor of Lagazpi city, he immediately started to make plans to talk to these two men claiming to be the lost American astronauts.

He would have to talk to these two men and make a personal judgment about whether or not they might in fact be who they claim to be.

If he decided, after talking to these two supposed lost astronauts, that they might really be who they claim, then he would contact the proper authorities in the United States.

He would then create a "leak" to the media because he was sure that he would be told that he would not have the authority to say anything to the media until given proper permission . . . if ever.

The message that he just read had to be hand delivered because of the sensitivity of it's contents.

On the other hand, now that he had read this message from the mayor, he could simply contact the Legazpi mayor via the telephone.

He left his office and went to the local telephone switchboard room with actual operators that handled all incoming and outgoing calls from his island where he was presently stationed as an ambassador to the United States.

He went to the supervisor of the switchboard operators.

He asked her if he could speak to her privately.

Of course, she immediately accommodated him with his request, and they went to her office down the hall.

Once inside the office, he quickly asked her if he could use a private line to contact the mayor of Legazpi city.

Once again, because of who he was, she did not hesitate to accommodate his request.

She told him to follow her to another room where there was only a single operator who sat there in this room, handling private secure calls.

She told this lone operator that she could take a break, and that she would handle her switchboard while she was the break.

The operator left the room quietly, and with much politeness because she recognized the Ambassador.

She smiled at his as she walked away.

He smiled back.

He then turned his attention to the supervisor, with a sheepish silent smile.

She smirked at him for an instant, not really liking to see flirtation with any of her staff while they were working.

She asked him to sit down in the chair where the operator had just been sitting.

He sat down like an obedient child, and waited for her to proceed with whatever she needed to do to get this call through to the mayor of Legazpi city.

He did not really pay to much attention to what procedure she actually followed to get the call through to the mayor, but after a few minutes, the call went through successfully.

On the other end of the line was the mayor of Legazpi city, waiting to hear the voice of the Ambassador.

The supervisor handed a phone over to the Ambassador.

She told him that he could start talking.

She stood there a few feet away, not moving.

He told her that he wanted complete privacy, and would she please leave the room.

He told her that when he was finished with the phone conversation with the Mayor, that he would simply put the phone down on the desk, and depart the room.

She said that she would wait outside so that he would not be interrupted.

He thanked her for that, and she left the room.

He picked up the telephone receiver and put it close to his ear, and started to speak.

"Hello mayor."

"This is the Ambassador to the United States speaking."

"I received you hand delivered message a short time ago."

"After reading the message, I contacted you as soon as I possibly could."

"The message that I read was very interesting, do you really think that it is true?"

The mayor of Legazpi city began to speak on the other end of the phone line.

"Hello Mr. Ambassador, it is an honor to speak to someone as important as you are."

"As the message that you recently read said, I do have two men here in my city, at a safe location, who both claim to be lost American astronauts from a space capsule that crashed in the ocean this year."

"I am not sure one way or the other if they are telling me the truth, but they are very adamant about contacting a representative such as yourself for verification."

"They do appear to be Americans."

"They both have very white skin, so I have figured out that they have not been here to my island for very long because they would have had their skin affected by the sun."

"As you know Ambassador, there are no planes that arrive here at my island, access to my island is only by boat."

"They do not carry any identification between them."

"I checked that out personally."

"I warned them that if they made you and me go through all of this trouble, and find out that they are wasting out times with lies, then they would be arrested and dealt with by law enforcement."

"This statement to them did not phase them at all."

"In fact they challenged me to proceed and that they would be able to eventually prove that they were telling the absolute truth about what they were saying."

"They also said that the United States would be very grateful for our efforts."

"So, I went ahead and started the process to find out whether or not these two men are being honest with me, or are making up an elaborate lie."

"So now I have done the best that I could do, and have contacted the proper person ... you ... who, if true, will be able to do the necessary and correct procedures to get these men safely back to where they need to be."

Silence filled the phone line for a few moments while the Ambassador collected his thoughts after hearing what the Mayor had to say.

The two men talked for a few more minutes, and came to a mutual decision that it would be best to relocate these two men to where the Ambassador was now located.

Arrangements were quickly made for the two supposed American astronauts to leave Legazpi the next day, via the ferry boat.

The Ambassador hung up the phone and set the receiver down on the table in front of him.

He opened the door to the outside hallway, and told the switchboard operator supervisor that he was finished with the secure phone call, and he thanked her kindly.

She gave the Ambassador a vaguely flirtatious smile back at him, much in the same way as the previous operator had when she was asked to go on a break by the supervisor.

It was common knowledge that the Ambassador was single man, and he was used to this type of treatment from many woman of the local population.

It was a daily occurrence for him to have woman flirting with him.

Of course, he enjoyed every bit of it.

He left the building, and proceeded back to his office.

He now had to contact various people from the United States, to tell them that there was a possibility that the two lost American astronauts might in fact be alive and safe on one of the many Philippine islands.

He spent the rest of the day, calling various people to pass on the information that he had so far from conversation from the mayor of Legazpi city.

He told them that once the two men, claiming to be the lost American astronauts, were safe on his island, and when he had a chance to personally interview them, he would then contact them and keep them up to date.

At that time, based upon whether or not there was strong evidence that this was all true, it would be up to these people that the Ambassador had contacted, to decide what to do next with these two men.

All anyone could do for now, was to wait until these two men had met, and talked to the Ambassador.

Darkness was quickly approaching, and so the Ambassador left his office, done with his work for the day.

Time to go do some of his own flirting with some local women in the many nightclubs of the city.

He left his office smiling.

Vernon Montague, and John Crevelli were contacted by the mayor, at the compound where they were safely housed, and told that they would be leaving the next day by a ferry boat to another island to meet the Ambassador to the United States of America.

They were both excited by this news, and called it a night.

Both men went to bed and fell asleep very quickly, knowing now that they would soon be on their way home to their friends and loved ones.

Joy filled both of their hearts.

CHAPTER THIRTY TWO

Arrangements were made by the employers of Rex Ruppert, and his partner, Spencer Ziegler, to have a team of three men travel to the island where Rex Ruppert was hiding, and on the run from the local authorities in a jungle.

They would not be given the go ahead to travel to this island for this assignment, until contact was made to these same local authorities who pursued Rex Ruppert, to try and make a deal for the safe transfer of Rex Ruppert off of the island.

Basically a bribe.

This team that they got together for the possible assignment of the rescue of Rex Ruppert were just basically on standby as a back up plan if the bribe did not work.

They felt confident that these authorities, who were poverty stricken, would be able to easily be bribed with the right amount of money offered to them.

If it was in fact true about the diamonds, and it appeared that it was indeed true, then they could keep increasing the amount of the bribe until they cracked with greed.

Everyone had their limits before succumbing to the feeling of need, and greed.

Each feeling was interrelated with each other.

More than likely, these authorities that they would offer the money too, would crack, and take a smaller amount of money than they would ever really realize that they could have actually gotten if they played a little hard to get.

The same mayor of Legazpi city was the first person contacted by these people of the diamond industry.

They were very serious people, with very serious money.

The answer No . . . was not ever an option with them.

They were always able to get anything that they wanted without much effort, because of the vast amounts of money that they had at their disposal.

This contact with this mayor would just be another example of how they could get what they wanted, by a little prodding of some money, and take advantage of the feeling of greed that all men harbored within them.

It took a little over an hour for these people to make actual contact with the mayor of Legazpi city.

The mayor had just finished making sure that the two men who claimed to be astronauts, had boarded the ferry boat, and departed for their meeting with the Ambassador of the United States of America.

He took the telephone call only a few minutes after he got back to his home from the ferry landing.

Meanwhile, Rex Ruppert was awake from a long night of moving through the jungle.

He was mosquito bitten on many areas of his body where skin was exposed and not covered by clothing.

He was very irritated by his situation.

All he could do was wonder if he was going to be captured, of rescued by people that were hired by his employer.

Anger swelled within him about the young boy escaping from him at the plateau of the volcano where the diamond cave was.

If he were to see this young boy right now, he would kill him as quick as he could blink an eye.

He was also very mad at himself for not being more careful at the cave of diamonds.

It was the greed factor, those diamonds made him drop his guard just enough to where he was not as careful as he should have been, and now he was on the run in this jungle . . . suffering, mentally, and almost physically.

He came upon a small creek.

This was in fact the same creek that the two astronauts had followed back to civilization . . . Legazpi city, while they carried the wounded Enrique.

Rex Ruppert quickly came to the same conclusion as had the two astronauts about this small creek of slow moving water.

It would lead to people at some point in time.

So, what he did was carefully follow this small creek, but he did it several yards away, walking parallel to it's direction of flow.

He wanted to find civilization, but at the same time not be found by the authorities.

He was sure that by now, there were most probably many people looking for him to capture him for what he had done to the man and the boy.

Onward he traveled, in silent paranoia as he walked.

He felt like all of the animals that surrounded him were watching him, and laughing at him.

He was tempted to shoot a few monkeys a couple of times that he had seen in the trees . . . chattering away loudly, seemingly directed at him from what they probably thought was a safe distance.

These monkeys did not realize that this man could have killed them in a second, and they would be in monkey heaven where he had earlier put Marcos's monkey friend "Kevvy."

Back at a medical facility, Enrique was treated for his wounds, and almost miraculously, it appeared that he would survive the mortal wounds given to him by Rex Ruppert.

Marcos was at his fathers side, happy that his father was going to live through this ordeal.

Enrique had become conscious early in the morning, and was finally able to speak with his son.

Marcos told him that he still had the diamonds back at their home stored safe away.

He told him how the Constable, and others, were out in the jungle hunting for the man who had shot him.

They had come back from the diamond cave last night when they discovered that Enrique was not lying on the ground dead.

After Marcos was safely back in Legazpi city, the Constable and his men had returned back to the jungle to continue searching for the man who had shot Enrique.

As soon as Marcos had returned back to Legazpi city, he quickly found out that his father was still alive, but barely.

His father was being operated on to remove the three bullets that had entered his body when he was shot by Rex Ruppert at the volcano.

Marcos went home to rest, because there was not anything that he could do while his father was in surgery.

He was contacted early in the morning, and told that his fathers operation had been successful.

Marcos was overjoyed with this news, and immediately went to the medical center to see his beloved father.

The Constable and his men had spread out in a large circle in the jungle and hoped that if Rex Ruppert was within this circle, they would be able to eventually capture him.

They meticulously walked slowly towards the center of this invisible circle, similar to tightening up a hang mans noose.

This technique would only work if the intended target were inside of this circle.

This technique had been used for many years to capture prey by hunters.

So now it was being used on a human.

Rex Ruppert was not aware that this trap had been set for him.

He continued to walk parallel to the small creek that he had found a while ago.

He was indeed within this circle that the constable and his men had created.

Two hours went by, then Rex Ruppert stopped in his tracks.

He could hear human voices.

This alarmed him.

He quickly had his gun out, and ready to shoot in an instant.

He went in the opposite direction of the voices that he could still hear not too far away.

He now started to run like a scared animal, breaking limbs of small branches from the trees as he ran haphazardly.

He kept looking back as he ran, hoping that whoever these people were, they had not discovered him yet.

Surely, these men were hunting for him.

Three of these people, the Constables men, had in fact heard the sound of Rex Ruppert starting to run through the dense jungle.

They silently continued what they were doing.

All of these men were professional hunters, and they now knew that they would eventually have this target trapped.

After Rex Ruppert had ran only about a hundred yards from these men, he could now hear voices of other people in front of him as well.

He changed directions once again, and started running away from these voices as well.

He went only about fifty yards this time, and then there were more voices.

He felt very paranoid now, fear crept through his large body.

This was an unusual feeling for him, he was used to inflicting fear on other people.

This negative sensation made him more desperate in his thought process as he continued to run from all of these voices in the jungle that seemed now to be all around him.

Desperately, he looked for a vantage point where he could make a stand for himself against these people . . . these hunters.

Word got back to the Constable very fast that the man had been discovered within the circle.

He gave orders to his men to continue what they were doing, and try to capture this man alive.

If they had to shoot the man, try to wound him.

But . . . if their life was in jeopardy, disregard that order of trying to wound him.

Rex Ruppert could not find any place to hide, he was trapped, and surrounded.

He was now within a circle that measured only about fifty feet across in all directions from where he now stood.

The Constable decided now that it was time for him to start making demands from this person to surrender peacefully if he wanted to live.

He started hollering these commands out to Rex Ruppert, even though he could not see him.

But he knew full well, that Rex Ruppert could certainly, by now, hear what was being said to him.

The Constable told Rex Ruppert that there was twenty two people with guns that had him completely surrounded.

Rex Ruppert was no fool, very dangerous, yes, but definitely not a fool.

He decided that he did not want to try to take on all of these armed people that surrounded him.

He came to the conclusion very quickly, that if he wanted to live through this, he would have to surrender, and maybe try an escape later.

He also thought that maybe his employer would be able to get him out of this mess too.

Either way, it was time to give up to these people.

He hollered back to the Constable that he was dropping his gun, and surrendering.

He said that he would not move.

He would remain where he was now standing with his hands held high into the air.

He emphasized that he was not trying to do some type of foolish trick.

Several of the Constables men could now see Rex Ruppert standing with his hands held high into the air as he said he would.

One of these men was tempted to shoot this evil white man who had shot his friend Enrique.

But he held back, knowing that he would get into a lot of trouble if he let his emotions take over, and do what he had an urge to do at that moment.

Three men came within a few feet of Rex Ruppert, guns aimed directly at his face.

It was very obvious that they were not bluffing with their guns.

They could see that Rex Ruppert had indeed dropped his own gun down to the ground a few feet away from where he was now standing.

One of the men picked up the gun, and backed away several feet from Rex Ruppert.

Two other men grabbed Rex Ruppert, one from the back, and the other from the side.

Three other men quickly grabbed Rex Ruppert as well moments later.

They held him firmly, and waited for the Constable to appear through the trees of the jungle.

Several of the men were now smiling as the Constable finally made his way to the capture fugitive.

The Constable took from his back pocket, a pair of handcuffs.

He handed them to one of his men, and then that man put the handcuffs on the wrists of Rex Ruppert within seconds.

Rex Ruppert was officially a captured man.

The Constable and his men started back to Legazpi city.

CHAPTER THIRTY THREE

At the same time that the mayor of Legazpi city was starting a conversation with a person from the diamond industry . . . (Rex Ruppert, and Spencer Ziegler's employer), an order was sent out to the three man team that would have been sent to rescue Rex Ruppert, to instead make their way to where Spencer Ziegler was, and eliminate him.

All that this person wanted now was to get what Rex Ruppert had in his possession . . . the GPS location of the cave of diamonds at the volcano.

The mayor told this person that the local law enforcement of his city were now involved in a manhunt in the jungle for a man who had shot one of their local people.

The man on the other end acted concerned, and said that he hoped that the person who had been shot would survive.

Of course he was 100%.

He did not really care if Enrique survived or not.

All he wanted was that GPS from Rex Ruppert!!

The mayor also knew that the man was not being truthful when he said that about Enrique.

The conversation continued on.

This man, who did not say what his name was, for obvious reasons, came out right away, and told the mayor that he was interested in paying a lot of money, if he could have this man that was currently being hunted in the jungle, transferred over into custody to his people, once he was captured.

The mayor balked at this request.

The mayor was a very honest man.

But this man who was talking to the mayor knew that all men have their limits before they succumb to greed.

He flat out threw a large number in dollars to the mayor.

"How about $2,000,000 dollars?"

"I repeat to you in case you think you misheard me, two million dollars."

"Now let me emphasize to you mayor, you have to make a quick decision about this offer."

"Time is definitely a very important factor."

The mayor felt light headed after hearing this from this stranger over the phone.

He decided that he would tell this man that he would wait and see whether this man actually did get captured, and while the wait was on, he would think about this offer.

The man on the other end was very persistent.

He upped the offer another million dollars.

The mayor almost fell out of his chair when the man did this.

Finally the mayor told this man to call back tomorrow, and he would have a definite answer for him about the offer of money in exchange for the man that was now being hunted.

The mayor did not know that the man in question had just been captured in the jungle by the Constable and his men.

He would find out this information before the day was over.

He was firm with waiting until the next day with this man on the phone.

The man finally realized that the mayor was being firm in what he was saying, and that he would have to wait until the next day to hopefully get what he wanted . . . the GPS information from Rex Ruppert.

The team of three men that were sent to deal with Spencer Ziegler were already on their way to his location that was only a matter of hours after a short airline flight.

After hanging up the phone with the mayor, he immediately contacted Spencer Ziegler to let him know that he was sending a team of three men to escort him safely back to where he was for a face to face meeting.

Within a few hours, the Constable and his men arrived with Rex Ruppert in Legazpi city, and promptly locked him behind bars at the Constable's police station.

The Constable contacted the mayor right away to tell him that he he captured the man who is suspected of shooting Enrique.

The mayor told the Constable that Enrique had survived the operation from the gunshot wounds, and that his son Marcos was at his side.

The mayor did not tell the Constable about the phone call that he had received, let alone the contents of that conversation.

He had to seriously think about what answer he would give that man, about the offer of money, a large amount of money, for the exchange of this captured man who now sat at the Constables station.

No matter what, he thought to himself, all would be well, and everything would return back to normal in a very short period of time.

Or so he thought.

CHAPTER THIRTY FOUR

There was a knock on the door of the room where Spencer Ziegler was staying.

He was expecting the knock on the door at anytime that day.

He had just woke up from a night where he had a very hard time sleeping.

He went over to the door, and opened it wide enough to let three large men into his room.

They glided into the room silently.

No expressions on their faces.

They almost looked robotic.

Silence filled the air.

This instantly made Spencer Ziegler feel nervous.

He did not like what he was feeling.

Instinctively, he knew that he was in danger.

So, he casually started to walk over to the other side of the bed to try to retrieve his gun that was tucked under a pillow.

These men instantly ordered him to stop.

All three of them pulled out of their pockets, very large guns.

All of these guns had silencers on the end of the barrels.

Spencer Ziegler froze in his tracks.

He started to plead with them that they were making a mistake.

He told them that he had talked to their boss, who was also his boss, and that the boss wanted them to escort him to meet him for a face to face meeting.

He pleaded with them to at least make a quick phone call to verify what he was now telling them.

It was all over in a matter of moments, all three men fired several shots from their guns into the body of Spencer Ziegler.

Spencer Ziegler collapsed in instant death, dead before his body even hit the floor.

One man opened up a briefcase on the floor, and looked inside. all of the money was there.

The assignment was now complete.

The three men picked up all of the spent bullet cartridges, the brief case that held the money, that had been offered to John Marin, for the information he said he had about where to find a new bonanza of diamonds, and then they calmly left the room.

As they left the room, one of the men left a "Do not disturb" sign on the door handle on the outside of this room where Spencer Ziegler's body now lay motionless . . . very dead to the world.

They contacted their boss as soon as they were at a lounge at the airport for a return flight back to where they originally departed from for this assignment.

Their boss was pleased.

That was one loose end taken care of.

Now it was time to call the mayor up, and put pressure on him to try and get to Rex Ruppert if he was captured.

He hoped that Rex Ruppert had been captured since he last talked to the mayor.

He called the mayor after drinking a glass of very expensive wine worth $700 for the bottle.

Cheap stuff to him, he was just thirsty, and needed to wet his lips before getting down to business, and getting rid of the last loose end . . . Eliminating Rex Ruppert, and acquiring the GPS location of that cave that supposedly had a large bounty of diamonds within it's interior.

The way he looked at the situation, He and his partners, if it was true about this diamond cave, they would make millions of dollars, maybe even a billion dollars, so what was a few million dollars to be offered as a bribe to get what he wanted?

It was, to him, practically like a normal business deal.

Strictly business.

He dialed the number for the mayors phone.

After four rings, there was answer.

It was the mayor on the other end of the line.

The mayor knew that it was the same man who was calling before he even answered the phone.

He spoke to this man very politely, trying not to show any nervousness that he had felt all night while he thought about the offer from this man.

It was a very large amount of money, but he just could not let the greed take him over.

He had decided that he would tell this man that he would not accept the monetary offer.

Little did he know about this decision was that greed would indeed at some point overwhelm his integrity.

Honesty would be destroyed totally.

So the conversation started.

The mayor spoke first.

"I have thought over what you said to me yesterday."

"I have decided that I cannot accept your offer, which is essentially a bribe, and I am not that type of person."

"I am an honest man, and well respected."

The other man felt slightly irritated by this quick answer back to him about the offer that he had made yesterday.

He spoke back at the mayor in a calm, and casual voice.

"So mayor, I can see that you are a man that will be a little stubborn with what I have offered you."

The mayor interrupted the man to speak again.

"I also wanted to tell you that we did capture the man who we suspect shot one of our local people."

"That person who was shot, did survive, thank God."

"He is currently in the custody of our local Constable, and is behind bars at the police station."

The man spoke back to the mayor after hearing this.

"Did this man have anything personal items in his possession?"

"Like maybe a small GPS device?"

"How about a laptop computer?"

The mayor answered back that he had been to the Constables station earlier in the morning, and that yes, he did notice that there were several items confiscated by the police.

He affirmed to this man that he did in fact notice a laptop computer, and another electronic device that said "Earth scan GPS" on the outside cover.

This excited the man after hearing this from the mayor.

The mayor did not tell this man on the phone that there were some very large stones that appeared to be diamonds in their raw form that were also confiscated.

In fact, these possible diamonds were put in a separate place away from the other confiscated items found on Rex Ruppert.

It was determined that this man had probably stolen these stones from someone.

They thought that this someone was most probably non other than Enrique.

This would explain why Enrique had been shot by this man.

Enrique would be questioned about this later when he was able to.

In the meantime, this man on the phone would not need to know about these stones, and he would not be allowed to speak with Rex Ruppert.

The man on the phone did not even care about any stones that Rex Ruppert might have had on him when he was arrested, there were plenty more of those type of stones where the confiscated stones came from.

His only desire was to get the GPS device that had the location of the cave where many more diamonds could be found.

He now thought of a different plan that might work, in regards to getting a hold of the GPS device.

He began to speak once again to the mayor.

"Well mayor, I do understand what your position is about being an honest man, so I will not try to convince you to turn over this man in exchange for the money that I offered you in our last conversation."

"What will you say to me if I say that you can still have the money that I offered you, and you would be able to maintain your integrity?"

This statement intrigued the mayor.

So, he asked the man what he meant by that statement.

The man spoke again, knowing now that his new plan might work this time with the mayor.

"I will still offer you the same amount of money that I told you yesterday, if you will simply give to me the laptop computer, and The GPS device."

"How does that sound mayor?"

"You could keep this man in your custody, and deal with him through your criminal court system, and you could make a lot of money for yourself by simply giving to me the items that I just asked for."

"Also, I would be willing to donate an extra million dollars to a local charity that you could choose."

"Maybe to build a children's recreational center, or something along those lines for the benefit of your local children."

"I would also like to offer some money to the victim who was shot to help him and his family improve the quality of their lives as well."

"So mayor, how does all of that sound to you?"

"It would be a completely honest deal . . . 100% honest."

The mayor came to the conclusion that there would be no harm to his integrity, and that his city would benefit very well from this offer . . . an honest offer, just to give this man a few electronic devices.

He pondered for only a few more moments, and answered back to this man on the phone that he would kindly accept the deal that was now being offered.

Arrangements were quickly made for all that was offered in the deal to proceed on as quickly as possible.

Rex Ruppert was now just someone who would pay for his crimes, and more than likely, remain behind bars until the day that he died.

CHAPTER THIRTY FIVE

The plane touched down at the airport in Hamburg, Germany. It had been a very long flight from the Philippines to Japan and now to Germany.

Vernon Montague, and John Crevelli were seated comfortably on this plane.

They were being escorted by the military police for the United States.

It had been determined that they were indeed the astronauts that they had claimed to be when they were found in the Philippine islands.

The mayor of that little city . . . Legazpi, had been very thankful to the astronauts about their efforts in getting Enrique to a doctor from where he had been wounded.

The mayor had made sure that they knew that Enrique had survived the operation, and was expected to lead a normal life.

Both of the astronauts were happy about Enrique's successful recovery.

They were sure that he probably would not live from the wounds of the gunshots.

In this case they were very glad that they had been wrong in their judgments about his survival.

The two astronauts were quickly whisked away to a military facility a few miles away from the airport.

They would be debriefed and interviewed very thoroughly once they arrived at the secure military base.

They were separated from each other so they could be interviewed without the chance of either man being able to influence the other about their ordeal since they had lost contact with the world.

The two astronauts had already talked about what they would say, and each man went back and forth as to whether they would tell the absolute truth.

The truth was in reality, a very unbelievable story.

They feared that if they told the truth, the real truth, that they would be ridiculed, and then be thought of as being certifiably crazy.

Delusional was another term that would probably be used about both men if they decided to tell the real truth.

On the other hand, both men were very honest men, and were proud of their respected integrity amongst their peers.

It was a very difficult decision for both men to make.

Up until yesterday, both men thought that it would be best to actually go against their ordinary nature, and flat out lie about everything.

They thought it would be best to keep it a secret between each other.

But . . . that was yesterday, both men carried a lot of pride within their souls, and today, they both mutually decided that they would tell the truth about everything, no matter what the final consequences turned out to be for them.

They both also came to this decision because they knew what the truth was . . . Yeshua . . . or Jesus, was going to make his return back to the surface of the Earth and be amongst humanity once again after almost twenty centuries had passed since he departed.

He had given this specific information to them when they were in his presence in Nevaehruo.

They were both completely convinced that the being that they had met called Yeshua, was in fact the being called Jesus.

The same Jesus that was crucified by the Romans on a cross, and whose death spurned the creation of a worldwide religion.

They realized what the initial repercussions would be for them when they told their unbelievable story, but it was true, and they were willing to put up with the mental stress from all of the naysayers that would not believe them.

Their retribution would come full circle for them in a positive sense, when Yeshua did make his return.

That return was supposed to be sometime this year, according to Yeshua.

Once he returned, both men would be able to simply say, without sarcasm, the old adage . . . "I told you so."

They would be the only people on the entire planet that would not act surprised when that glorious day came for humanity.

His return back to humanity would shock everyone . . . believers, and non-believers alike.

The respect that the astronauts would lose for now, would be regained, when Yeshua stood before the people of the Earth once again!!

They were both curious about how Yeshua would be able to convince the skeptics that he was indeed Jesus.

They both thought that it would have to be something spectacular, or even an unbelievable event for sure.

Maybe he would have to show people that he could do what was deemed as impossible . . . possible.

There had been tales told in the past about his seemingly impossible acts that had been witnessed by people of the Earth.

He had easily demonstrated, without much effort, very unbelievable acts for both astronauts.

They were not magic tricks, or even illusions, they were things that he was able to do because he had the power do those things.

It seemed as if he had the power to do anything he well pleased at any particular time.

So both men were convinced that Yeshua would indeed really come back to Earth this year, and he would do something very unbelievable, that would very quickly convince humankind, that he was in fact the being that they worshiped . . . Jesus.

So now both men were separate from each other for the first time since they embarked on their mission to outer space and back then to Earth.

Since they had both agreed to tell the absolute truth, and deal with the consequences, they would not have a very hard time at all in telling separate stories that would be very identical.

Vernon Montague sat in a chair near a small table, in a well lit room that was so bright that his eyes squinted slightly.

He could see across the room, a large mirror mounted on the wall.

Obviously, it was a two way mirror.

Vernon Montague sat in the chair waiting for whoever was going to show up to interview him.

In another room, not to far away down the hallway, John Crevelli also sat in a similar room with a similar set-up, including the obvious two way mirror on the wall.

Neither man felt nervous about their upcoming interviews.

In fact, both men were actually very anxious to start telling their unbelievable stories.

The door to Vernon Montague's room opened wide.

In side of the room stepped two people.

One male and the other a female.

They both looked very studious with their glasses, and like doctors because of the white jackets they were wearing.

Vernon Montague started to stand up from the chair to shake hands and greet them, but the man insisted that he could remain seated.

The female did not say a word yet.

There were two chairs across the table from Vernon Montague.

Both of these people sat down in these two chairs.

They both had "plastic" smiles upon their faces, the same as the phony grins that politicians use to try to make people believe that they are genuinely in a pleasant moment with themselves, but in reality are quite the opposite in most cases.

The pretend game of acting like one is in a good mood is often played by people that have a hidden agenda that is hidden behind that fake smile.

In this case, these two people that sat across from Vernon Montague were most probably the types of people that could be put in this pretend game.

The man introduced himself first, and then the female finally spoke, and introduced herself as well.

She had a voice that made her sound older than she appeared to be.

Her youthful appearance made her look like she was probably about twenty five or a bit younger, but if you were to close your eyes and listen to her talk, you might imagine a woman that was a few decades older.

After their introductions to the astronaut, the man simply, and to the point, asked Vernon Montague if he would please tell his story about where he and his fellow astronaut had been, and what they had done since they disappeared in the Pacific Ocean.

Vernon Montague was now smiling, because he knew that he was going to absolutely wrangle the brains of these two people that sat across from him.

He already knew that they were going to either think he was mentally unstable, or a very good at telling untrue stories.

He cleared his throat before speaking.

"What I am about to tell you, I promise you, will be very unbelievable to both of you."

"I will also guarantee both of you that my partner, John Crevelli will tell a story that will be almost identical to what I will tell both of you."

"Afterwards, I am sure that all of the people that heard our stories, will undoubtedly think that we coached each other ahead of time to tell the same stories."

"Both of us will be willing afterwards, to take a polygraph examination to determine if either of us were being deceptive during our interviews."

"I will also say right now . . . we will be determined at that time, that we were both telling the absolute 100% truth."

"I also want both of you to think to yourselves, as you hear me telling what happened, Why would this man make up such an unbelievable story?"

"I assure you both, I have no ulterior motives, and do not have anything to gain in a positive sense, to fabricate an untrue story."

"I do not feel like wasting my time, or yours, when I take the time to tell this story to both of you."

"Believe me, I do not want to ruin my professional career because I decided to lie about what everyone is curious about."

"Where were we?"

Vernon Montague laughed out loud at this question.

"What did we do?"

He laughed again at this other question.

"Well . . . here we go with the story."

Both people that sat across from Vernon Montague shook their heads in silence to indicate that they were ready to hear the entire story from him.

"Me and John braced ourselves for impact with the surface of the water of the ocean."

"Neither of us were sure that we would survive that impact."

"We were both scared for our lives as the space capsule plunged downwards towards the ocean's surface."

"I was actually, silently, praying to God at that moment."

Vernon Montague laughed out loud again after saying this.

He regained his composure, and continued to speak once again to these two people.

"The capsule hit the water, the "G" forces and impact with the oceans water made me lose consciousness."

"I am suer that the same happened to John as well."

"The space capsule started to sink down below the ocean's water at an incredible speed."

"Surely, the capsule would at some point, implode, but amazingly it did not."

"I guess those Chinese engineers had their act together when they built this particular space capsule."

"I do not know for sure how far down we sank below the ocean, but I assure you that it was several miles at the very least."

Both people that sat across from the astronaut as he spoke, looked at each other in silence.

They continued their silence as Vernon Montague paused for a moment before starting to speak again.

He could already detect doubt from these two strangers in front of him.

"The capsule, somehow was sucked into a cave system, deep beneath the floor of the ocean."

"The space capsule traveled in this cave system for quite awhile, bouncing off the walls as it continued downward."

"It was worse than any amusement park ride that I ever experienced in my life."

"Me and John were getting pretty banged up during this freefall in this cave system."

"My mind was racing with all sorts of different thoughts, most of them were about the horrific death that I was about to experience at a given moment."

"It did not look like God was going to answer my prayers."

He chuckled after saying this.

"I honestly lost track of time, because it was completely dark as we traveled inside of this underwater cave system."

"But . . . eventually, the capsule became airborne once again, and splashed yet again in another body of water."

"It was like we went over a giant waterfall, and splashed down on a humongous lake down below."

"We could now see light."

"But, of course it was not sunlight from our Sun, it was some type of artificial light."

"I new this almost instantly."

"Me and John sat there for an undetermined amount of time inside of the capsule."

"We could not believe that we had actually survived this ordeal up to that point."

"Finally, we were able to look through the window of the capsule and see what was outside."

"What we saw . . . was quite unbelievable."

"On the shoreline nearby, there was a very large number of people dressed in white clothing."

"They appeared to be of all the various ethnic groups that we all recognize."

"I felt a spooky feeling when I realized that they were looking at us, and they all looked like they were just as surprised as we were at that moment."

"Who were these people?"

"Me and John finally realized that we had to exit the capsule, and meet these people on the shoreline."

"As we climbed out of the capsule, these people started to back away slightly and spread apart to create a pathway from the shoreline, and backwards a few hundred feet."

"We did not see anything that would make us feel like we were going to be harmed by these people."

"We now noticed a man, who had very dark skin, he looked like a black man, wearing the same white as everyone else."

"He stood in front of all of these people as if he were their leader."

"So me and John started to walk towards these people, slowly, and cautiously."

The two people listening to Vernon Montague remained silent . . . and already skeptical.

They already had thoughts that this astronaut was mentally unstable, but they needed to hear the whole story anyway.

So they continued to listen to this fantastic story from Vernon Montague.

"Me and John finally made our ways to the beach and stopped to see who if this black man would be the person to greet us."

"We stood there silently waiting."

"Nobody approached us, or even said a word to us."

"All they did was stand there and stare at us silently."

"Finally, this black man did take a single step in our direction, stopped, and then spoke to us."

"He was very polite and made us feel comfortable right away."

"He gestured us to follow him up the pathway created by the people around him."

"We followed him with no fear or paranoia."

"After we were relaxed in a comfortable setting, this black man told us where we were, and who he was."

"I know by now, you already probably think that I am crazy, but this is what really happened."

"John will tell you the same story."

Vernon Montague continued to tell the entire story, not leaving out a single detail. It took him over two and a half hours to complete his story to these two people.

He finally finished telling these two people everything that he could possibly remember in regards to the ordeal that he and his fellow astronaut John Crevelli experienced since the space capsule disappeared.

He was totally exhausted, and asked if he could go and get some rest.

The two people did not bother to ask him any questions at this point in time because everything was recorded, and as suspected by Vernon Montague, there was indeed some people behind the mirror on the wall who were witnesses to his entire story.

There would be plenty of time later on to ask any questions, but first, all the information collected from this fantastic story had to be sifted through and analyzed.

They told Vernon Montague that he could go and get some much needed rest.

He was led out of the room by two military sentries and back to his assigned room.

They closed the door behind him.

The door was locked.

John Crevelli had already finished telling his story to other people in a separate room, a short time ago, and had been escorted to a cafeteria by sentries to eat because he said he needed something to eat.

It was agreed by all of the staff of people that had interviewed the two astronauts that the astronauts would have to remain apart, and put into custody until further notice.

They were initially diagnosed as mentally unstable.

The two astronauts were not aware of any of this information.

After a few days, the two astronauts were once again taken to separate interview rooms, and once again there were two people inside of these rooms to talk to them.

The people were different this time.

The staff, after much analysis of the two astronauts stories, came to the conclusion that they had came up with their stories while they were on that small Philippine island.

The staff was convinced that the part of the story where they talked about this black man called Yeshua ... or who we call Jesus, was supposed to come back to Earth and meet humankind once again, and this was supposed to happen this very year . . . 2012.

Staff thought that for sure, the two astronauts had access to a computer, and went online.

Once online, they probably read about the ancient papyri that was recently found.

Those papyri had been put online by a world renowned scholar for everyone on the planet to read.

If one were to believe the contents of those papyri, one could be led to believe that a man called Yeshua, or Jesus would be returning to Earth in the later part of this year . . . 2012.

Apparently, these two astronauts have come to believe this story that they obviously had to read online, because their stories match what is said in the ancient papyri.

The staff informed both astronauts of their belief that they had read the unbelievable story online, and were repeating the story back to the people who were interviewing them.

They also told the two astronauts that it was their belief that this unbelievable story was being told to the interviewers instead of what the actual truth really was.

They flat out told the two astronauts that they were either being deceptive, and telling this fantastic story to avoid telling what actually happened, or the two astronauts were mentally unstable at this point in time because of the trauma they experienced while they were missing.

The two astronauts argued with the interviewers about their conclusions.

They became very loud, and it only made them look even more like they were mentally unstable, as staff was suggesting.

Both astronauts asked what would it take for them not to be thought of as mentally unstable.

They both wanted to go home, and back to their private lives.

They were told that this would not be possible at this time.

Anger flowed out of both astronauts as the staff answered their question as to what it would take to be deemed not mentally unstable.

The simple answer was that the two astronauts would have to tell the truth.

The astronauts were very frustrated because they had indeed told the absolute truth to these interviewers.

The astronauts did know ahead of time that this would probably happen if they told the actual truth, which they did, so they were now prepared to experience all of the consequences by sticking to their stories.

They were both confident that Yeshua would eventually return to Earth, just as he had told both of them.

Yeshua's appearance would be the catalyst to believe their stories.

CHAPTER THIRTY SIX

Roger Tusk sat comfortable in his plush chair waiting for the two Presidential candidates to enter the room for their scheduled debate that would be aired throughout the world.

He was almost giddy at the thought that he would be asking a question to both men that would totally catch them off guard.

It would be a question that neither man would have had time to practice answering.

The thought of seeing both of these men, squirming in their seats, trying to figure out how to answer this one particular question, really made Roger Tusk feel more powerful than the two men vying to be the President of the United States for the next four years.

He could not make the smile on his face go away.

Finally, after the President, and his challenger were finished receiving make-up on their faces for the television cameras, they entered onto the stage.

First on stage walking towards a podium was the challenger.

He was followed a few seconds later by the current incumbent President.

Both men now stood at their respective podiums, waiting for Roger Tusk to begin with some questions for them to answer.

Roger Tusk spent the next forty five minutes asking both men various questions ranging from the Economy, and Healthcare, to Immigration, and National Defense.

Both men had plenty of time to answer all of these questions with their normal talking points that had been heard many times during the campaign season.

Both of these candidates had very confident, almost smug looks upon their faces.

Finally . . . the time had come for one final question to the two candidates before the debate would be concluded.

Roger Tusk looked at both men with a smile, and started to speak very coyly.

"I have one final question for both of you to answer and then we will be finished with this debate."

"I know that both of you men have heard about the ancient papyri that was found this year, and subsequently had a very thorough analysis done with them by several renowned experts from the appropriate fields, to accomplish the task of translating the ancient language that was written upon the papyri for modern day people to understand."

Both men looked back at Roger Tusk quizzically, no clue as to where this question might be going.

Already, both men lost their looks of confidence, and now they both showed an obvious uneasiness between them.

Roger Tusk continued.

"These translations have been put online for all to read, and come up with their own opinions."

"The very well known Professor Ntangku put these translations online, and ever since these translations have been online, it seems like everyone is going crazy about them."

"I am sure that both of you have heard about these translation."

Both men shook their heads to affirm that they had indeed heard about these translations online.

"So . . . there is one thing that is mentioned in these ancient papyri that is the most popular question amongst nearly all of the people that hear about it, or actually take the time to read the actual translated text."

"There is mention of a man called Yeshua."

"This man is supposed to actually be Jesus."

"Supposedly, the name Jesus did not even exist during the time that he was supposed to have walked the Earth."

"This man called Yeshua in the translations is supposed to return back to Earth this year."

The translations say the exact date."

"This exact date is . . . December 21, 2012."

"That date is not to far away from today."

"So here is my question to both of you pertaining to what I have just described."

"I'll ask the Presidential challenger to answer this question first, and then the President can finish the night with his final answer to this question to the people of his own country, and the people of the world as well."

"Do you believe that Jesus will in fact return back to Earth on December 21, 2012?"

Roger Tusk waited for an answer from the Presidential challenger, who was now very obviously uncomfortable.

He had the look of someone that was scared, and lost.

Roger Tusk felt internal elation upon this sight across from him.

This powerful man looked frozen.

Roger Tusk urged the man to speak.

Finally after several moments had passed, he tried his best to answer this unusual question.

"I will definitely have to go on record that it is my belief that the translations are nothing but a bunch of garbage written by a delusional man of those times."

"I do not believe that Jesus will return on December 21, 2012."

"That would barely be a month after I win this upcoming election, and I will not have an embarrassment of going along with this atrocious prediction hanging over my head when I am sworn into office as the new President of the United States of America."

"I am not going to waste my time anymore with any of this nonsense about Jesus coming back this year."

Silence reverberated within the large expanse of the room.

Roger Tusk looked over towards the President and gestured to him to please answer the same question.

The President did not waste to much time before he answered the same question as his challenger.

"I will say right off the bat, I am a strong believer in our Lord, the savior, Jesus Christ."

"I have actually taken the time to read what was posted online by Professor Ntangku."

"I am sure that my opponent has not done this."

"It is a hard question for me to answer, because on the one hand, I really do hope that Jesus does in fact return back to the Earth to face humanity this year."

"I have been hoping for this my entire life since I discovered our Lord Jesus."

"But . . . that papyri was written almost two thousand years ago."

"I find it very hard to believe that someone could say with any positive certainty that this wonderful event would actually happen on an exact date almost twenty centuries into the future."

"So I have to honestly say that I am very skeptical that this wonderful event will actually happen this year, as the ancient papyri has said it would."

"If this event does actually happen, I will be one of the first people to admit that I was incorrect in saying what I am saying tonight."

"I will invite the Lord Jesus to the White House."

"I have no more to say at this time on this particular subject."

"God Bless the United States of America!!"

The debate ended within a few minutes after the President finished speaking to Roger Tusk.

Roger Tusk was very pleased with himself.

He had a smile on his face that stretched completely across his face as he signed off of the air for the night on worldwide television.

CHAPTER THIRTY SEVEN

Vernon Montague, and John Crevelli sat dazed in their separate rooms.

Both men had just finished watching the Presidential debate hosted by Roger Tusk.

A few hours later, both men were finally allowed to see each other once again.

They sat and talked to each other for the next three hours about what they had told the interviewers.

As they already knew, the same questions had been asked after they finished telling their stories.

Also, they were not surprised when they heard from each other that they had told almost identical stories.

Both men knew of the consequences that awaited them.

They had discussed this prior to even leaving the small Philippine island.

They were surprised that they were being treated like prisoners.

They had not done anything wrong to warrant this type of treatment.

All they wanted to do at this point was to go home to their friends and loved ones.

Did their loved ones, or friends even know that they were alive?

They did not know the answer to this question because they had not been allowed to try and make contact with those people.

Even a man locked up in jail gets the right to make at least one phone call.

But this was not the case with these two astronauts.

The next day, they both decided to go together to talk to the highest authority at the facility where they were presently located.

They were given permission to talk to the Commanding Officer of the Base.

A short time later, both men were led to his office by sentries.

He welcomed them into his office, and asked them to sit down and make themselves comfortable.

Both astronauts sat down in plush high back chairs facing in the direction of the Commanding Officer.

He started talking almost right away.

"I have been told by the people that interviewed both of you men separately, that you tell a story that is downright hard to believe."

"I have watched the videotapes of these interviews, and I have to be completely honest with you men, I don't believe the fantastic story that came out of your mouths."

"I do not understand why both of you would decide to be so deceptive."

Vernon Montague started to talk without asking permission.

"Sir . . . we were both telling the truth."

"I know that our story sounds unbelievable, but it is the absolute truth."

"Are you going to keep both of us as prisoners because we are telling this story to you?"

"We did not break any laws."

"I want to call my loved ones, and friends."

"They think that I am dead."

"That is not fair to me, or the people that care about me."

"I won't speak for John, but I am sure that he feels pretty much the same as I do."

The Commanding Officer answered these questions in a kind respectful tone of voice.

"Mr. Montague, and Mr. Crevelli, I have no intention of keeping both of you men here on my Base against your wills."

"We just had to get the interviews from both of you."

"All we wanted to know was what in the Hell happened to both of you from the time the space capsule entered the Earth's atmosphere and then the splash down in the Pacific Ocean."

"We were worried about what happened to both of you after splash down."

"After the space capsule disappeared, there was a massive search to find you men, and the space capsule."

"But both of you and the space capsule vanished."

"What were we to think?"

"Then, out of nowhere, both of you reappear on a small Philippine island."

"Then you both tell a fantastic story that would make people either think one of two things about you."

"Either you are not telling the truth, for what reason, we do not understand, or your both mentally unstable due to a traumatic experience that caused you both to be deceptive after going online and viewing the ancient papyri that was found this year in some cave in the desert."

"I had a discussion earlier today before you men requested to talk to me, to everyone involved with this debriefing process."

"I have given orders to have both of you released from custody after you leave my office."

"You will both be free to go and do as you both please."

"I just want to warn you though, if you both go and tell other people what you have told me and my staff, I am sure that you will get the same reaction as we have given to both of you to this point."

"They will think that your not being truthful, of your mentally unstable."

"Nobody can force you to tell what really happened out there in the Pacific Ocean, but we can only hope that one day, and I hope that it is very soon, one day you will both tell the true story as to what really happened when that space capsule hit the surface of the Pacific Ocean."

"Of course, there is going to be a huge media blitz when both of you return back to your lives with your friends and loved ones."

"Everyone thinks that both of you men are dead."

"So it will ultimately be your choices as to how you will proceed once you leave this base."

"You are both free to leave anytime you please."

The Commanding Officer sat there silently, waiting for another reaction from the two astronauts.

Moments later, both men stood up, and thanked the senior officer for his decision to let them leave freely.

They shook hands, and left his office.

Both men were now elated that they would finally be able to go home.

Both men went to the nearest phones to start making the calls that their friends and loved ones never in their dreams ever expected to receive.

Both men spent the next several hours crying and talking on the phone with people that cared the most for them.

CHAPTER THIRTY EIGHT

It seemed like every channel on the television, and every radio station was talking about the miraculous return of the two astronauts who were thought to have died somewhere in the Pacific Ocean.

But . . . amazingly, the talk was more about what they were saying, than their return, after supposedly being dead.

Already, both men had been on major networks, and had been interviewed several times.

Both men keep telling the same amazing, unbelievable story.

The story was upsetting to a large amount of people, mainly the religious types.

Even the Pope himself had gotten word of their unbelievable story, and the Vatican officially went on record, calling the two astronauts mentally unstable.

Roger Tusk was also elated about this new development.

It fit in with the question that he had now asked a growing number of high ranking politicians, and various famous people throughout the world.

The question was the same as the story that the two astronauts were now telling to the world.

Professor Ntangku, and her colleagues that worked with her on the ancient papyri project also took notice of the two astronauts story.

The world was definitely buzzing about what the two astronauts were saying in their interviews.

Their story never changed after several interviews with a number of different media outlets.

It was always the same, Yeshua, or who is now called Jesus, would return to Earth on December 21,2012.

Of course they were often ridiculed by many who heard what they were telling everyone, but that did not faze them even a tiny bit.

They were setting themselves up for either being the biggest fools in recent memory, or they would be lauded as very brave honest men who were not scared to go ahead and tell their story, even through all the criticism they received.

Professor Ntangku and her colleagues who worked on the project were now having their own discussions as to whether there might be something to their discovery.

What if it turned out to be true?

What is Yeshua . . . Jesus actually did make his return on the date predicted?

None of them were ready to commit to saying that they in fact believed that this would actually happen in December of this year.

On the other hand, none of them would go in the other direction either, and say that they did not believe it would happen.

They pretty much had a wait and see attitude . . . remaining neutral to all inquiries of belief to the most popular question that not only Roger Tusk, but what seemed like what everyone was asking nowadays.

There were times when Vernon Montague and John Crevelli thought to themselves while they were experiencing extreme amounts of criticism . . . where is Yeshua when you really needed him.

He could, with a wave of a hand, convince everyone how real he actually was.

But both men would quickly catch themselves during these tough moments, and remind themselves that they would have the last laugh when Yeshua did indeed show up in December of this year.

World leaders, famous people ranging from sports to movies stars, and normal people from all walks of life were talking about what these two astronauts were saying publicly . . . over, and over again.

The military that each astronaut represented was also being asked a ton of questions about the astronauts as well.

The astronauts were actually becoming a public embarrassment to them.

But there was really nothing that the military could do, the astronauts were just using their rights of freedom of speech, as they knew they could under the laws of the constitution of their country.

Unfortunately for their friends, and loved ones, their was also much ridicule as well that they had to put up with.

There was teasing at workplaces for the adults that were close to the astronauts, and even the children were teased by other kids when they were at school.

It seemed like there was a very large percentage of people that were non-believers of the two astronauts story.

It was disheartening to the two astronauts when even some of the people that were closest to them, started to avoid, or even shun them because they did not want to be known associates to them.

Residual negativity by association.

They found out, for sure, who the people were that really did in fact care for them.

These were the people that would put up with the criticism, and ridicule from the non-believers.

For now, they had to go through the clouds of sadness, but eventually, they knew that those clouds would turn into a sunshine of happiness.

CHAPTER THIRTY NINE

The Mayor of Legazpi City was nervous as he paced the room, waiting for the arrival of two men who would be picking up the items confiscated from Rex Ruppert, who was still incarcerated in the jail at the Constables station.

There had been an arrangement already set-up between the Mayor, and these men who it tuned out, were people that represented the diamond industry.

So much money, and the benefits that the children of his city would receive was just simply wonderful.

Also, this man . . . Rex Ruppert would be able to be prosecuted in his jurisdiction, and punished accordingly.

That pleased the Mayor as well.

At first, the Mayor, and the Constable, had decided that they would not mention the fact that they had found some very large diamonds along with the items that were going to be turned over to these two people.

They did changed their minds though, when they found out that these two people were from the diamond industry.

These diamond people were probably here to get the diamonds as well as the other items that they specifically requested.

It was certainly not a coincidence that some large diamonds were found in the personal items of this person that they had in custody, and that now there was diamond industry people here in this little city out in the middle of the Pacific Ocean.

Large diamonds . . . people from the diamond industry?

More than likely, definitely not a coincidence.

For now, the Mayor would honor and complete this prearranged deal for all parties involved.

Everyone would benefit from this wonderful deal, except of course . . . Rex Ruppert.

He would be the big loser in this case.

Nobody seemed very concerned about this fact.

There was a knock at the door.

The Mayor almost fell down when he heard this knock.

The diamond industry people were here.

The Mayor walked over to the door and answered it as casually as he possibly could without showing any outward excitement or anxiousness.

Two men stood their in suits that must have easily cost thousands of dollars each.

Both men had dark sunglasses upon their face, so dark in fact, that there was no evidence of eyes behind the dark lenses.

But, as soon as they walked into the Mayor's home, they took off their sunglasses to show respect.

They held out their hands, and bowed their heads slightly, showing more respect for the moment.

The Mayor introduced himself, and then the two men did the same back to him in very pleasant voices.

The Mayor motioned for the two men to get comfortable in two "Butterfly chairs" across from a small table and another chair made of mahogany.

All three men were seated, and then the Mayor rand a small bell on the table.

In the room came a young woman.

She walked over to the Mayor silently, and stopped in front of him, waiting for instructions.

The Mayor asked the two men if they would like something to drink.

Both men said that they would like to have some beer.

The Mayor motioned with his hand to the woman, and she quickly went and retrieved several bottles of beer, and set them on the table.

After a few minutes, the Mayor cut to the chase . . . "So, are we still going to go ahead with the deal that we worked out before your arrivals?"

One man replied back to this question.

"You may have noticed that we did not bring a briefcase that might carry the amount of money that was agreed upon for the deal."

"This is for security purposes Mayor."

"Once we have all of the items that we came for, and a chance to at least talk to our former employee for a few minutes, we will transfer the amount of money that we agreed upon into a bank account of your choosing."

"Also, we will sign a legal binding contract that will be for the building of a children's center . . . at our expense of course."

"I forgot to mention one thing over the phone though."

"Along with the computer, and GPS device, there are a number of precious stones in raw form as well."

"We want to take those stones as well."

"Do you have a problem with that Mayor?"

The Mayor did not waste any time answering this question.

He had already practiced the answer many times in his head while he waited for their arrival.

"All we have to do is go over to the Constable station, and you will be able to get everything that we agreed upon."

"Also, I do not have a problem with you meeting with the prisoner for a few minutes."

"As far as the precious stones?"

"We did in fact find some diamonds in raw form in the prisoners possessions."

"I do not have a problem with giving those to you as well."

Both men looked over at each other with pleased expressions on their faces.

The three men sat there for another half of an hour, and then the Mayor offered to finally take them over to the Constables station to complete the deal.

The two men quickly agreed to the offer from the Mayor.

It did not take very long for the three men to arrive at the Constables station.

Once there, they went in and sat inside of the Constables office.

The Mayor introduced the two men to the Constable right away.

Over in the corner of this office on a small desk was all of the items that had been confiscated from Rex Ruppert upon his arrest.

The only exception was the diamonds.

The diamonds were stored in the Constables desk, under lock and key.

The Constable had his own desk top computer on his desk.

The Mayor asked the Constable if the two men could use the computer so the money could be transferred to the Mayor's bank account.

The Constable did not hesitate.

In an instant, he was to his feet, and moving out of the way, so one of the two men could start using the computer as the Mayor had asked.

One of the two rose to his feet and walked over, and sat down at the computer.

The other man asked if he could please talk to the prisoner . . . Rex Ruppert.

The Constable motioned the man to follow him out of his office, and back to where the jail cells were located.

This man . . . unknown to the Constable, had inside the palm of his hand, a tiny custom engineered syringe with one dose of a deadly toxin that could kill a human within a few hours after entering the bloodstream.

The plan was to inject Rex Ruppert with this toxin as they shook hands when they greeted each other.

The man would want to have privacy when he attempted to do this.

Once the Constable and this man were in the jail cell room, he asked the Constable if he could talk to the prisoner alone.

The Constable unlocked the cell to where Rex Ruppert was located, and relocked the cell door when the man was inside of the cell.

The Constable walked away, and said that he would return in a few minutes.

This would be plenty of time for this man to carry out his secret plan of murder.

This specially engineered syringe was so small that Rex Ruppert would not even be able to feel the injection once administered during the handshake.

Within a few minutes, the victim ... Rex Ruppert would feel sleepy, and not show any effects of being injected with a highly toxic death potion.

When the next day came, the victim would not wake-up.

He would be dead, and there would not be any traceable evidence of the deadly potion within the body.

Rex Ruppert was all smiles when he saw the man with the Constable.

He knew this man very well.

He had been hired on several occasions by this man to do dastardly deeds.

He walked over and stuck out his hand to shake.

The man quickly grabbed Rex Ruppert's hand with the hand that held the tiny syringe, and used his other hand to hold the other side of Rex Ruppert's hand for a very firm, and what appeared to be a very friendly handshake between the two men.

The deadly toxin was injected into the bloodstream of Rex Ruppert instantly.

As planned, he did not feel a thing.

There was not even a drop of blood that was visible from the injection sight.

Part of this deadly potion had a blood clotting enzyme mixed into it so as to prevent any blood from exiting the small wound.

Of course, Rex Ruppert thought that this man was here to basically rescue him from this ordeal that he was in, but the man quickly gave the bad news to him, along with the deadly shot of toxin.

Rex Ruppert was crushed, he sat down in total bewilderment and just stared straight ahead.

He knew better than to argue, or plead with this one particular man.

The only thing that Rex Ruppert said to this man before he left his cell was that he had diamonds in with his possessions when he was arrested.

The man simply said to Rex Ruppert as the Constable opened the cell door to let him out . . . "I already know about the diamonds, they will be in my possession in a few minutes . . . good luck Rex."

The Constable walked the man back to his office.

Once they were back at his office, he could see that the Mayor was standing behind the man that was sitting at the computer.

The Mayor had a huge smile on his face.

The Constable realized that the money had been transferred into the Mayor's bank account.

The man at the computer asked the Mayor if he was satisfied.

The Mayor said that he was very happy.

The man then rose from the chair and asked as he walked across the room . . . "I guess this is everything?"

The Constable walked over to the desk and unlocked the drawer.

Inside of this drawer he pulled out a brown bag.

He told the man that was now across the room looking at the confiscated items . . . "This is also yours as well."

The other man collected this brown bag from the Mayor, almost snatching it out of his hands, like someone who was desperate.

He opened the bag, and pulled out a large diamond.

He walked over to his partner and handed it to him with a smile on his face.

The other man smiled instantly.

The GPS device was on, and he could see that there was indeed a marked location on the screen.

He quickly went on the laptop computer to see where exactly this GPS location was.

To his delight, it was at a volcano on this very island.

Both men marveled at the diamonds within the brown bag.

As a gesture of happiness, and for the purpose of being able to get more favors from the Constable and Mayor in the future, the one man with the GPS device handed each of them a diamond as a gift.

He next asked the Constable if he could use the printer in his office.

The Constable quickly gave permission to this request.

The man printed out a document, as he had previously promised the Mayor, that was made up by lawyers stating that the following contract was a binding contract upon receiving signatures from all parties.

This was the document for the building of the children's center.

All four men in the room could not sign this document quick enough.

Their signatures were on the document within one minute between the four men.

What the Mayor and Constable did not realize was that now that their signatures were on this document, this man would be able to transfer these same signatures to other documents that the mayor or Constable might not ever see with their eyes.

There would be other documents made up by lawyers that would give these diamond industry men permission to bring their company to the island and start mining for the diamonds at the GPS location . . . the diamond cave where these large diamonds were found.

They would have 100% sole ownership of all of the diamonds mined from this GPS location.

CHAPTER FORTY

It was now the middle of December . . . 2012.

Yeshua was starting to prepare for his return trip back to the surface of the planet.

He was waiting for one of his brother's from another part of a distant galaxy to arrive.

This brother was one of his brother's who would normally be delivering souls when there was a shortage in Nevaehruo.

This would normally coincide with all of the "UFO" sightings from around the planet when this type of delivery was being made to Yeshua.

As evil people's souls on the planet Earth turned into dust to float endlessly in the air, or grains of sand laying on the beach, the number of good souls would become low in numbers.

This was something that had been done with all of Yeshua's brother's for thousands of years when ever the amount of souls got to a low level.

On this particular occasion, there would not be a delivery of souls from this brother.

This brother would come to Earth to watch Nevaehruo, while Yeshua was on the surface of the planet for his time of judgment with the human population.

This had been planned almost two thousand years ago by Yeshua.

Yeshua's brother finally did arrive to Earth that same day.

Of course, as usual, there were human witnesses that observed his space craft, and they . . . as usual, reported to various authorities that they had seen a "UFO."

Yeshua's brother came alone with an empty space craft, not carrying a single soul as was the norm.

This brother had done this duty for Yeshua on a few prior occasions over time, for various reasons.

There were times that this brother had to carry a large number of souls to deliver to Yeshua on Earth.

One such occasion was when the "Bubonic plague" ravished Europe during the "Dark ages."

This was when over half of the population of Europe was decimated by the plague.

Other times were when there had been evil men of the world, recorded in human history, who had decided to try and wipe out an entire population of people.

A couple of these examples were in Cambodia and Germany.

These two "Genocides" were busy times for Yeshua to request from his brother, more souls to be delivered to Earth.

There was a different plan from Yeshua this particular time for the human population of the planet Earth.

It could be compared to what humans call . . . "Spring cleaning."

He would return to the surface of the planet in just over a week on the calendar date of . . . December 21, 2012.

On this day, he would make an entrance that would be absolutely unbelievable to the human population of the planet.

It was time to follow through with a plan that he had envisioned for many centuries.

Yeshua was not very satisfied with how the people of the planet were treating each other, and how they were totally disrespecting the actual planet that they live on.

All of the natural resources were being depleted at a rate that was unacceptable to Yeshua.

There were far to many evil people roaming the planet who were causing harm to good people, and the wonderful planet Earth.

It was now time for a complete transformation for all of these unacceptable things.

Evil would be destroyed.

Good would be rewarded.

A new way of living would begin with a new set of rules to help insure that what has happened to the planet Earth in the past two thousand years would not occur ever again.

It would definitely be judgment day for the people of the planet Earth when Yeshua made his return, as was written by his friend Ossismi twenty centuries in the past.

Even though there had been now, for several month's up to this present time, a forewarning of the arrival of Yeshua, there were really only two people on the surface of the planet Earth that felt in their hearts that he would truly arrive to face humanity.

These two people . . . Vernon Montague, and John Crevelli.

These two astronauts had been telling the people of the Earth that Yeshua was indeed going to arrive on December 21, 2012, but they were being ignored and ridiculed by most people.

Yeshua would be ready for his return in only a few more days.

Would the people of the planet Earth be ready for his actual arrival?

The two astronauts would not be surprised of his return.

The rest of the people of the planet would certainly be shocked and surprised that he really has actually made his return!!

Change for the good was fast approaching.

CHAPTER FORTY ONE

The ferry pulled up to the dock at Legazpi City.

Minutes later, a team of seven men disembarked the ferry to the shore.

These men were from the diamond industry.

Two of these men had been here before, making a deal with the Mayor, and the Constable.

One of these men now had in his possession, some paperwork that gave the companies that these diamond representatives were a part of, full rights to mine the cave of diamonds located on the volcano.

The paperwork signified the exact GPS location for these legal rights.

Of course, these paper works were actually fake papers, made up from the signatures that were acquired at the previous meeting with the Mayor and Constable.

These seven men immediately went to the Constables station.

Once there, they wanted to talk to the Constable, and see Rex Ruppert.

Another officer greeted them with news that they did not expect to hear.

He told them that the prisoner . . . Rex Ruppert, had mysteriously died the day after they had left the island.

This was not unexpected news, what was unexpected to hear from this officer was that the Constable had resigned his position and retired.

The Mayor of the city had also left his position as the leader of their city, and retired as well.

Both men had packed up their belongings, and departed the island to relocate to other more favorable places.

The diamond industry people knew exactly why this happened.

Both the Ex-Mayor and Ex-Constable were given diamonds.

The Mayor also had some money from his bank account.

He did not take all of the money when he left, just what was meant for him.

The rest of the money was kept for the city's treasury to be used for whatever was decided would be best for the city.

The children's center was already in the process of being built on the outskirts of the city.

Upon hearing this news from this officer, the man with the mineral and property rights papers, showed the papers to this officer who was now the acting interim Constable until an election could be held for the position.

The officer looked over the papers carefully for almost fifteen minutes.

Finally, he handed the papers back to the man who had given the papers to him to look at, and commented that the paper work seemed to be all in order, and legal.

But . . . he said it in a tone of voice that suggested that he might be slightly skeptical of their authenticity.

One of the man noticed this, and immediately took over.

He asked the officer if there was a "fee" that had to be paid to him for processing the papers.

The officer looked at him after this statement.

A moment later, a small smile appeared upon his face.

He understood what this question meant . . . a friendly bribe that nobody would ever know about.

He told the man that there was indeed a "fee" that would have to be charged for processing.

Another man reached into his wallet and pulled out a wad of money that made the officer's eyes almost pop out of their eye sockets.

This man peeled off almost a third of the amount of money that made up this wad of cash.

He asked the officer if this would be enough to cover the processing fee.

The officer reached out with his hand immediately and took the money from the man in silence.

The diamond industry men then left the Constables station and made preparations to travel to the GPS sight where the diamond cave was located.

They now knew that there would not be any complications in regards to them starting their initial prep work for future mining operations.

The diamonds that had been given to them by the Constable when they were last here, were inspected very thoroughly by their own experts in the field.

Their conclusion was that the diamonds were of the highest quality ever seen in the diamond industry.

Those diamonds were also among the very largest they had ever laid their eyes on in their entire careers in the industry.

They were obviously excited about starting a mining operation at this new location on this tiny South Pacific island.

What they did not know was that the person who had originally found the diamonds in the cave . . . Marcos, had left the island with his father Enrique a few weeks ago.

This was news that did not concern them.

Marcos and his father were terrified about the possibility of having another deadly episode brought upon them by other men who were affiliated with Rex Ruppert.

So they took their diamonds and left their beloved country altogether, and traveled to Europe to resettle, and to hopefully experience better qualities of life for both of them.

The diamond industry men went and got hotel rooms for the night, they would be leaving for the cave once they had acquired enough supplies from the locals, and had enough to last them while they were doing their prep work at the diamond cave.

All of the men with this small team were very anxious, and excited that they were about to go to a location that would yield them enough diamonds to make them richer than they had ever imagined they would ever be.

All of a sudden, for almost twenty seconds, the ground beneath their feet shook tremendously.

It was a sizable earthquake.

There had already been a number of smaller earthquakes in the past few weeks, but this trembler was by far the largest yet.

All of the men had looks of surprise, and fear was also present within them.

Nobody admitted to being scared by the trembler, but the fear, and now slight doubt was amongst them.

Silent thoughts of safety at the cave were now something that they would all be thinking about.

Nevertheless, they continued on preparing for their journey to the cave for their prep work . . . Greed overrode all doubts and fears

CHAPTER FORTY TWO

Tioto and Trevor both witnessed the large earthquake that Legazpi City had just felt beneath their feet.

The trembler was measured at 5.5 on their instrument panel.

Most of all the previous tremblers were much smaller, with measurements of between 2.2 and 2.6.

It was now time to contact the Philippine authorities, and call for a mandatory evacuation of the island where a volcanic eruption was now considered imminent within a few days by Trevor's estimates.

Tioto agreed with this calculation.

Tioto contacted a former colleague of his who now worked for the Philippine government for the monitoring of all possible volcanic eruptions that might occur within the vast number of islands in the Philippines.

It did not take very long for Tioto's former colleague to go into action.

Volcanic eruptions were a very serious matter that the people of the Philippines understood all too well.

There had been much death caused by previous volcanic eruptions in the past.

After contacting the President of the Philippines, she gave an order for an immediate evacuation of the island where the volcano was located.

The Philippine Navy was called into action to help with this mandatory evacuation ordered by their President.

Their would be no exceptions, everyone would have to leave the island until the eruption was over, and it was deemed safe for people to return.

The men of the diamond industry did not know about the order now given by the President of the Philippines.

Even is they did, they would more than likely ignore the order, because greed had taken them over completely.

There was no acting Mayor of Legazpi City at the moment.

The Interim Constable was left in charge of making decisions for the small city until an election could be held.

He was contacted by a government official who informed him of the Presidential order of evacuation of the island.

He was told that the Navy would be there to help him that very same day.

He was told to start informing all of the people of Legazpi City about the mandatory evacuation of the island.

There were also other cities located on this island who also had to be evacuated as well.

Their local officials were also contacted and given the same instructions from the President.

An hour later, the diamond industry men departed their hotel rooms to go find some supplies that they would need for their trip to the diamond cave.

All around them, they could see people running as if their lives were in danger.

They stopped one of these people and asked him why everyone was running.

He did not speak English, and ignored their question and ran away.

The men immediately hurried over to the Constables station to talk to the acting Constable.

As they arrived at the Constables station, the acting Constable was just exiting the station.

They stopped in front of him and asked him why everyone was running, in apparent fright.

The acting Constable informed the diamond industry men that a mandatory evacuation of the island had been ordered by the President of the Philippines.

He told these men that they were also included in this mandatory evacuation.

He also told the men, before they could ask why the evacuation was being ordered, that an eruption from the volcano was considered to be imminent at any time.

The men looked at each other in varying degrees of surprise, and anger about the new turn of events.

They asked the acting Constable if they could please talk to him in the station for a few minutes privately.

He looked at them for a second, and then agreed for a very short discussion with these men.

Almost immediately upon entering into the Constables station, one of the men pulled out a gun that had a silencer attached to the end of the barrel.

He pointed the gun at the acting Constable, and ordered him to walk into his office.

They went into the office together in silence.

The man with the gun instantly shot the acting Constable in the back of the head.

He fell to the floor, very much dead.

This man put his gun away and went over to the body and retrieved a set of keys from a pocket.

He next went over to the door of the office and walked through and shut it behind him, and then took one of the keys and locked the door.

The diamond industry men then left the Constables station, making sure to lock it up as well.

They quickly went around the city as everyone was scurrying about in various levels of panic, and collected as much supplies as they possibly could under the circumstances.

They did not get as much as they would have wanted, but they were able to get enough to at least make the trek to the diamond cave.

They left immediately after getting this small amount of supplies.

They went into the jungle, following the GPS device towards the massive volcano that rose high above their heads in the distance.

Nobody noticed their departure . . . nobody really cared.

CHAPTER FORTY THREE

Roger Tusk was a happy man these days, he had received a lot of publicity because of his questioning of various well known people throughout the world with his one simple inquiry.

Did they believe that Jesus was going to return on December 21, 2012?

He had scheduled one final interview.

He had tried, almost desperately, for the past two and a half weeks to locate the two astronauts that had been spreading their story about how they were convinced that who they called Yeshua, but everyone called Jesus, was in fact going to return back to Earth in December.

The two astronauts had kept a low profile as the predicted date of Yeshua's return neared.

They were simply tired of all of the criticism that they were receiving from their claims about Yeshua.

Ridicule followed them everywhere that they went.

They were very recognizable throughout the world . . . unfortunately, in a negative way.

Roger Tusk was finally able to locate the two astronauts, and convinced them that he would hold a respectful interview with them at a private location of their choosing.

They earthquake that had happened, and the ordered evacuation by the Philippine President was not a news story that was transmitted in many areas of the world.

It was treated like a story that was not very important.

The story nowadays that everyone was talking about was what the two astronauts had been telling everyone since their return from the South Pacific.

Would this man called Yeshua really return as the two astronauts were claiming?

This was the simple question that Roger Tusk wanted to ask.

The only difference with this interview with these two astronauts as compared to interviews with others, was that he would expand his questioning after the first inquiry about Yeshua actually returning.

The three men met in a hotel casino in Reno, Nevada.

The hotel room was fifteen stories from the ground below.

They entered the hotel room and made themselves comfortable while Roger Tusk set-up his equipment.

Finally after a few minutes, Roger Tusk informed the two men that he was ready to start their interview.

He started with the normal, very predictable question about whether they still believed that Yeshua was going to return only now a very short time from now.

As they have in every interview, they had the same identical answer . . . yes.

Roger Tusk went on to ask them several other questions.

The astronauts answered all of his other questions without hesitation.

His last question to them was if they would be accessible for another interview with him if Yeshua did indeed actually made his return back to humanity.

They could not give him a definite yes or no for that last question.

He pressed them as to why?

They answered that they did not know what Yeshua was going to do when he came back, and that they did not know themselves what they were going to do either.

The interview came to an end.

Roger Tusk bid them farewell, and hurried off to get this new footage on air to the public as quickly as possible.

Vernon Montague, and John Crevelli decided that they would stay for the time being where they were at and relax until the day when they were sure that Yeshua would make his return . . . December 21, 2012.

Later on that same night, they both watch their interview with Roger Tusk.

At many different places around the globe, there were many powerful people who were also watching this latest interview.

All of them . . . 100% of them, simply shrugged this latest interview off as something that did not have to be taken very serious at all.

What would they do if Yeshua actually did make his return?

None of these people took that question serious enough to even take the time to come up with any type of plan.

The clock ticked towards the predicted date . . . slowly and inevitable.

CHAPTER FORTY FOUR

The day finally came.

December 21, 2012 was officially here.

All of the people on the island where the volcano was threatening to erupt had been evacuated, with the lone exception of the team of men from the diamond industry whose greed had taken them on a journey to the cave of diamonds on a plateau of the active volcano.

There had been several large rumblings in the past twenty four hours.

These men simply ignored the warnings.

The thought of getting their hands on some more of the diamonds from the cave was something that had now totally consumed their very souls.

They knew it was now dangerous to still be going to the diamond cave, but they just could not stop themselves at this point in time.

People from around the world anxiously waited for the supposed arrival of this man called Yeshua.

There were actually, in several places, parties being held called "Jesus returns" parties.

Of course there was the usual amount of people walking the streets in many places as well that carried the "end of the world' and "Jesus is here" signs.

It was still being treated as a big joke to the vast majority of people of the Earth.

Several hours passed, and there still was no sign of the return of the great savior.

People eventually started to make the usual comments, especially the majority of the mass media, that it was now just another day as usual.

Their were comments of belittlement towards the two astronauts who had made the people of the world watch this date.

All of the non-believers, and naysayers had smiles on their faces.

The Pope went on national television to make the official announcement, that the Vatican had been correct all along with their stance, that this was not going to happen, as the two astronauts had claimed for months before this day.

The two astronauts sat in their hotel room watching all of the negative criticism about their claim of Yeshua's imminent arrival.

What all of these people did not realize was that the day actually had come.

Yeshua had already departed Nevaehruo several hours ago, leaving one of his brothers, to watch over everything while he was gone.

As Yeshua traversed through the cave system, the volcano was getting close to erupting with a huge devastating blast of molten lava.

At the same time that Yeshua was traveling through the cave system to the exit opening out to the surface of the Earth, the team of diamond industry men had finally arrived at the cave.

They were delighted to see that the GPS device had been 100% correct.

It had led them right to the opening of the diamond cave.

They quickly went inside of the cave to start examining what they were hoping to find . . . more diamonds!!

Almost instantly, they were able to see easily with their eyes, that the walls of the cave was littered with a very large amount of diamonds.

It was also easy to see that a large amount of these diamonds were very large in size.

All of these men were like little children unwrapping their presents on Christmas day.

They were not aware that Yeshua would be at their location in a short period of time from now.

These men hurriedly started to take many of these diamonds out of the cave wall, and depositing the stones into large canvass sacks normally used by Army soldiers in the field.

Two more hours passed.

Yeshua was now on the same level as the diamond industry men who were still carving diamonds out of the cave wall.

He could hear their voices now.

He was now only less than a hundred feet from where they were.

He stood there for a moment watching these men in the shadows.

They did not see him standing where he was.

They were to preoccupied with fulfilling their greedy interests.

All of a sudden . . . it happened!!

The ground shook tremendously!!

The volcano erupted massively!!

All of the men inside of the cave stumbled in different directions.

Two men fell over to the ground.

The only one that was not affected at all was . . . Yeshua.

He stood their firmly, not even moved an inch by the large shaking of the volcano.

Lava started to exit the volcano high into the air, and traveling down the side of the mountain.

The cave system, from below Yeshua, was starting to quickly fill up with molten lava as well, traveling up and out of the entrance to the cave.

It would only be a matter of a few minutes before this molten lave were to pass the area where Yeshua now stood.

Yeshua walked out of the shadows, and came face to face with the men inside of the cave.

They all looked over at him in shock and curiosity.

Standing before them, they could see a black man.

He was dressed in a white hooded robe with a red piece of dress cloth . . . a sash . . . that was draped over the front of his body.

One of the men hollered over to Yeshua rudely . . . "Who in the Hell are you?"

He continued speaking rudely.

All of the men quickly retrieved their firearms that they had on their bodies.

"Get your ass over here!!"

Yeshua did not verbally answer this man yet.

He only smiled slightly.

One of the men decided that he was just going to shoot this man that stood before them.

He pulled the trigger on his gun.

It did not fire a bullet.

The other men tried to shoot their guns as well.

They had the identical results with their guns.

All of their guns would not fire a single bullet!!

How was this possible?

All of the men now tried to run over to this black man who still stood before them silently, still smiling slightly at them.

None of the men could move at all.

The only body part that they could move was their heads.

They were still able to speak, even though the rest of their bodies were completely paralyzed.

Their bodies were as solid as statues.

Frozen, and embedded into the ground that they stood on.

All of these men started to scream in horror about their new situation.

Finally, Yeshua started to walk towards the men, and when he was a few feet from their location, he once again stopped.

He spoke to them.

"You men are evil, I will not tolerate any evil, anymore."

"You will soon live upon this earth anymore as human beings."

"You will become a part of this Earth . . . very soon."

"It is time for me to talk to the rest of the people of the Earth."

"Their judgment day has arrived."

"I have already passed my judgment upon all of you evil men."

Yeshua started to walk towards the entrance to the diamond cave, and as he did this, lava started to come into the area of the cave where all of these men still remained frozen like statues.

Yeshua kept walking at a slow normal pace, unconcerned about the lave that looked like it was going to engulf him in a matter of moments.

The frozen diamond industry men screamed for their lives to no avail.

The molten lava quickly passed by them and melted them into nothing.

They became a part of the lava flow.

They were now a part of the Earth, as Yeshua had told them moments before.

As the lava came upon Yeshua, he spread his arms out to his sides a few inched with his palms outward.

There were very visible scars on each wrist.

As he stood there with his arms out, the lava started to spread away from his body.

None of the lava even came close to touching his body.

Remarkably, none of his clothing was catching on fire from the extreme heat either!!

The lava passed by Yeshua and continued it's destructive path out of the cave, and down the side of the large mountain.

Yeshua walked another fifty feet, and then stopped again.

He still had the same posture.

Arms held out at his side, with his palms out.

He had a caring look upon his face that seemed to radiate love and peace at the same time.

At this exact moment . . . Humanity was now meeting Yeshua . . . Jesus for the first time in almost twenty centuries.

CHAPTER FORTY FIVE

At this exact moment when Yeshua stood there outside of the cave while lava from an erupting volcano passed by him, untouched, many unbelievable things were happening on the entire planet Earth simultaneously.

Professor Ntangku sat at her desk, looking at the screen of her laptop computer.

All of a sudden, am image came onto the screen.

The image was of Yeshua standing outside of the cave of the erupting volcano.

All she noticed at first, before careful examination was a black man in a white robe, and red sash, standing with his arms spread out to his sides.

She could also see that there was what appeared to be a flow of molten lava passing by this man.

She was amazed to see that the lava was not touching him, and his clothing was not catching fire.

As she looked even more carefully, she noticed the scars on each wrist.

She looked down at his feet, and also noticed scars on both of his ankles.

A quick thought crossed her mind for a fleeting moment.

Could it be him?

She now looked at his face very carefully, and then noticed a series of scars going across the top of his forehead.

Professor Ntangku was absolutely stunned.

She now remembered a few details that were written in the ancient papyri that she had translated.

It was the description of Yeshua.

"Skin of ebony."

"Hair like the wool of a sheep."

Her and her colleagues had thought at the time of reading this particular translation, that it described a dark skinned black man.

She tried to convince herself that maybe this was a Hollywood hoax, with special effects, because of what day it was, and all of the commotion about the prediction of Yeshua's arrival.

Was this a fake movie being transmitted on her computer?

She could not get her computer to do anything else except show this image on the screen.

She decided to call some of her former colleague on the landline phone in her office.

She called Dr. "Darny."

He answered on the first ring of the phone.

Instantly, he asked Professor Ntangku if she was listening to any radio station.

She answered that she was not.

She walked over to a radio on another table nearby and turned it on.

No matter what station she turned on the radio, they were all talking excitedly about what she was observing on her computer screen.

Dr. "Darny" told her that he was also looking at the same image as she was on his cellphone.

Apparently, from what is being announced on all of the radio stations, this image of this black man outside of a cave with molten lava surrounding him untouched is appearing on all screens throughout the planet.

As he was explaining this to Professor Ntangku, he did not actually realize the magnitude of what was actually happening, in regards to this image.

He thought that only all of the computer, television, and cellphones were broadcasting this image.

It went far beyond that.

Every screen on the planet was broadcasting this video image.

There were unbelievable things happening.

Such as . . . Television repair businesses that had several televisions that were not even operating, missing parts, and even unplugged . . . these also had the video image on their screens as well!!

Impossible!!

Department stores that sold computers, notepads, cellphones, and televisions . . . all had this video of Yeshua!!

Even all of the unopened boxes that held these electronic devices were playing this video image while still inside of the box!!

All of the movie theaters in the world that were playing movies to movie patrons?

Yes . . . even these screens were showing this video image instead of the movie that they had been watching!!

The large monitors throughout the world in large business and entertainment districts, like Broadway, and Wall Street to name a few . . . These type of screens as well.

Professional sports stadiums had the video image on their large screens!!

Even the radar screens on the Philippine Navy ships that were offshore on the horizon, witnessing the volcanic eruption, had this image as well!!

They had just finished the operation of evacuation all of the people from the island.

Even junkyards that had various broken monitors from televisions, and computers . . . yes . . . the same video image!!

The impossible was happening.

Every single screen, whether working, or not functional, had this same image showing.

News of this unbelievable event could not be broadcast on any screen because of this video image.

So, the only way that word was getting around about what was happening throughout the world, was by radio transmission.

Almost all eyes of the world were now watching this video image, whether they wanted to or not.

Yeshua now had humanities undivided attention.

For the moment, nobody actually realized for sure, who this man actually was.

There was a few exceptions though.

Professor Ntangku, and Dr. "Darny" were now convinced between them, that this person on the screen was in fact Yeshua, or his modern day name . . . Jesus!!

Vernon Montague, and John Crevelli were absolutely elated by what they were now watching from their hotel room.

They 100% knew that this was Yeshua!!

Why? . . . because they recognized him!!

All of the critics who had made them feel like liars, or crazy, would now have to face the reality that they had made a huge mistake in doubting the integrity of the two astronauts.

Yeshua stood where he was for what seemed like an eternal amount of time.

He remained silent.

Sounds of explosions all around him could be heard.

Yeshua wanted to make sure that all of the people of the planet who were now witnessing his return, would be able to figure out who he was without telling them yet.

The Pope was one of the people who was watching this event.

His mouth was wide open in shock.

He, like Professor Ntangku, noticed the obvious scars on Yeshua's wrists, and ankles.

The doubt that had been permanently embedded within his mind, was now starting to quickly dissipate into true belief!!

In fact now . . . many people, religious, and non religious, were also now noticing the scars, and the unbelievable fact that this man was not being harmed by the molten lava.

Because of the fact that the arrival of Yeshua/Jesus had been in the news now for several month's, to happen on this very day, as told by the ancient papyri, there was now a large amount of people who were now coming to the conclusion that this man before them was the man who was crucified on a cross, by the Romans, almost two thousand years ago . . . Jesus has returned!!

This revelation throughout humanity on the planet quickly spread.

The eruption of this particular volcano was unknown to most of the world.

People were curious as to where this volcanic eruption was happening on their planet.

Tioto Fujiaka and Trevor Johnson knew that this volcano was erupting in the South Pacific on the island of Luzon.

The Philippine people throughout their chain of islands were also aware of where this eruption was taking place.

Other than these particular people, there were not to many others who knew where this volcanic eruption was occurring.

There were many world leaders at the moment, scurrying about, realizing who this person might in fact be, and trying to locate telephone landlines for communication purposes.

It took almost a half of an hour for the majority of the people on the planet who were witnessing this event on a screen nearby them, to actually realize, that this is what had always been told would happen someday . . . the second coming of Jesus Christ!!

Yeshua was now ready to speak to all of humanity.

CHAPTER FORTY SIX

The entire world came to a virtual standstill, anticipation of what Yeshua would say to them.

He started to walk again.

As he walked, he started to speak.

When he spoke, all languages of every type, was heard from his mouth.

No matter what ethnicity, he could be understood in their native tongue.

"I am Yeshua."

"Modern day man has given me the name of Jesus."

"The name "Jesus" did not exist as a word in the time that I last walked the surface of this planet."

"The image of me that was created by the religion that was spawned after my departure is one of a man with white skin color."

"This creation by this religion also shows a white person with different colored eyes, and different type and color of has as well."

"The image that your eyes see right now are the real true images of who you have renamed "Jesus.""

"As you can see, I have dark skin, almost black, and my eyes are almost as dark as my skin."

"My hair is very comparable to the wool of a sheep."

"This is the image that people of this planet should have been looking at since my departure."

"Modern day terminology would be that I am called a "Black" man."

"If there are any people who are watching me right now who might doubt what I am saying . . . think for a moment, how is it possible that I am not being burned alive by the lava that flows from this volcano?"

"Notice that my clothing is unharmed."

"How is it possible that all of the devices on this planet that have screens, are able to project what you are now watching?"

"Even devices that do not function at all, show what you are now watching."

"The people of the Earth are now witnessing the impossible."

"This is the only way that I can convince you at this long awaited moment, that I am truly the person that you call Jesus Christ."

Yeshua turned his arms outward once again.

"Do you see these scars on my wrists?"

He looked downward, and pulled his gown slightly apart.

"Do you see these scars on my ankles?"

He pointed to his forehead.

"Do you see these scars across the top of my brow?"

"These are the scars from when the Romans, almost twenty centuries in the past, nailed spikes to my wrists, and ankles, to two crossed pieces of wood."

"You now call these pieces of crossed wood . . . the cross."

"The scars on the top of my brow were from thorns of a bush wrapped around my head as I was beaten by the Romans."

"I did not intend for a religion to be created from my death as a human."

"All I ever really wanted was for the people of the Earth to lived with each other in peace, and respect the planet that they live on."

"I had hope upon my departure, that all of humanity would change to make a better world to live in."

"I have been a witnesses of how humanity has not lived in peace with each other."

"I have also been a witness to the total disrespect of their planet."

"The people of this planet have become a type of people who no longer deserve to live anymore."

"I have come back today to pass my judgment upon the human population of this planet."

"I will not change my decision."

"I have decided that there will by a new start, and new rules for humanity to live by."

As Yeshua said these words, the population of the planet cringed with fear.

If it was true what this man, apparently Jesus, was now saying, mankind was now in trouble.

Serious trouble.

Yeshua continued to speak as he started to walk again.

"I am very disappointed about how out of control the people of this planet have become."

"I am not happy about the selfishness that has engulfed the entirety of humanity."

"Evilness has consumed a large amount of the people who live upon this planet."

"Before I depart once again, I am going to make sure that evilness is destroyed, and any future evil will be recognized and destroyed as well."

"When I was alive on this planet, almost twenty centuries ago, I had a wife."

"Her name was Mary."

"She had a child after my departure."

"This was a child that I fathered."

"She escaped with my friend Ossismi to a place that is now called France."

"Ossismi, was a friend of mine who had the responsibility of writing everything that he witnessed about me while I was alive."

"Ossismi helped my wife raise our child."

"This child grew-up to adulthood, and continued on my legacy of descendants."

"Today, there lives upon this planet, many people who are my descendants."

"They carry within them, my blood."

"There is a reason why I am mentioning my descendants who still live upon this planet . . . today."

"They will be the new caretakers of this planet, and make sure that all of humanity that survives upon my departure will become what I had always hoped for."

"The first thing that I am going to do is to have all of my descendants identified . . . now."

"All of my descendants will now have a symbol of a cross become visible on their palms of their hands."

"Look at the palms of your hands."

"All of the people who can now see a symbol of the cross on the palms of both of their hands, are my descendants."

"The next thing that I am now going to do is to explain the new rules that humanity will live by, under the supervision of my descendants, Earth's guardians."

"It is actually very simple."

"Life will be lived in a more simple manner."

"Love and peace with each other will be the normal practice for all of humanity."

"The Earth will once again be respected."

"I will transform the planet back to where I believe the human population will be able to live a more simple and peaceful life."

"I am going to destroy all of the evil that is now present on this planet."

"All of the evil people who now live upon this planet will now become frozen like statues."

"They will only be able to turn their heads, and speak through their mouths."

"I will then make these evil people become either the dust that floats through the air, or the grains of sand that is common on the surface of the entire planet."

"Look around you."

"Do you see these evil people now?"

People started to look around them as Yeshua had suggested.

There was in fact, many people that were like what Yeshua had said they would be.

Frozen where they stood, or where they laid.

All that these evil people could do now, was to turn their heads, and speak out of their mouths.

It was an amazing sight to behold for the people with good souls to witness this.

There was evilness all around them.

Yeshua began to speak once again.

"Now that you are able to see the evil people around you, watch them as they transform into dust or sand."

As he said this, all of the evil people upon the entire planet became particles of dust, or grains of sand.

The only remaining people left on the planet were people that did not harbor evil within their souls.

Many people started to cry in fear, anger, and despair.

Some people did not realize that some of the people that they trusted were in fact evil people.

After the shock of witnessing this magnificent event upon the evil of humanity, people once again turned their attention to Yeshua as he spoke to them.

They were in tremendous shock as they stood there listening to this powerful being.

Was he even human?

He looked like a black human man.

But his powers were obviously not human.

Yeshua explained to the remaining human population their actual history of how they evolved on this planet many thousands of years ago, before returning to explaining how people would now live upon this planet.

He explained how his race of beings traveled here to this planet a very long time ago, and transformed the animal on this planet that most closely resembled a humanoid . . . the ape.

They implanted a gene from their very own gene pool, and put it into the genes of this ancient ape.

Over time, this ape evolved into different species of primitive apes throughout the planet.

There was a continuos evolution of this ape species for many thousands of years.

Once this species had evolved enough, Yeshua's race of humanoids returned to the planet, and gave knowledge to these primitive humanoids.

They gave only enough knowledge to help them survive better, and evolve into better beings.

Unfortunately, there was another gene in the original ape gene pool that harbored what is now called . . . evil.

This evil has been present from then until now.

People were shocked to hear all of this new information from Yeshua.

What could they do but listen.

After explaining to the human population their actual history, he went back to talking about what he is now going to do with the human population that is left alive on the planet.

"I am going to leave my descendants in charge of making sure that humanity lives peacefully with no more evilness."

"I am going to implant a gene inside of the gene pools of all of the people that I allow to live."

"This gene will make the person, if they have evil within them when they have reached the age of ten years from the time of their birth, turn into dust or sand, as you all have witnessed today with the evil people that had surrounded you."

This statement shocked the people of the Earth.

What about the people that were older than ten years?

Yeshua answered that question next.

"I am sure now that you might be wondering about what if you are already older than ten years?"

"Those people will departs the Earth upon my departure."

"They are good souls."

"They deserve another chance to live again at another time in the future."

"I will take these good souls, and they will go to a wonderful safe place until they are reborn once again in the future."

This statement once again startled the remaining people of the planet.

Yeshua continued to speak.

"I am going to spread my descendants out throughout the world on all of the livable continents, and give to them young innocent children who have not reached the age of two years."

"These descendants will take care of these children, and teach them love and peace as they grow to adulthood."

"They will teach them how to respect the planet that they live on."

"I am going to give my descendants the power to heal."

"I am going to make all knowledge that has been written to disappear from everywhere on the planet."

"There will be a new beginning for all of humankind."

"There will not be any religion taught to these children."

"I will leave only one book on the planet."

"My descendants will teach these children from this book."

"This book will be called the "The teachings of Yeshua."

"I have prepared this book personally, throughout the time, that I was gone from the surface of this planet."

"I am going to get rid of all that man has created."

"I am going to return back to Earth, all of the resources that have been used by man."

As Yeshua said this last statement, everything started to go back to the Earth.

All of the different chemicals that make up all things created by man, started to dissipate back to the Earth.

Everything dissolved back into the Earth, except for the screens that were now showing this video image of Yeshua.

Buildings, cars, ships, airplanes, weapons, everything . . . started to dissipate back to the soil of the planet where they originally came from.

As this was happening, people were relocated to areas of safety.

All of this actually happened fairly quickly, unbelievably, only a few minutes for this total transformation to occur.

Once again, the people of the earth were stunned.

Yeshua, as he said he would do, started to relocate all of his descendants to various places throughout the world.

These people were just as shocked as the rest of the population.

Many of these descendants did not want to have this responsibility, so they were instantly turned into dust or sand and returned to the Earth.

One look at the planet Earth now was an amazing sight to behold with ones eyes.

The planet looked almost barren.

The only things that remained that had not disappeared yet were just enough screens to continue showing this video image of Yeshua.

There was no sign of anything that was created by modern man anywhere.

Yeshua set up places around the globe where his descendants would live and raise the new generation of people on the planet.

These children were still young enough to not have any real knowledge about the past.

These sites were set up with all of the essentials needed for proper survival.

All disease was permanently eradicated from the planet for humans, and animals.

The descendants, as Yeshua had said, would have the power to heal as needed.

Yeshua made an exception with a small amount of non descendant adults, who would have the opportunity to live for the rest of their lives.

Among them still lived two particular people on the planet, that were lucky enough to garner this opportunity . . . Vernon Montague, and John Crevelli.

He made it a special point to make this statement to the people of the planet.

The two astronauts were stunned by this.

They did not understand why they had been chosen as some of the few non descendents that would remain living, but they did not object to this reality.

They felt very thankful of Yeshua's decision.

They were saddened by the fact that they were going to lose all of their friends and loved ones, unless they happened to be descendents of Yeshua.

The spouses of the descendents were also allowed to live as well, alongside their life mates.

Besides these few chosen people that were non descendents of Yeshua, only a certain amount of children would be chosen to live and be raised by the descendents, or guardians of the Earth.

Each descendent was given the responsibility to take care of these children.

The amount of descendents, that finally were chosen to stay on the planet to be guardians of the planet, and teachers of the new generation of humanity was . . . 82,359 people.

This number included all of the chosen children of all the different ethnic groups, and non descendents.

Yeshua was finally through with what he had to say to the people of the planet.

It had never been his intention to stay of the surface of the planet for very long.

His plan had always been to come back to the surface, address the people of the planet, and follow through with everything that he had planned to do.

He did not want to watch any unnecessary suffering from the people with the good souls, as they came to realize that they would not be alive for much longer on their planet.

He felt a need to at least explain a few things, but not waste too much time while doing so.

It was now time to take all of the good souls from the people not chosen to continue living upon the planet.

Instantly, Yeshua took all of these good souls and transferred them to Nevaehruo where his brother waited.

As these good souls arrived at Nevaehruo, Yeshua's brother transferred them into special containers inside of his spaceship.

These good souls would help to replenish other worlds where the supply was needed.

After all of this was completed, Yeshua turned around, and walked back into the cave system with his arms still spread to keep the molten lava from touching any part of him.

As he started his journey back to Nevaehruo, all of the screens that had showed his video image disappeared as he did within the cave system.

A very short time later, he was back in Nevaehruo alongside his brother.

He his brother farewell.

His brother went into his spacecraft, and left Nevaehruo, on his way to another planet that needed a new supply of good souls.

These good souls that were now leaving the planet where they were born had in fact been able to realize that making an effort to be good, respect their fellow people, and the Earth as well, would now be rewarded with a chance to live again . . . someday . . . somewhere, without the memories that they ever even lived on a planet called Earth.

Yeshua was now hopeful that humanity would finally become what he had always wanted.

He would use all of the time of the future, monitoring the results of his latest efforts for the humans who now live on the planet.

He will remain in Nevaehruo, replenishing the planet with good souls as is needed.

So . . . is this the End?

Or is this a new beginning for humanity?

The answer to these questions will only be known in the distant future . . . hopefully . . . love, and peace for each other, and respect for the planet Earth . . . will finally prevail for all of humanity.